Annie Burrows has been writing Regency romances for Mills & Boon since 2007. Her books have charmed readers worldwide, having been translated into nineteen different languages, and some have gone on to win the coveted Reviewers' Choice award from *CataRomance*. For more information, or to contact the author, please visit annie-burrows.co.uk, or you can find her on Facebook at facebook.com/AnnieBurrowsUK.

Discover more at millsandboon.co.uk.

THE CAPTAIN CLAIMS HIS LADY

Annie Burrows

MILLS & BOON

First published in Great Britain 2018
by Mills & Boon, an imprint of HarperCollins*Publishers*
1 London Bridge Street, London, SE1 9GF

Large Print edition 2018

© 2018 Annie Burrows

ISBN: 978-0-263-07507-6

FLINTSHIRE SIR Y FFLINT		
C29 0000 1219 797		
MAGNA	£14.99	

FSC ... ertified
m ... ement. For
... k/green.

YY

New Year, New Life—
welcome to the world, Alfie!

Chapter One

Captain Harry Bretherton ducked his head as he entered the waterfront tavern and ran his eyes swiftly over the occupants of the low-ceilinged, smoky taproom. He hoped that none of his former crew members were drinking here on this dank October night. For the meeting being held in the back room was supposed to be a secret.

Grinding his teeth, he strode through the room that swarmed with dockers and sailors, wondering what on earth the Marquess of Rawcliffe had been thinking, arranging to hold his meeting here, of all places. He certainly hadn't been living up to his nickname of Zeus, the all-knowing, not by a long chalk.

He'd even picked the most memorable of his footmen to stand guard at the door to the back room. Though Kendall was wearing a drab coat and slouch hat, he still managed to look every inch the footman to a marquess.

Harry looked the man straight in the eye as he drew near, wishing he knew exactly what orders Zeus had given him. If it came to a fight, he wasn't at all sure he'd be able to get past Kendall. The footman was over six feet tall and extremely muscular, as well as being utterly loyal to his employer. And it had been a long time since Harry had been in his best form.

He'd just have to hope he could bluff his way past.

'Good evening, Kendall,' he said, in what he hoped looked like a confident manner.

'Wasn't expecting you here tonight, sir.'

No. He wouldn't. Zeus had arranged the whole affair with Ulysses without consulting him, let alone inviting him to take part. If he hadn't overheard a couple of conversations between Lady Rawcliffe and Lady Becconsall, he might never have discovered what their husbands had been planning.

Behind his back.

'Only had orders to let three naval officers in, sir,' Kendall explained, a touch defensively. Harry drew himself up to his full height and lifted his chin slightly, utilising the single inch he had over

Kendall to its full effect. There weren't many men the footman had to, literally, look up at.

'Three *other* officers, besides myself,' Harry improvised quickly, 'I dare say that was what His Lordship meant.'

'Oh, I see, sir.' Kendall looked relieved. But then he wouldn't have wanted to test his strength against a man who'd been a guest in his employer's home, any more than Harry had wished to start a struggle that would probably have escalated into a full-scale brawl within seconds. He might be an officer, but he was navy. And Kendall clearly wasn't. The man had never looked more like a footman than when he opened the door to let Harry past.

Having successfully cleared the first hurdle, Harry stepped into the back room.

The four men who were seated round the sticky, blackened table went quiet. Zeus, who was at the head, made his feelings about Harry's presence known by narrowing his eyes and thinning his lips.

By way of reply, Harry looked at each of the other men seated at the table in turn, before training his eyes on Zeus and raising his eyebrows.

These were the men Rawcliffe deemed acceptable to carry out the investigation into the murder of their former schoolfriend? A drunkard, a bully and an inveterate gambler? Personally, Harry wouldn't trust any of them any further than he could throw them. Which wouldn't be all that far, these days.

Rawcliffe met his expression of disbelief with one of bland defiance. Their staring match might have gone on indefinitely, had not Captain Hambleton drained his tankard, slammed it down on the table and belched.

At which point, Rawcliffe wrenched his gaze away from Harry and shot Captain Hambleton an expression of disdain so cold it practically sent a sheet of frost across the tabletop.

Captain Hambleton met that icy gaze with the kind of aplomb that came naturally to a man who'd spent years honing it under fire. 'Are you going to carry on informing us about the service you wish one of us to perform on your behalf, my lord, or are we waiting on anyone else?'

Harry made the most of the opportunity Captain Hambleton had unwittingly provided, to pull up a chair, sit down on it and fold his arms across his chest.

'I may as well proceed,' said Rawcliffe, with resignation, having looked at each of the men now sitting round his table with varying degrees of repugnance. 'You already know that the service I require from whichever of you I choose is not for the faint-hearted, or squeamish. I made that perfectly clear when I approached each one of you. The task will necessitate acting in a way that many...' he turned briefly in Harry's direction, his eyelids lowering fractionally '...would consider dishonourable. If that perturbs any of you, then I urge you to leave now, before I make my final selection.'

Nobody moved. But then none of the other men had all that many scruples. Lieutenant Nateby was a brute, renowned for flogging men under his command on the flimsiest pretext. Lieutenant Thurnham was so deep under the hatches, because of his addiction to gambling, that he was willing to do just about anything to stay out of debtor's prison. And as for Captain Hambleton, Harry rather thought his conscience had long since been pickled in alcohol.

'Just how do you plan on making your final selection,' Harry challenged him, 'from this pool of... *talent*?' He could not keep the scorn from his voice. Or the anger. Rawcliffe should never have brought strangers into this. Especially not men like these.

'How about drawing straws?' sneered Captain Hambleton.

'Yes,' said Lieutenant Thurnham eagerly. 'Place it in the hands of fate.'

'Are you sure you only want one man for your... task?' Lieutenant Nateby said, twirling his brandy glass round and round. 'If it is as difficult and dangerous as you were suggesting before Captain Bretherton joined us,' he said, darting a rather sardonic smile at Harry, 'then it might be easier to accomplish if two of us joined forces.'

'No,' said Lieutenant Thurnham. 'That would mean splitting the fee. Unless you would pay each of us the same amount you mentioned?'

'This is a job for one man, working alone,' said Rawcliffe repressively.

'Oh, well then,' said Lieutenant Thurnham with a shrug, 'let us draw straws. Save you the pain of making the decision about which one of us to pick.'

Rawcliffe already knew which one of them he should pick. Dammit, Archie had been one of his oldest friends. If anyone had the right to hunt down his murderer and bring him to justice, it was he. Rawcliffe and Becconsall had no business hiring men to do the job. Not when they knew he, Harry, would have done it for nothing.

'A sensible solution,' said Rawcliffe, infuriating him still further. 'Kendall!'

His footman poked his head round the door. 'Yes, my lord?'

'Procure four straws. Three cut short and one left long. Then come back and present them to these four gentlemen one at a time, in the prescribed manner.'

'Yes, my lord,' said Kendall, leaving at once.

Harry clenched his fists on his lap. All five men at the table sat in silence, broken only by the grating noise of Captain Hambleton dragging the ale jug across the table, then refilling his tankard.

Good god, did Rawcliffe and Becconsall really consider such a fellow preferable to him? To bring their friend's murderer to justice? True, Harry had felt, and looked, a mere shadow of his former self when he'd first returned to England. And, admittedly, he'd been drinking too much. But even foxed, and at half-strength, surely he was more suitable, not to say reliable, than any of these three?

Kendall returned after only a brief interval. Though heaven alone knew where the fellow could have found any straw in this neck of the woods. He made as if to hand the bunch of straws over to his master, but Rawcliffe held up his hand.

'No, it is better if you present them to the candidates for the post. Less chance of anyone accusing me of cutting a sham, should they be disappointed.'

'Seems fair,' said Thurnham, holding out his hand.

'Hold hard,' said Captain Hambleton. 'We should do this according to rank.'

Kendall raised his brows in a manner that wouldn't have looked out of place in a drawing room. 'We will do this,' he said repressively, 'according to who's nearest the door. And that's this fellow.' He extended his fist in the direction of Lieutenant Nateby, who gave his senior officer an insolent grin before plucking out one straw.

It was hard to tell whether it was short or long compared to those still clenched in Kendall's fist. The only thing anyone could tell for certain, when Nateby held it aloft, was that it was about four inches long.

'Have I won?'

If he had, then why was Kendall offering the remaining straws to Lieutenant Thurnham? The straw he drew was of the same length as Nateby's. Which meant that Kendall must be still holding a much longer one.

Kendall held out his fist to Harry. 'Your turn, Captain,' he said.

Harry studied both remaining straws carefully, his heart pounding sickeningly. He had to pull out the long straw, he just had to. He'd been robbed of too much, these past few years. His command, his liberty, his health, his self-respect and, finally, his timid, yet loyal, friend Archie. He couldn't lose the right to avenge him, too. It would be…well, the last straw.

He closed his eyes, briefly, took a deep breath and laid hold of one of the two remaining straws clutched in Kendall's fist. And tugged at it. And kept on tugging as, slowly, the length of it kept on emerging.

He breathed again. He'd got the long straw. And the job.

Kendall ushered the other three men out of the room, amidst much grumbling and cursing. Leaving him alone at the table with the Marquis of Rawcliffe.

A man who claimed to be his friend.

'I can't believe,' Harry growled, 'that you could even *consider* hiring anyone else. I was the obvious candidate all along.'

Rawcliffe's thin mouth clenched into a hard line. 'No, you were not. I thought you heard me explaining that this task will entail acting in a dishonourable fashion. And you are not a dishonourable man.'

'You have no idea what kind of man I am nowadays.'

'We didn't give you the nickname of Atlas for nothing. You—'

'You see? You are basing your judgement on the boy you used to know at school. You have no idea how much I may have changed since then. And don't bring up the letters I wrote bragging about my so-called heroic exploits. Most of them were a pack of lies.'

'You stayed with me for weeks this spring. Until I married Clare—'

'And you didn't notice how much brandy I got through? Or how keen I was to sponge off you? Are those the actions of…?' He stopped and ran his trembling fingers through his hair, slightly stunned by the fact that he was deliberately trying to persuade a man he was dishonourable, as though it was an asset, when, ever since his release from his French captors, he'd been wallowing in the certainty he was no longer of any use to anyone.

'You ceased sponging off me, as you like to put it, the moment you knew I was to marry. I know that since then you have been living in extremely reduced circumstances, quite unnecessarily, I might add—'

There he went again—trying to attribute noble motives to account for his actions. When the truth was that since their marriages, both Rawcliffe and Becconsall had been so nauseatingly happy Harry could hardly stand being anywhere near either of them. Or their frilly little wives.

'Look, Rawcliffe, while you've been living in idleness for the last dozen years, I have been sailing all over the world fighting England's enemies. I've employed whatever means necessary to destroy them. *Whatever* means. There isn't a dirty trick I haven't resorted to, if it has meant preserving the lives of my men, or slaughtering our foes. Didn't you think I'd be prepared to go to the same lengths, to bring Archie's murderer to justice?'

'To be frank, no, we didn't. You didn't seem to care about anything much, beyond getting to the bottom of the next bottle.'

That took the wind out of Harry's sails. Even though the jibe had been well deserved.

'Look,' said Harry, 'when you and Ulysses started getting all worked up over the disappearance of some jewels, I admit, I couldn't get the slightest bit interested.' What did he care about the baubles that hung round the necks of fat, old, rich women, when out there, on the high seas, men who deserved so much better were daily being ground to pulp by cannon or shredded by flying splinters? Especially when he knew that those same pampered matrons would turn their noses up at the odour those men produced, due to a combination of their hard work and lack of sanitary conveniences? 'And I could see that Ulysses was just looking for an excuse to impress Lady Harriet, anyway. And that when you went off on that search for the thief, it was a way to relieve the tedium of your existence. In the same way, when Archie went down to Dorset to visit that old relative of his, who seemed to be implicated in some way, I just thought it would do him good to stop hanging on your coat-tails and prove himself.'

Now it was Rawcliffe's turn to flinch. At least, he began to tap his forefinger on the stem of his wineglass, which was the nearest he ever got to displaying agitation.

'But somebody killed him,' Harry continued. 'That changes everything.'

'Not quite everything. To be frank, neither of us think that you have the stomach to employ the stratagem which Ulysses and I have deemed necessary.'

'Haven't the stomach for it?' That was one thing about himself he'd never doubted. He might have done a lot of foolish things, but nobody could deny he'd fought like a tiger to try and mitigate the results of his mistakes. 'I am no coward.'

'It isn't a question of cowardice. And don't repeat your excuse about me not knowing you any more. You have been back in England for several months, during which time I have had ample opportunity to discover what kind of man you have grown to be. You were the only one of us, remember, who made any attempt to defend poor Lady Harriet, when we found her in the park, alone, at dawn. The only one to treat her with respect.'

'Well, that's different. A female...alone...'

'Well, that's just it,' said Rawcliffe with a touch of impatience. 'The task of bringing Archie's murderer to justice is going to involve deceiving a female. A gently born female. It is at the very heart of the plan Ulysses came up with. And unless I'm very much mistaken, seducing a gullible virgin is not something you would be comfortable doing.'

'Seducing a...?' He shook his head. Then looked at the straw clutched in his fingers. 'It's too late now. It appears to be my fate.' And anyway, could anything he did make him despise himself more than he already did?

'Damn fate!' Rawcliffe slapped his open palm on the table, in a display of emotion that was so uncharacteristic it made Harry jump. 'I don't have so many friends I can afford to lose another one.'

Just like that, Harry understood why Rawcliffe had held this meeting in secret. Had made plans with Becconsall behind his back, too. People might assume Rawcliffe was cold-blooded and unfeeling, but he wasn't. It was all a façade. Behind it beat the heart of a man who detested injustice. He hadn't changed all that much since he'd been a boy at Eton, either. Not deep down, where it counted. At Eton, they'd given Rawcliffe the nickname of Zeus, not simply because he out ranked them all, but because he really was a natural leader. Just as they'd nicknamed him Atlas, because not only was he bigger and stronger than anyone else in the school, but he'd been willing to take on the burdens of those who needed his protection. And Becconsall, the third of their band of brothers, had been Ulysses. So named for his cunning and intelligence.

He'd never forged friendships like the ones he'd

formed at that school, even though he'd been there for such a comparatively short time.

'Seducing a gullible virgin doesn't sound all that dangerous.'

'Going to visit an elderly relative didn't sound all that dangerous when I let Archie go and do so, either, did it? The point is, there is somebody down there in Dorset who is cunning enough to plan the theft of jewels in such a way that it took years, in some cases, for the theft to even be discovered. And with the connections that enabled him to introduce jewel thieves into the houses of members of the ton, in the guise of ladies' maids. That person is also ruthless enough to commit murder in order to keep his crimes from being discovered. So we need someone as cunning, and as ruthless, to withstand him.'

'I have already declared myself willing to do whatever it might take. Even to the point of seduction. Though to be frank, whatever female you have selected for this process would fare better with me than with the likes of Thurnham or Nateby. I, at least, won't debauch her.'

Rawcliffe looked at him for a second or two, his face blank, though Harry knew it was a mask he adopted to conceal what he was thinking.

'And Archie,' Harry continued, 'was not only a civilian, but a scientist. He had no idea how to spot a liar, or a rogue. Whereas I am not only an experienced fighting man, but have lived in close quarters with some of the most despicable criminals on earth. Men who chose to serve in the navy rather than go to the gallows.'

'There was a good reason,' said Rawcliffe thoughtfully, 'why I sought candidates for the job amongst other naval men. The ability to handle a boat might come in handy.'

Harry's heart picked up speed. 'There you are, you see? And you can trust me, which you could not do with the others. They would not have had the zeal I can bring to the table.'

'You are still not fit for active duty, though, are you? If it comes to a fight…'

'I am much stronger than I was. Getting stronger every day. And anyway, isn't it better that our enemy underestimates me?'

Rawcliffe's cool grey eyes narrowed. 'Actually, in one way,' he said thoughtfully, 'your physical condition *is* an advantage. It will provide the perfect cover for you to be in Bath. Where the young lady who is pivotal to the investigation is currently staying.'

Harry leaned back in his chair. The job was his.

'Why don't you just tell me what dastardly plan you and Ulysses have cooked up between you? And then let me decide if I'm the man to carry it out.'

Or not.

Chapter Two

Lizzie took the cup of water from the hand of the footman who had just drawn it from the pump and turned hastily. The rooms were particularly crowded this morning and she'd been queuing for what felt like an eternity. Grandfather would certainly think so. Waiting in his chair by the fireplace, he would be tapping his cane on the floor by now, his temper rising with each second that passed.

Though it wasn't even as if he'd wish to leave once she'd brought him his daily dose of the water which was supposed to be the cure for his gout, since so many of his cronies were here for the season. He'd be gossiping for ages long after he'd downed his medicinal cup of water, while she would have to stand behind his chair, still as a statue lest he accuse her of fidgeting.

Nevertheless, she'd annoy him less if she made it look as if she'd completed this errand as quickly as she could.

As she stepped back to make her way out of the throng pressing round the pump, her shoulder caught on something. Something that felt rather like a brick wall. And which said, *'Oof!'*, just before she heard the distinctive sound of a cup clattering to the floor.

'Oh, no…oh, dear,' she said, turning to make her apologies to whoever it was she'd just stumbled into. And finding herself on a level with a very determined chin. Above that was a full-lipped mouth and above that was a rather blunt nose, sprinkled with freckles. And above that, a pair of the bluest, saddest eyes she'd ever seen.

'I'm so sorry,' she said, her cheeks heating, though the Lord alone knew why. She had to apologise so often for blundering into someone or something that she ought to be used to it by now. It was just that this man was so…tall. And so solid. Most people would have staggered back under the force of her weight, applied directly to their midriff. Or even fallen right over. In fact, it was a miracle, given that the place was full of the frail and elderly, that she hadn't knocked anyone over yet this season.

But this man hadn't budged as much as an inch.

Which meant they were standing far too close to each other.

She took a hasty half-step back. Immediately his facial features blurred into a pale oval topped by a neat thatch of closely cropped black hair.

'Your cup...' she began with mortification. It would be of no use attempting to pick it up. She had no idea where it had gone and her eyesight was too poor to bother making a search. 'I shall go and fetch you another...'

As she made to move, something that felt like a wooden vice gripped her by the elbow.

'Oh, no, you don't,' said the large man, in a firm voice. 'I mean, that is to say,' he said in a much lighter tone, 'you have no need to fetch me another. No need at all.'

'But I—'

'No,' he said, in that same firm tone. Then he leaned in and murmured, 'You have just saved me from a terrible fate. Do not, I beg of you, undo your good work now.'

'A terrible... My good... What?'

'I know the water is supposed to be good for my

health, but…' He shrugged. With a pair of shoulders the width of a mantelpiece.

'Oh,' she said. Or rather, sighed. Yes, the sound that had just come out of her mouth had definitely contained far more sigh than sense.

'May I,' said the enormous, solid man, 'be permitted to know your name? So that I may render due gratitude to my redeemer?'

She wasn't sure, afterwards, if it was the slightly mocking allusion to scripture, or the jocular tone of his voice, but she suddenly felt as if she was making a bit of a fool of herself, standing so close to a man she didn't know, and feeling all… Well, she wasn't sure what she was feeling. Only that she'd never felt anything like it before.

And also, that no matter what he was making her feel, she really ought allow him to keep hold of her elbow in that proprietorial manner.

She lifted her chin.

And promptly thought better of saying anything cutting. He'd been so forgiving of her clumsiness. Shouldn't she return the favour by forgiving his forwardness?

'It is…' No, she couldn't simply give him her name. That was not at all the proper thing to do. Why, he could be anybody.

'Miss…?' he prompted her.

She ought to step away from him. Why couldn't she? 'Step,' she finished. For it would indeed be a misstep to act in such a fast manner.

'Miss Step?' His dark brows raised. He shook his head. 'Are you quite sure?'

'Yes, I…' She glanced in the direction of the fireplace and her grandfather's chair. 'In fact, I ought to be…'

'Because you have the distinct look of the Cheevers family.'

'Cheevers?'

'Yes, I have the distinct impression you are, decidedly, Miss Cheevers.'

He ran the two words together so that it sounded as though he'd said mischievous. Her breath caught in her throat. Good heavens, was he…teasing her? *Flirting* with her? No, no, he couldn't possibly be doing that. He'd looked sensible, when she'd been close enough to make out the expression on his face.

'I am not being mischievous,' she retorted. And then, heaven alone knew why, she succumbed to the temptation to add, 'You are clearly Miss Taken.'

He laughed. The sound erupted from his mouth as though it had taken him completely by surprise.

'No, no, I am no sort of Miss at all. Though clearly you believe I have committed a Miss Demeanour, by being so bold as to ask for your true name.'

'It was a piece of rank Miss Conduct.'

'No, not so bad as that. It was, perhaps, a touch Miss Guided.'

'Which was why I felt obliged to use a Miss Nomer.'

'I understand completely. But believe me, by attempting to be Miss Terious, you have only made me more determined to uncover your true identity.'

Somebody nearby cleared their throat. And she realised that the pair of them were creating a rather substantial obstacle to people trying to reach, or move away from, the pump.

The tall, blue-eyed man bowed from the waist. 'Forgive me, Miss Teak, but I really should be moving along.'

'Oh,' was all she could think of say, as her spirits plummeted. Of course, a man like that was not going to stand around playing word games with the likes of her for any length of time. She might have amused him, for a moment or two. But he had eyes in his head. She was tall, she was ungainly and she had no dress sense. She didn't think her face was actually ugly and her hair was the kind of silver blonde that men might go into raptures over, if it sprouted from the head of a smaller, dainty woman.

But she wasn't. And it didn't.

By the time she'd thought all those things, he'd vanished into the throng. Though she would have thought a man like him would be visible above the general run of people, being a full head taller than she was.

Her wretched eyesight. If only Grandfather would permit her to wear spectacles when she went out. But Grandfather didn't hold with them. And she didn't have the heart to defy him. He'd been generous enough to her over the years. Indeed, if it wasn't for him…

She sighed, and, her cup of supposedly health-giving water held firmly in her hand, made her way back to the spot where she'd left Grandfather, holding court over a group of Bath widows and old cronies.

'Who were you talking to, miss?' Grandfather scowled at her over the rim of his cup as she handed it to him.

'I have no idea,' she admitted wistfully. 'He didn't give me his name.'

'I should think not. In my day a gentleman waited to be introduced before speaking to a lady.'

'Well, I did blunder into him and knock his cup of water out of his hand.'

'Oh. I see. Like that, was it?' And with that, he turned back to Mrs Hutchens and took up from where they'd left off gossiping, having clearly dismissed the entire incident.

Which was a bit depressing, actually. For a minute or two, Lizzie toyed with the idea of saying that, no, it wasn't *like that*. That the tall, blue-eyed man had flirted with her outrageously. Showered her with compliments, then asked her to elope with him.

But saying any such thing would only have earned her a sharp reprimand. Grandfather knew she wasn't the kind of girl that gentlemen ever flirted with. The only thing that might tempt a man to look beyond her gargantuan build, and her clumsiness, was an enormous dowry.

And Lizzie didn't have a penny to her name.

Still, there was nothing to stop her from reliving the encounter in her mind. And imagining the expressions that might have been flitting across his face as they were bantering with each other. Why shouldn't he have looked at her with admiration?

Why couldn't her dazzling wit have managed to chase the shadows from his eyes and make them twinkle with laughter?

Grandfather rudely interrupted her daydream by poking her in the leg with his cane.

'Come on, girl, stop wool-gathering!'

It was time to leave.

'Yes, Grandfather,' she said meekly. But instead of trailing behind him, shoulders drooping at the prospect of facing the next stage in the daily round of Bath life, Lizzie imagined she was balancing a pile of books on her head. Because ladies were supposed to glide, gracefully, wherever they went.

And for once, Lizzie could see the point of trying to do so.

Because, who knew *who* might be watching her?

Chapter Three

'And of course,' said Lady Mainwaring, 'I told *her...*'

Lizzie kept her head tilted to one side, her eyes fixed in the general direction of Bath's most garrulous widow, while her mind wandered freely. It was one of the benefits of having such poor eyesight. People didn't expect her to look as though she was focusing intently on them when they cornered her and tried to interest her in the latest gossip.

She did make sure she smiled at Lady Mainwaring though, because the plump little woman was one of the least terrifying of the Bath set. Lizzie was certain that she gossiped about her the moment they parted company, but she never actually said anything unkind to her face, the way so many of the other dowagers did. Lady Mainwaring had never asked her why she didn't smarten herself up, for example, or recommended modistes who would know how to counteract her faults, or sigh and pretend to sympathise with the difficulty of finding eligible young men in Bath these days. She was too keen on keeping Lizzie up to date with what everyone else in Bath was doing.

'Excuse me,' said the Master of Ceremonies, bowing to both ladies and making Lizzie jump. She hadn't noticed him approaching, so intent had she been on convincing Lady Mainwaring she was listening to her account of her latest altercation with one of the other dowagers.

'I have here a gentleman I would wish to recommend as a dancing partner, for you, Miss Hutton.'

'For me?' Lizzie couldn't have been more surprised if he'd told her she'd just won the lottery. Especially since she'd never purchased a ticket.

'Permit me to introduce Captain Bretherton, of His Majesty's navy,' said the Master of Ceremonies, smoothly ignoring Lizzie's less-than-gracious reaction, and waving to someone who, presumably from the direction of the waving, was standing just behind him.

'Captain Bretherton?' Of the navy? She peered beyond Mr King's shoulder and saw an immense figure loom up out of the golden candlelit fog. And her heart skipped a beat. It was the man from the Pump Room that morning. It had to be. For there surely couldn't be two such tall, broad men in Bath at present.

'Miss *Hutton*,' said a voice she recognised at once. A voice that sent strange feelings rippling through her whole body. Making her feel a bit like a pointer quivering in the presence of game. 'I am charmed to make your acquaintance.'

'Eep!' That was the noise which escaped Lady Mainwaring's mouth as Captain Bretherton stepped closer and bowed over her hand. Which also, co-incidentally, expressed exactly what Lizzie was thinking.

'Captain Bretherton,' said Lizzie, dropping into a curtsy. Causing Lady Mainwaring to stagger a little as Lizzie's elbow caught her in the midriff.

She really ought to practise curtsying more often. She had never mastered the art of controlling her elbows. It was hard enough to get her knees to dip to the approved level, while keeping her balance. Spreading her elbows wide helped her not to stagger in the rising portion of the curtsy, she'd discovered. And Lady Buntingford, who'd been the one attempting to teach her *all that a lady needed to know*, had said that she supposed that at least it meant she could perform the whole manoeuvre relatively smoothly, even if nobody and nothing within range of them was likely to emerge unscathed.

'Allow me to escort you to the ballroom,' said Captain Bretherton, as a large, gloved hand swam into view.

She took it, grateful that she couldn't see the expression on his face. The poor man must be regretting having asked her to dance, now that he'd seen how clumsy she was.

'You are very brave,' came tumbling out of her mouth. And then she blushed. That was just the sort of thing she ought not to tell a man, just before he danced with her.

But then, what did it matter, really? Once he'd spent half an hour stepping over the bodies she'd no doubt strew across the dance floor, he would never come anywhere near her again.

Oh, dear. It had been so pleasant daydreaming about her encounter with him this morning. She'd actually been *witty* for a few moments. But now she had a horrid feeling that she was only ever going to be able to cringe when she looked back on what was likely to happen during the course of the next half-hour.

She felt his arm, upon which she'd rested her hand in the requisite manner, stiffen.

'Brave? What do you mean?'

'To ask me to dance,' she confessed miserably.

'Indeed,' he said. 'But it was the only way I could think of to get an introduction. Wondering what your name could really be has been tormenting me all day.'

'Oh, well, if that is all, we don't need to go through with it. We could just go to the tea room...'

'Tea won't be served for another hour at least,' he said swiftly. 'And...er...'

'You have no taste for cards? Neither do I. In fact, Grandfather won't even buy me a subscription for the card room. Says it is a waste of money.'

'Playing cards at all is a waste of money,' he said grimly.

She shot him a startled look. And, since the crowded room obliged them to walk very close together, she could see the clenched plane of his jaw quite distinctly.

'Besides, I would much rather dance with you.'

'Really? But I thought...'

'Thought what?'

'Well, I was just going to say that, this morning, I thought you looked quite sensible.'

A bark of laughter escaped his lips. But then he turned his head and looked down at her.

'Sensible and brave. My, my. Two compliments in such rapid succession. Miss Hutton, you will turn my head.'

'No, I didn't mean, that is…' She felt her cheeks heating as her thoughts, and her tongue, became hopelessly tangled. How she wished she had more experience of talking to men. Well, single men, who'd asked her to dance with them, that was. Then she might not be making quite such a fool of herself with this one.

'I will make a confession,' he said, leaning close to her ear so that his voice rippled all the way down her spine in a caressing manner.

'Will you?' She lost her ability to breathe properly. It felt as if her lungs were as tangled as her thoughts.

'When I looked in upon the ballroom, earlier, and saw how few people were actually dancing, and how many were watching, my nerve almost failed.'

'Well, it is just that there are not that many people here who are fit enough to dance. But they do enjoy watching others. And then…'

'Giving them marks out of ten, I dare say,' he finished for her.

'Yes, that's about it. And I'm terribly sorry, but—'

'Oh, no,' he said sternly. 'You cannot retreat now. We are almost at the dance floor. Can you imagine what people will say if you turn and run from me?'

'That you've had a narrow escape?'

'That *I've* had…' He turned, and took both her hands in his. 'Miss Hutton, are you trying to warn me that you are not a good dancer?'

She nodded. Then hung her head.

She felt a gloved hand slide under her chin and lift her face. And saw him smiling down at her. Beaming, in fact. As though she'd just told him something wonderful.

'Then, you are not going to berate me when I tread upon your toes?'

'I… Is that what your dance partners normally do?' When he nodded, ruefully, she welled up with indignation. 'How rude.'

'I shall remind you that you said that, after you have suffered the same fate.'

'I suspect that you will be too busy regretting having asked me to dance at all to remember anything I said beforehand.'

'Oh? Why is that?'

'Because I have no...' She tried to wave her hands to demonstrate her lack of coordination, only to find them still firmly clasped between his own. 'And people do try to get out of my way, but...'

'I can see that this is going to be an interesting experience for both of us,' he put in.

'And for the spectators.' The walls would probably soon be resounding to the screams of pain from the other dancers and the laughter of those watching her mow her way through the others in her set like a scythe through ripened wheat. At least, that was how her very last dance partner had spoken of her performance after he'd returned her to her seat, mopping his brow. It was funny how people assumed, because she couldn't see very well, that she couldn't hear, either. They seemed to think they could talk about her freely, and often very rudely, and get away with it.

And because it was easier to pretend she hadn't heard, than to confront them and make a scene, Lizzie had learned to keep her face frozen into what another local youth had described as being very like that adopted by a cow when chewing the cud.

And what a cud he was.

'Yes,' he said, turning and leading her on to the dance floor where she could see the dim outlines of other people forming a set. 'Let us give them something worth watching.'

Chapter Four

Harry's cravat felt too tight. And sweat was trickling down between his shoulder blades, giving him an almost uncontrollable urge to scratch at it. Or tear off his neck cloth.

It was pretty much the way he'd always felt before going into battle. The determination to go through with the grim task in spite of knowing that whatever strategy he followed, there were bound to be injuries. This time, to a young woman who would have no idea she was a deliberate target.

He gritted his teeth. He'd told Rawcliffe he'd do whatever it took. And once he'd learned how pivotal Miss Hutton was to the success of their scheme, he'd assured both him, and later Becconsall, that he was the best man for the job. Rawcliffe had assured him that this part of it would be simple, that Miss Hutton would be so grateful for any attention any eligible young man might give her, she would fall into his hands like a ripe plum. Which might be true, but he would wager that neither Lieutenant Nateby nor Captain Hambleton would be sweating like this if either of them had drawn the long straw. Or be feeling as though, at any minute, one of the assembled Bath gossips would point the finger and expose him as an impostor. Nor did it give him any comfort to reflect that the only one of the candidates Rawcliffe had summoned to that interview who would have been having a harder time, at this precise moment, would have been Lieutenant Thurnham. Because it would only have been due to his struggles to resist the lure of the card room.

Not one of the others would have been wrestling with their conscience. Not one of them would have had any qualms about laying siege to Miss Hutton's heart, or conquering it, and then, when she'd served her purpose, walking away from her without a backward glance.

He scowled across the ballroom at the few other couples milling about as he gave her arm a squeeze. His conscience with regard to Miss Hutton might be smarting a bit, but he was fully committed to seeing this mission through to the bitter end. Therefore he had to persuade Miss Hutton that he was a genuine suitor. A suitor so smitten that he would not be able to part from her when the time came for her to leave Bath. By then, hopefully, he would have wormed his way into her affections to the extent that she would extend an invitation to spend Christmas with her and her family in Lesser Peeving. From which vantage point he would be able to continue the investigations Archie had been conducting in that area. Investigations which had resulted in his death.

He swallowed as he glanced down at the crown of Lizzie's head, the droop of her shoulders. He'd felt sorry for her before even meeting her, because of the plan to deceive her into believing she'd captured his heart. But now he had met her...well, she was so utterly defenceless against him that when she had placed her trembling hand upon his sleeve, just now, revealing her dread at the prospect of having so many spectators mocking the way she danced, he experienced a bizarre sensation of wishing he could somehow protect her.

When he was the one she needed protecting from.

He ground his teeth. He'd always hated seeing anyone take advantage of those weaker than themselves. But he hadn't felt such a strong surge of indignation on anyone's behalf since the day he'd come across Tom Kellet cowering behind the buttress in the fives court. Back then, he'd been able to wade straight in and dispatch the beefy bullies who'd been taunting him. And assure the lad, who'd later gained the nickname of Archie, that he was no longer alone, that he, Harry, would always stand by him. Back then, his actions had given him a sense of self-worth he'd never known before. He'd discovered that he was not a 'good-fornothing' after all.

Right now, Miss Hutton looked as though she could do with having someone to stand by her, too. Even if it was the very man who was responsible for luring her out on to the dance floor where she was afraid she was about to make a spectacle of herself.

Which didn't surprise him actually, not when he recalled the way she'd knocked his cup of water from his hand at their first meeting. The way she'd very nearly sent her companion flying when executing the most awkward curtsy he'd ever seen, outside the theatre. It just went to confirm Lady Rawcliffe's description of her as an awkward giantess. He'd dismissed her evaluation, up 'til then, because Lady Rawcliffe was one of those tiny, dainty, fairy-like females who always got a crick in their necks when attempting to look him in the face. The kind who always made him afraid he'd accidentally crush them if he turned round too quickly without first taking note of exactly where they were standing. But now he saw that Miss Hutton herself believed all those things Lady Rawcliffe had said of her. To the extent that she was discernibly trembling at the prospect of stepping out on to the dance floor, when other females would have been looking on it with anticipation.

Just as he was sweating with his own nerves. Which gave him an uncanny sense of kinship with her. He knew what it felt like to be robbed of the kind of pleasure most people took for granted, right enough. It had happened first in his childhood, when his family had fallen apart. And then when he'd been taken out of school just as he'd begun to find his feet. And again when the French had taken him prisoner. Each time he'd hated that feeling of being weak and helpless in the face of cruel fate and no longer able to partake in the activities others enjoyed almost by right.

She darted him a glance that was half-trepidation, half-despair as they took their places in the set. He heard the murmurs going through the assembled crowd of onlookers. Saw people nudging each other and looking in their direction. And probably speculating on the likely outcome of having two giants attempting to weave in and out of the band of pygmies who formed the rest of their set.

He wanted to tell her she wasn't going to have to face it alone. That he would protect her from the stares, the gossip, the sniggers. But how could he? It was his fault she was going to have to endure it all.

But one thing he could do. He could show her that though they were not cut from the same cloth as most people, that didn't mean they had no right to enjoy themselves. For the next half-hour he would do his level best to provide Miss Hutton with the fun that seemed so sadly lacking in her life, from what he'd both learned and observed of her so far.

'You know,' he remarked casually, 'when at sea, it is a general principle that the smaller, nippier craft treat the larger, ocean-going vessels with respect.'

'Respect?' She cast a doubtful look round the others who'd come on to the dance floor before them and who could now not retreat without looking craven.

'Yes. If they don't want to get broadsided, then they take jolly good care to keep out of the way.'

'That is a nautical principle, is it?'

'Yes. An eminently sensible one. And one which ought to hold true on the dance floor.'

'Are you trying to say that if you step on my toes, it will be my own fault?'

Before he could deny he'd meant anything so unchivalrous, the musicians were striking up the opening chords and everyone was curtsying or bowing to the other members of the set.

'No,' he just had time to say, 'I was referring to the others.'

And then they were off.

And he soon discovered that Miss Hutton was nowhere near as bad at dancing as she'd led him to believe. She did appear a bit reserved at first, a little awkward about the way she moved her limbs, but to make up for it, she had a very good ear for music. She stepped out firmly on the beat, never missing a step. Which meant he didn't have to worry that she might not be in the place he expected her to be at any given moment. True, her steps were a bit longer than those of the other ladies in the set, and most of the men, too, but they matched *his*. What was more, when he took her hand in the turns, she returned his grip with such strength that he soon lost his usual dread that he might accidentally snap one of her fingers. He could also swing her round without worrying about the risk of whirling her right off her feet and out through one of the windows.

After a while, he noticed that she was starting to look much less nervous. And by the time it was their turn to gallop down the inside of the set, hand in hand, she was actually smiling.

'You were right,' she said as they waited for the next couple in the set to gallop down the centre. 'About the smaller craft giving the larger ones a wide berth.'

'And they have ample space to do so tonight, since this is the only set in a room designed to hold several, by the looks of it.'

'Yes, not many people come to Bath for anything other than to play cards and drink the waters, these days. Oh, and gossip. And reminisce about how much more fun it used to be when they were younger.'

They stepped smartly sideways as the next couple in line reached the head of the set and began their skip down the middle of the room.

'It must be very dull for you,' he observed.

She shrugged. Darted him a shy glance. 'Not tonight.'

And then she bit her lower lip, her face turning red.

His stomach contracted. Though he ought to be pleased at having made such an impression on her in such short order, the truth was he'd forgotten all about Rawcliffe's scheme, for a while there. He might have asked her to dance in order to further that scheme, but he'd wanted her to enjoy herself because... Well, he'd just wanted her to enjoy herself, that was all.

Now, her blushing response to him reminded him how very vulnerable she was, all over again. The perfect mark for Rawcliffe's scheme.

He ground his teeth. If there was any other way...

But, according to both Rawcliffe and Becconsall, when they'd filled him in on the mission, there wasn't. The village where the man lived, who they suspected of being responsible for Archie's murder, was impregnable from a full-frontal attack, tucked into an inlet that was backed by sheer cliffs and approachable from the sea only by means of a narrow, rock-strewn channel. They'd never be able to get in openly, and search for the evidence they needed to bring him to justice. Visitors to the surrounding area were watched, too. From what Rawcliffe had been able to discover in the short time he'd stayed at Peacombe, a nearby seaside resort, that had been Archie's mistake. He'd been too open about what had led him to go to that area. Had spoken to someone who had reported back to someone else, who'd promptly had him killed.

Stealth was the answer. Going in under cover of a lot of smoke. And Miss Hutton was the means of providing it.

'You may think that these men I was interviewing,' Rawcliffe had told him, when the others had left the supposedly secret meeting that night, 'were a set of rogues, but one thing you cannot deny is their appeal to the gentler sex.' Harry had only had to reflect for a moment or two before agreeing. Especially since he knew a little about each man's exploits in that area. 'Moreover,' Rawcliffe had continued dispassionately, 'from what Clare has told me, Miss Hutton will jump at the chance for a match that will provide the means to escape her grandfather's tyranny. Giving her fiancé the perfect opportunity to haunt the place for as long as it takes to find the proof we need to bring Clement Cottam to justice.'

'Right-hand star,' shouted the dance caller, jerking him out of his reverie.

Miss Hutton grasped his hand firmly. But the

other lady in their foursome kept her own hand timidly under her own partner's so that the star never fully meshed. Which meant that when they began to circle, he and Miss Hutton, whose steps matched perfectly, were in danger of overtaking the other two. When Miss Hutton made as if she was going to slow down, he gripped her hand tighter and shook his head, reminding her that it was for the others to keep up. And, after one brief moment when he saw panic in the other lady's eyes, she did indeed speed up, obliging her partner to do the same. In short order, their little legs were positively twinkling as they put on a spurt of speed that left them red-faced and panting by the time the figure ended.

Luckily for all concerned, the orchestra brought the performance to an end soon after. Everyone in the set bowed to everyone else and tottered away from the floor. Leaving Miss Hutton and he standing there alone, as if in possession of the field.

Oh, to the devil with his conscience! And Rawcliffe's schemes. He seized Miss Hutton's hands.

'I say,' he panted. 'Would you like to do that again?'

She blinked. 'You cannot mean that.'

'I jolly well can. I don't think I have ever enjoyed a dance more.'

She peered up at him, as though perplexed.

'But we disrupted the others. We didn't…keep time.'

'We kept perfect time. We just kept a bit more of it than the others, that was all.'

She tipped her head to one side, as though assessing his viewpoint. 'That's as may be,' she then said, pensively. 'But I don't think anyone else will return to the dance floor while we remain on it.'

He glanced round the other occupants of the ballroom, who were, indeed, looking a bit reluctant to return to the floor while they still stood there. 'Lightweights,' he said scornfully. 'It wasn't as if I trod upon anyone's toes. Nor did I knock anyone over.'

'Have you ever done so? Knocked anyone over, I mean? I know about the toe-crushing.'

'Not actually.'

'I have,' she said dolefully.

'How did you manage that?'

'Swung him round with a bit too much enthusiasm.'

He couldn't help grinning at the image she conjured up for him. 'You can swing me round with as much enthusiasm as you like,' he assured her. 'And you will never manage to knock me off my feet.'

She eyed him in an assessing manner.

'Come on,' he urged her, 'let's dance again. And this time, no holds barred. Let's just enjoy ourselves, for once, without worrying about what damage we might do.' Or what the future might bring. 'And then I shall escort you in for tea.'

'You…you…' She gazed at him as though he was some kind of marvel. 'You are going to set tongues wagging,' she finished, though he was pretty sure that was not what she'd been going to say.

'From what I can gather, they wag anyway,' he said scornfully. And then noted the little furrow between her brows. 'Does it bother you?'

She lifted her chin. 'Not tonight. Besides, I won't hear it, will I, if I am on the dance floor, or supping tea with you.'

But she would have to face it the next day. And the one after that.

Poor Miss Hutton.

Not that he was going to permit sympathy for her to stop him from his pursuit. And conquest.

Too much depended on it.

Chapter Five

Lizzie had never woken up, while in Bath, with a sense of anticipation. And she'd always regarded their daily attendance at the Pump Room as just a part of the grindingly dull routine she had to weather. But this morning, her heart was beating double time as she helped Grandfather out of his sedan chair.

Would he be there today? Captain Bretherton? He'd come yesterday, to drink the waters. Although she couldn't think why. He was the strongest man she'd ever met. Which was probably why she'd enjoyed dancing with him so much. For the first time, she hadn't felt oversized and gangly, and unfeminine. Not at all. She'd felt…

Well, if he was here today, she could ask him what on earth he was doing, drinking the foul waters, when he was so…

She felt a blush coming on and ruthlessly turned her thoughts in another direction. The last thing she wanted was for anyone to notice how susceptible she was to Captain Bretherton and start quizzing her about him.

And if he was here, she was going to speak to him in a sensible fashion. Not stammer and blush, and sigh. Absolutely not. She'd start, she'd decided earlier—after ransacking her wardrobe for a gown she would actually like him to see her wearing, before realising she didn't possess one—by asking him why his doctor had sent him to Bath to drink the waters. For there was nothing most invalids enjoyed more than going into great detail about their ailments. While he was describing a set of symptoms that would probably make her shudder, she wouldn't have to come up with anything witty or interesting by way of response. She wouldn't have to do anything but listen. And by the time he'd recounted the history of whatever ailment he had, he probably wouldn't appear so...god-like. Which would be a good thing, because it was blasphemous to think in those terms about a mere mortal.

But how else to account for the fact that she became a different person whenever he drew near? A wittier, more graceful version of herself. Who could actually dance? It was nothing short of miraculous.

Ouch!

She winced at the blow from Grandfather's walking stick.

'That's the third time I've asked you! What's got into you, girl?'

'Nothing, Grandfather,' she replied penitently. 'I was wool-gathering. I do beg your pardon. I—'

'Never mind excuses. Snap out of it. And go and fetch me my cup of water. It's what I bring you for, after all. Go on. At the double!'

'Yes, Grandfather.' Lizzie made her way across the crowded Pump Room to join the queue at the fountain. If he was here, he would have to come and find her. It wasn't the done thing for a lady to seek out a gentleman. Even if she could pick him out from the crowd, which she couldn't.

She fingered her reticule, wishing she had the courage to make use of the one item that would have put her on an even footing with all the other people here. But she hadn't.

She sighed.

He wouldn't come to look for her. Even though he'd said he'd enjoyed their time together last night, she mustn't pin her hopes on him still being in the same frame of mind today. Men with god-like attributes such as he possessed surely did not waste more than one evening upon any one female. Why, he might not even still be in Bath. He—

'Good morning, Miss Hutton.'

He was here! And bowing to her. And speaking to her. At least, he'd said good morning. Which meant— Oh! She ought to make some kind of reply.

'Ah. Oh. Um.' Yes. Very witty. That would really impress him. A wave of embarrassment flooded her, making her cheeks flame.

'It's deuced hot in here, isn't it?' he said. Oh, how kind of him to come up with a valid reason for her to blush!

'Don't know why they need to have a fire blazing,' he said, 'with all the crowds jostling to get in.'

'Grandfather always takes a seat as near to the fire as he can, while I go to fetch his water,' she managed to say, though her tongue felt a bit too big for her mouth.

'Rheumaticky, is he?'

Which reminded her, she had meant to quiz him about his own ailments. With the twin aim of getting him to do most of the talking, while toppling him from his pedestal.

'It's his broken bones. He had a few injuries during his years of active service. And he claims draughts set them off. Is that why you are here? Were you injured? I mean, that is, you are in the navy, are you not?'

'I did have my fair share of injuries,' he replied, as the queue shuffled forward. And fell silent.

'And is that why you have come to drink the waters?'

The queue shuffled forward again before he had made any reply. Which made her fear he had picked up some nasty disease which he couldn't mention in female company.

Well! That would make her think less well of him. Sailors were notorious for seeking…comfort…in whichever port they happened to be. She ought not to know about it, but—

'It is a bit complicated,' he finally said. 'I had yellow jack when I was in the tropics, which left me… not in prime twig, shall we say,' he finished saying on a huff of a laugh. 'And then I was taken prisoner by the French.' He plucked at the front of his jacket, making her aware that it hung a bit loose on his big frame. 'I lost so much weight while enjoying their hospitality that when I finally came back to England my friends said I resembled a scarecrow.'

They reached the head of the queue. The footman handed them each a cup. They stepped aside.

'I say, Miss Hutton, I don't suppose you would care to knock this out of my hand again this morning?'

'It won't do you any good if you don't drink it.'

'I don't think it will do me any good if I do,' he said glumly. 'To be honest, I think I will gain more benefit from sticking to my daily swim in the stuff.'

He swam? Oh, how she wished that Grandfather would grant her permission to do the same. But she wasn't ill. And so there was no need for him to waste his blunt on any such treatment for her.

And then a horrid thought assailed her. It sounded as though he was explaining why she would not be seeing him again.

'Are you telling me you will not be attending the Pump Room again?'

'What? No. It is just...' He bent his head, as though studying the cup he held in his hand. Then, with one swift movement, he raised it to his mouth and tossed back the entire contents in one go.

Then shuddered. 'To think people drink this willingly.' He shook his head.

'But...you just did.'

'No. *That...*' he grimaced '...was my punishment.'

'For what?'

He turned away from her for a moment, presumably to dispose of his cup. 'My sins,' he said, turning back to her, 'are too numerous to mention. Let us instead talk of you.'

'Me?' Her voice came out in a squeak.

'Yes. I want to know everything,' he said in a determined voice, 'there is to know about you.'

'Well that won't take very long. I am really very boring.'

'Not to me, you aren't. Have you any idea what it was like, to dance with a partner who...matched? Most women make me feel big and lumbering and awkward. But not you.'

'Oh.' She felt another blush coming on. And, before she could stop her unruly tongue, she heard herself admitting, 'It was the same for me, too. That is, most men make me feel big and lumbering and awkward.'

'Can you wonder, then, that I want to get to know you better?'

'I... I...'

Her feet, by this time, had carried her back to her grandfather without her even taking note of where she was going. And since he was by her side, he'd fetched up there, too.

'Who's this? Eh?' Grandfather was glaring up at them from under lowered brows.

'Captain Bretherton,' said Captain Bretherton, bowing.

'And just what do you think you're doing with my granddaughter? Eh? Young jackanapes.'

'I was thanking her for taking pity on me last night and dancing with me.'

'Taking pity on *you*? That's a likely story.'

She wasn't sure if she imagined it, but Captain Bretherton seemed to stiffen. His voice was certainly a bit cool when he said, 'Miss Hutton, now that I have restored you to your grandfather, I shall bid you good day.'

Her spirits plunged as he disappeared into the throng. That was probably the last she'd see of him. He might say he wanted to get to know her better, but no man, at least none with any pride, would stand for being addressed as a jackanapes.

'Didn't take long to get him to take to his heels, did it?' Grandfather was glaring in the direction of Captain Bretherton's retreat. 'Though I warned you about fellows of his stamp, yesterday. What do you mean by dancing with him, eh?'

'Well, he asked. And I didn't have any reason to refuse…'

'That's the trouble with places like this. Full of strangers. Anybody can pass themselves off as marquesses or dukes…'

She took a breath to object. Grandfather's eyebrows lowered even further. 'Or call themselves captains,' he persisted. 'Ten to one he never got nearer a regiment than walking past a parade in Hyde Park.'

'Well, no, but then he is in the navy. He…'

'Playing on your susceptibilities is he, because of Sam?'

Lizzie flinched. Firstly, the chances Captain Bretherton knew she'd even had a brother, let alone one who served in the navy, were so remote as to be laughable. And secondly, why would he play on her susceptibilities?

'Just let him know you don't have a dowry, next time he comes sniffing round. Then we'll see what his motives really are.' He rapped on the floor with his cane. Though he might as well have struck her with it again.

'Very well, Grandfather,' she said, with as much meekness in her voice as she could muster. 'Next time I see him, the first thing I shall do is tell him I am penniless.'

She hadn't thought it was possible for his eyebrows to get any lower, but they did. And he thrust out his jaw, as though he was trying to decide whether she was being sincere. But, after a moment or two, he leaned back in his chair, with a 'hmmph', and then turned his shoulder to carry on the conversation in which he'd been engaged before.

Lizzie took up her station behind his chair, her chin up, her gaze fixed straight ahead. She wasn't trembling, although the entire episode would have humiliated any girl who hadn't grown inured to such scenes over the years. She told herself that Grandfather probably meant well. That he was trying to protect her, in his own, inimitable fashion. That Bath *was* the kind of place that did attract men on the lookout for gullible heiresses, or so Lady Buntingford had told her. And that it didn't matter what they looked like. A practised seducer would make his intended victim feel as though there was something special about her. Something that only he, out of the whole world, could appreciate. Make her believe he truly loved her. So that he could get his hands on her money.

So, the sooner she informed Captain Bretherton that she had none, the sooner she would know whether his interest in her was genuine.

Or not.

Chapter Six

He strode from the Pump Room, his fists clenched. No wonder Lady Rawcliffe had said Miss Hutton would jump at the chance to escape her grandfather, if that was an example of the way he treated her. The old man should have taken an interest in the stranger who'd escorted her back to his side, not driven him away. After insulting her, in front of all the other Bath quizzes, by insinuating that no man could possibly have asked her to dance for any reason except from pity.

He'd had to walk away before retaliating in kind. Which wouldn't do his prospects any good. You couldn't get into a stand-up row with a man, then ask for permission to court his granddaughter. Or a sit-down row, anyway, since the old man hadn't stirred from his chair.

He whipped off his hat and ran his fingers through

his hair. Since today was Tuesday, he wasn't going to be able to see Miss Hutton tonight and attempt to offer her any comfort. Because it would be cards in the Assembly Rooms. Still, since he'd already told her his aversion for games of chance, she wouldn't expect to see him. She wouldn't think her grandfather had scared him off.

Would she?

It felt as if a month went past, rather than just a day and a half, before he was entering the Assembly Rooms again. For on his return from his daily swim, he'd found a muscular young man waiting for him outside the door of his hotel room, bearing a message from Rawcliffe and Becconsall. They'd decided he needed a bodyguard, apparently, and had sent Dawkins to perform that duty, under cover of being his valet. It had taken some time for them to discuss strategy. By the time they'd reached an understanding it had been too late to attend the Pump Room. So he was chafing at the bit by the time he entered the room where he hoped he might find her attending the Wednesday night concert.

And it wasn't all to do with furthering his quest to find Archie's killer, either. Even if he never got any further with Miss Hutton, he simply had to convince her that he hadn't danced with her out of *pity*. Although he did feel a bit sorry for her, in some respects. She really needed someone to give her a bit of confidence, so that she could blossom into the kind of woman any man would be proud to call his wife.

Any man but him, that was. He might have agreed to pose as an eligible bachelor, but he didn't really have anything to offer any woman. He'd returned from France a hollow shell of the man he'd once been. And even *that* man hadn't been in any position to take a wife. He had to live on his pay. Which meant that not only would his wife have to struggle just to get by, but she'd be doing it alone, because he'd be away at sea.

He scanned the room for a glimpse of her. She should be easy enough to spot. She stood head and shoulders above every other female, and most men, in any room. And her silvery hair was very distinctive, too. He'd certainly had no trouble picking her out from the crowds in the Pump Room, that first time.

A smile tugged at his lips as he recalled the moment she'd backed into him, with such force she'd knocked the cup of water from his hand. And the sudden, surprising flare of attraction that contact

with her body had provoked. Surprising, because
he hadn't felt any such stirrings since the day he'd
fallen into the hands of the French.

But not unwelcome. For one thing it was proof
that he was recovering, physically at least. For another, it meant that in one respect he would not be
deceiving Miss Hutton at all. He was genuinely
attracted to her.

Ah, there she was. His heart lifted. And not just at
what she might represent in terms of vengeance for
Archie. She looked stunning with the candlelight
gleaming on her silvery hair. He couldn't take his
eyes off her. Indeed, it wasn't until he was within
a few feet of her that he noticed the older woman
standing with her. The same one who'd been with
her the night he'd asked her to dance.

He bowed to them both, wondering how he was
going to be able to detach her from her chaperon.
'Miss Hutton, it is a pleasure to find you here tonight.' And it was. He didn't have to feign delight.
He was delighted to see her again.

Though she didn't appear to feel the same. On
the contrary, she was looking at him as though he
was an unexploded shell that had landed at her
feet. Until the lady at her side nudged at her with
her bony elbow.

'Oh. Yes,' said Miss Hutton with one of her frequent blushes. 'Lady Mainwaring, this is… Well, he says his name is Captain Bretherton.'

'My name *is* Captain Bretherton.' Or at least, that was part of it. He never used the part of his title that referred to his earldom, since the title had never been of any use to him whatever. What use was insisting on being addressed correctly when the title denoted nothing but shame? When it was hollow? Since his father, the previous earl, had left things in such a shambles that his trustees had not even had the money to keep him in school.

'Lady Mainwaring, charmed to make your acquaintance,' he said, a touch untruthfully, since he heartily wished she'd take herself off so he could have Miss Hutton to himself.

'Well, it's equally charming to meet you, too,' simpered Lady Mainwaring. 'But you will have to excuse me. I see somebody just over there to whom I simply must speak.' And just like that, his view of her capsized. Instead of being pleased he'd dispensed with her so easily, he was indignant that she'd abandon her charge with such alacrity. Leaving her at the mercy of a man she didn't know. He could be a cold-hearted seducer for all Lady Mainwaring knew.

In fact, his conscience muttered, he wasn't that much better.

'Miss Hutton,' he said. And then foundered. He gritted his teeth. Captain Hambleton wouldn't have been at a loss right now. Even if he had been three sheets to the wind. And as for Lieutenant Nateby...

'I think I had better inform you,' said Miss Hutton, flinging up her chin, 'that I have not a penny to my name.'

That was her grandfather's doing, he supposed. 'Your financial status,' he said with a touch of indignation, 'has no bearing on my interest in you.' Perversely, the moment the wariness started to fade from her eyes, guilt started twisting at his vitals. He might not have any intention of robbing her, but he did have an ulterior motive for pursuing her. And her grandfather must have detected that something was not completely genuine about his interest.

For some time there had been a discordant noise forming a background to the general hubbub, but now the strains of a recognisable tune began to dominate.

'Would you care to sit and listen to the music?' he asked her, grasping at the opportunity to turn their conversation away from the murky subject of his motives. 'Or would you prefer to take a turn about the room?'

Miss Hutton shifted from one foot to the other, her eyes troubled. He could almost see her slipping from his grasp.

'Please, Miss Hutton,' he said, taking a step nearer, obliging her to raise her head a fraction to look him in the eye. 'Please believe that I am no fortune hunter.' He could swear his complete innocence of that crime, even if he was guilty of others in relation to her. 'I told you that you and I match, did I not? Like...' He searched desperately for inspiration. And came up with, 'Atlas and Phoebe. Do you know anything of Greek legend?'

'A little,' she said, warily.

'They were Titans,' he explained. 'Titans all governed heavenly bodies. In the case of Atlas and Phoebe, it was the moon. And with your silvery hair, I just thought...'

She tilted her head to one side. 'What does Atlas have to do with anything?'

'Oh,' he said, taking her elbow and scanning the seating area for a couple of vacant chairs, since, as he'd got her engaged in conversation, he might as well take steps to ensure she couldn't escape with any ease. 'Atlas is a nickname some school friends gave me. On account of me being so much bigger than the rest of them.'

Her eyes ranged over his frame. But then a little pucker appeared between her brows. 'Why not Hercules?'

'Well,' he said, steering her in the direction of the back row of chairs, 'we were only schoolboys, after all. And they seemed to think I was trying to take the weight of the world on my shoulders. On account of me being averse to seeing bigger boys bullying the smaller, weaker ones.'

'Oh,' she said again, only this time her expression definitely softened. He'd finally hooked her interest. Now all he had to do was reel her in.

'And then it stuck, you see, after I went into the navy, since Atlas had a whole ocean named after him.'

'The Atlantic!'

'That's it. Excuse me,' he said to a lady occupying the end chair of the row in which he wished to sit. 'Are those seats taken?' He indicated the ones in the rest of the row. She frowned. Jerked her eyes to the two rows in front of her which were completely empty.

He smiled at her. 'It would be most remiss of me

to sit in front of you, since my partner and I would no doubt block your view of the orchestra.'

She eyed their combined height, and bulk, speculatively, then, with a waspish expression, got to her feet and stalked away. Leaving the entire back row free for him and Phoebe.

That was, Miss Hutton.

'She may not have been all that interested in seeing the orchestra,' Miss Hutton pointed out, as he ushered her into a chair. 'Not many people do pay all that much attention to them, after all. She was probably just resting her feet for a moment.'

'Well, now she can rest them elsewhere,' he said, settling himself beside her. 'Do you have a programme upon you?' He glanced down at her lap, on which she'd placed her large and rather lumpy-looking reticule. She shook her head as she clutched at it. And then she averted her head and gazed in the general direction of the orchestra, a tide of pink creeping up her cheeks.

And damn it if he had any idea what to say to her, now he had her all to himself. With nobody to overhear.

Rawcliffe had been right. He wasn't cut out for this type of work. He was a man of action, not words. Were he standing on the deck of a ship, preparing to go into battle, he'd know what to do. His mind would be assessing the enemy's capabilities, with one eye to the wind and the tide. Weighing up the strengths and weaknesses of his men, his supplies.

But here, on a spindly chair, in a stuffy room, with an orchestra plunking out a backdrop to the conversations of the other, mostly elderly concertgoers, he was at a bit of a loss.

And what did that say about him? That he was better at orchestrating acts of violence, in order to smash his enemies to a pulp, as part of man's endless quest for conquest, that was what.

And once this interlude with Miss Hutton was over, once he'd brought Archie's killers to justice, that was the world he'd have to go back to. A world in which he'd had to treat men like so much cannon fodder, rather than as human beings with any intrinsic worth. He was a warrior, not a lover. A man of action, not of sentiment.

So, rather than trying to find words, he reached for Miss Hutton's hand, where it lay tangled with the strings of her reticule. And let that action speak for him.

She blushed, but did not pull it away. On the contrary, as the music swelled and throbbed, she tucked it under the folds of her skirts. Taking his hand with it.

And his own heart swelled and throbbed along with the violins as they sat, secretly holding hands.

The tide was turning in his favour.

Chapter Seven

Whatever could have put that grim expression on his face? Sitting this close, she could see him much better than when they were standing up and they had to preserve a decorous distance from one another. She could see the muscles clenching in his jaw, the grim line flattening his mouth and even the bleakness in his eyes. And just as at the first time they'd met, she wished she could do something about it.

When he reached for her hand, therefore, it felt like the most natural thing in the world to grasp it and offer him what small comfort she could. Even though it was not at all the thing.

Though what did it matter, as long as nobody found out?

Her heart tripped over itself as she not only formed such a rebellious thought, but also took action to ensure that it bore fruit. Concealing their linked hands took but a second, as she rearranged the folds of her unfashionably voluminous skirts.

His own breath hitched. Though he made no sign that anyone else could detect, she was sure he gave her hand a little squeeze.

Golly, but she'd never felt so wicked in her life! Was this really stumbling, stammering Lizzie Hutton? Sitting holding hands with a *man*? Practically in full sight of a room full of people?

If she'd been the kind of girl who giggled, she'd be giggling right now. Never had she felt so…*giddy.* Or so in tune with a piece of music. Whenever the violins soared, so did her heart, as she revelled in the feel of his hand clasping hers, his response when she'd told him she wasn't an heiress.

When the instruments groaned and wept, she found herself biting her lower lip and wondering when it was all going to end. And if people would carry the tale back to Grandfather about the way they were sitting so close together. If such talk would send him into retreat. After all, he surely wouldn't want his name linked too closely with a girl he'd only known a matter of days.

The musicians did not finish their piece until Lizzie was so wrung out she could understand why some people actually wept during certain performances. And though it was not because of their skill, but because of the man next to whom she was sitting, she knew she ought to join in the applause that was breaking out, politely, all round the room. Only, that would mean she'd have to let go of his hand.

While she was still hesitating, he gave her hand one last squeeze and then released it. Which meant she *had* to let go. She couldn't very well keep clinging to his hand, not once he'd started clapping, could she? Even though it felt as though his action had cast her adrift.

She forced her eyes to look in the direction of the musicians and lifted her own hands to clap, which she did with considerably more energy than anyone else. Hopefully, then people would think she'd been moved by the power of the music, if they noticed she was upset. Especially since she had no reason to be sad. She'd never been completely alone in the world. She'd always had some member of family to take her in. It was ridiculous to feel as though she'd never been more alone, in all her life, when she was sitting in a room full of people.

The applause soon died away. Long before she'd pulled herself together. So when Captain Bretherton turned to her and asked if she'd like to go to the tea room and take supper, she had to bite her tongue.

Supper? How could he sit there talking about tea, and supper, in that reasonable, casual tone, as though holding hands with her had meant nothing?

Though perhaps it had meant nothing. Perhaps he was the kind of man who held hands with females, clandestinely, all the time. What did she know of him, really? What kind of man he was?

And he *was* a man, not a demi-god, even if some people did call him Atlas.

'I had better go and see if Grandfather wants anything first,' she said. Even though what she wanted was to spend the rest of the evening with him. Holding hands again. Or even more…

She looked at his mouth. What would it feel like to kiss him? To have him kiss her?

The longing that tore at her insides was so fierce she could see herself flinging herself at him, right there in the concert room, and scandalising the rest of the concert-goers. Panicked, and confused by the strength of her reactions to a man who was virtually a stranger, she leapt to her feet, with the result that the chair upon which she'd been sitting overturned with a crash. Everyone turned to stare, of course. And then a wave of laughter rippled round the room. Closely followed by a chorus of comments. She couldn't hear the actual words, but she knew the kinds of things they'd all be saying.

That Miss Hutton. Always so clumsy. So awkward. I wonder why that handsome officer is paying her so much attention?

The handsome officer in question bent forward to right her chair at the exact moment she did the same. With the result that they clashed heads. To the increased amusement of everyone else in the room.

'Please, Miss Hutton, allow me,' he said, placing one hand on her arm and pushing her firmly, but gently, aside.

'I… I…' She raised both hands to her cheeks, which were flaming hot. 'Th-thank you, but I really do need to return to my grandfather.' With that, she turned and fled.

He'd pushed her too far, too fast, holding hands like that. He hadn't thought she'd minded. He hadn't been holding on to her all that hard. She could have pulled her hand free at any time. But she hadn't.

Perhaps it had only hit her, what she'd done, when

the music had finished. It had been a rather powerful piece, one that tugged at the emotions. Perhaps she'd been carried away with it and not realised how—what was it girls said of such behaviour?—*fast* she'd been, until it came to an end?

Damn, but he hoped he hadn't ruined everything.

He couldn't pursue her into the card room. The old Colonel would simply send him packing, again.

He'd have to hope he could catch her at the Pump Room again. And reassure her that his intentions were honourable.

Only, it felt a bit too soon to start speaking of marriage. She was bound to become suspicious of him, if he appeared to have come to such a momentous decision after knowing her only a few days.

He had to be more patient with her. Allow her to get used to him. Reassure her that nothing she did was going to put him off her. Make her believe that everything she did fascinated him.

Which wouldn't require any acting at all, come to think of it. She was such an intriguing bundle of contradictions. So bold one moment, in the way she'd hidden their clasped hands. Then so timid, darting away from him like a startled fawn.

He didn't think he'd ever grow tired of her. She would be endlessly fascinating. Like the sea. Even her eyes, now he came to think of it, put him in mind of the colour of certain parts of the Mediterranean. A colour you never saw anywhere else. Or at least he hadn't thought so.

An elderly couple strolled past, amused expressions on their faces. Which brought him up short. Made him realise he'd been standing stock still, in the middle of the room, gazing after Miss Hutton like a...

He plunged his fingers through his hair and made a beeline for the exit. Tomorrow. He'd seek her out at the Pump Room and continue his counterfeit courtship of her tomorrow.

But the next day, neither Miss Hutton nor her grandfather put in an appearance at the Pump Room.

Nor did they show up at the fancy ball that night.

He paced the floor of his room, later, wondering how to proceed. It was just possible, he supposed, that her grandfather had taken a turn for the worse and couldn't stir out of doors. He might have some genuine illness for which he was seeking treatment in Bath, rather than merely coming here to gossip with his cronies.

He'd simply have to wait and see if the old fellow recovered. He wasn't yet on familiar enough terms with Miss Hutton to just call upon her and enquire after her grandfather's health. Not taking into account the way Colonel Hutton had taken an instant and irrational dislike to him.

'Shall I snoop about a bit, sir,' Dawkins asked on the second morning he returned from the Pump Room without seeing her, 'and see what I can find out? After all, that's why Their Lordships sent me down here. To be an extra pair of eyes.'

'No.' The very idea of letting someone spy on Miss Hutton revolted him. 'I will ask some of her acquaintance, openly, what they know of her whereabouts.'

'Ah, yes, playing the role of smitten suitor. Very clever.'

No, it wasn't *clever*. It was just…the obvious course to take.

The next day, when he attended the Pump Room and joined the queue to purchase a cup of the disgusting water that was supposed to be helping restore him to health, he spotted Lady Mainwaring. She would be the perfect person to approach, since he'd met her first in Miss Hutton's company. If any-

one knew what was going on in the Hutton house-
hold, it was likely to be her.

'Good morning, my lady,' he said, sweeping her
a bow.

'Good morning Captain,' she replied, according
him a nod, rather than a curtsy.

'I was wondering if you knew how Colonel Hutton is faring?'

'*Colonel* Hutton?' She gave an arch smile. 'I
would have thought your interest was in his granddaughter.'

'Yes. Well…but…it's just I haven't seen either of
them for a day or two. So I assumed he had taken
a turn for the worse.'

She pursed her lips. 'His temper certainly has.
According to Mrs Hutchens, who lives just across
the way from his lodgings, he was in a rare taking. Ordered his bags packed and his horses put to.'

'Horses?'

'Yes. He's gone home. Cancelled the lease on
his lodgings and asked for his money back. Quite
the commotion, there was, with the leasing agent,
over that, since the agent refused to reimburse him
a single penny.'

He wondered how on earth the woman knew

such things. Thought it best not to ask. But to just be grateful she did.

'Home, to Dorset?'

Lady Mainwaring's eyebrows shot up. 'Yes. My goodness, it didn't take you long to discover where Miss Hutton hales from, did it?'

Well, no, but then he'd known it before he'd even set foot in Bath. Not that he was fool enough to correct Lady Mainwaring's assumption.

'Did your friend happen to find out why they left?'

She shook her head. 'You would think, with that parade-ground voice of his, that she would have been able to make out just the gist of it, wouldn't you? But even the cook he hired with the house hadn't been able to discover why they all left so suddenly. But then by the time she came into work on Thursday morning, the agent was there and the battle in full swing.'

Thursday morning. She'd left Bath the very day after the concert.

Was it a coincidence? Or could it be a result of his own behaviour? Could someone have seen him holding hands with her and told her grandfather?

That was the trouble with making a daring move.

The rewards could be great, but sometimes the risks meant the end result could be catastrophic.

Though, in this case, he could see a way to come about. He'd simply adapt the plans Rawcliffe and Becconsall had drawn up. They'd instructed him to cajole Miss Hutton into inviting him to spend Christmas with her at Lesser Peeving. Instead, he would move his pursuit of Miss Hutton to the next level by going down to Peacombe, a little seaside town which boasted a hotel or two. And from where he could beat a path to her door.

Chapter Eight

'Good afternoon, sir, and welcome to the Three Tuns,' said an oily-looking man who put Harry in mind of an exceptionally crooked tavern keeper he'd had the misfortune to have dealings with in Naples. All smiles for paying customers, all double-dealing behind the scenes. 'How may I help you?'

'I want a room for myself and my manservant.'

'A room?' The landlord looked confused.

'This *is* an hotel, is it not?'

'Yes, of course it is, I just…' The landlord replaced the confusion with an ingratiating smile. 'We do not usually get many visitors so late in the year.'

'Which means, I hope, that I can have my pick of rooms.'

The landlord ran an appraising eye over Harry, from the gold braid on his hat, to his battered and

scuffed boots, judging the cost and age of everything he saw. Harry pretended not to notice.

'Since I suffer from,' Harry said, 'that is, since I
may have need of my manservant during the night,
I will want a large room, in which you can place a
truckle bed, or one with a dressing room in which
one can be placed.' Though Harry didn't think
whoever was responsible for Archie's death was
likely to try sneaking into his room and stabbing
him while he lay sleeping, Dawkins had insisted
they take no chances.

'May I ask how long you are considering staying with us?'

'A week to begin with. After that, it depends
upon how my...business in the area progresses. I
take it you require payment in advance? For the
first week, that is.'

Harry didn't wait for the landlord to answer, he
just pulled out the roll of folding money Rawcliffe
had handed him 'for expenses' before leaving London, peeled off one note and handed it over.

The landlord didn't appear to even glance at it
before palming it and making it disappear somewhere within the folds of his own coat.

'I believe you would be most comfortable in our
first-floor suite,' he said. 'It has a sea view, which

some former occupants…' he leaned in as though sharing a titbit of gossip '…a marquess and his new bride, remarked upon most favourably.'

Just as he'd thought. The man was a rogue. The marquess and bride to whom he'd referred had to be Lord and Lady Rawcliffe, who *had* come to Peacombe earlier that year. There couldn't be any other marquess eccentric enough to have attempted to take his bride to such an unfashionable destination for her bride trip. But when Rawcliffe had stayed down here, he'd rented an entire lane full of cottages to house himself and his retinue, according to Becconsall, who'd found it highly amusing. Nevertheless, he could not let on that he knew. He wasn't supposed to have any connection to Rawcliffe at all, let alone be so close to him that he knew where he'd spent his honeymoon. So he took the man up on the other part of his statement.

'I have seen quite enough of the sea during my career to date,' he said curtly, hoping the landlord would draw the correct conclusion about his background. Since he was not going to be a guest of the Colonel and Miss Hutton, he and Dawkins had come up with a revised plan to explain his presence in Peacombe. They'd then written to Rawcliffe to inform him that Harry would drop a steady stream of crumbs of information, as though unwittingly, in order to control the gossip that his arrival in the small seaside town would engender.

So far, he thought he'd done a fair job of announcing that he'd been in the navy and had more money than sense.

'Very good, sir. My name is Mr Jeavons,' said the landlord with a smug bow. 'It will not take long to prepare our best suite, for you. Jones,' he said, indicating a servant in a green apron, who'd been lounging against the doorframe of what appeared to be the entrance to a public taproom, 'will take your luggage up.' Jones pushed himself off his doorframe and made for the pile of cases Dawkins had just deposited on the stone flags. 'If you would not mind just signing our guest book?' He gestured to a leather-bound journal propped open on a shelf beneath the main staircase.

Harry obliged. Once Jeavons had glanced at the entry, which included his title and gave his estate in Scotland as his main address, the manager became even more obsequious.

'Permit me to guide you to our reading room, where there is a fire by which you can warm yourself, my lord,' he said, inching in the direction of a corridor which led into the bowels of the large, rambling building which occupied one entire side of the market square.

'Captain Bretherton,' Harry corrected him.

'As you wish,' said the landlord subserviently. 'We have the London papers, as well as a large stock of books in our lending library. People—that is, the *better* sort of people—come from all over the locality to borrow books or simply to take coffee. In fact, I am not ashamed to confess that the Three Tuns has become the centre of the social life in this part of Dorset, since I made the improvements.'

Harry glanced round the deserted foyer, into which a little rain was gusting through the door which still stood open behind him.

'Ah, if only you had been here during the summer months. Then you would have been able to enjoy concerts, and balls, as well as the very best of society.'

'I was not up to dancing, during the summer,' because he'd rarely been sober enough to know his left foot from his right. 'Though my recent sojourn in Bath,' he continued, hoping Jeavons would pick up on the fact he was posing as a semi-invalid, 'has worked wonders.'

'Ah,' said Jeavons, with dawning comprehension. Finally. 'You have been taking the waters. Did someone you met there recommend the health-giving properties of our own spring? Though it is not,' he continued before Harry had a chance to make any sort of response, 'as conveniently situated, I am sure that you will find the walk along the recently constructed promenade along the sea front, followed by the climb up through our beautiful cliffside gardens to reach the source, most beneficial to your health and well-being. And when you drink it—'

'All I wish to drink, for the present, is some of that coffee you mentioned.'

'Of course, of course,' said Jeavons with a deft bow. 'Please follow me to the reading room, where I will serve you myself.'

He set off along the corridor he'd pointed out before and Harry followed, with Dawkins close on his heels.

The room to which Jeavons took them turned out to be far more appealing than Harry had expected from what he'd seen of the Three Tuns so far. There were plenty of comfortable-looking chairs arranged round various-sized tables. A pair of sofas flanking a cheerfully crackling fire. Newspapers and journals displayed on slanted-topped tables set beneath the windows to catch the light.

But what really caught his interest was a large, framed map, displayed on the wall between those windows, with the legend 'Peacombe' picked out in bold red lettering.

He shrugged off his overcoat and dropped it casually, the way he'd seen Rawcliffe do, so that his 'valet' had to step forward briskly to catch it. He then strode to the map and peered at it intently.

'This is very interesting,' he said. 'I have been hoping to visit an acquaintance of mine while in the area, but was not completely sure where he lives. Could you possibly point out to me where, precisely, in Lesser Peeving I might find Colonel Hutton? And tell me where I might hire a gig to take me to him?'

'Colonel Hutton?' For a moment there was what looked like a flicker of alarm in the landlord's eyes, though it was gone so quickly that anyone who hadn't been looking for it might have missed it. The landlord licked his lips. Took a breath. Closed his mouth. Put on a servile expression.

'If you wish to visit Colonel Hutton, I can arrange for a driver...'

'No need. My man here can drive me, providing there is a suitable vehicle.'

'I shall see what can be arranged. When would you be thinking of visiting the Colonel?'

'As soon as humanly possible,' he said firmly. 'Today would not be too soon.'

'A matter of urgency, is it?'

He wasn't imagining the landlord's look of anxiety this time. His voice had even risen by about half an octave. If he could grow so alarmed at an unknown naval officer marching into town and demanding to see the local magistrate at once, it stood to reason he was hand in glove with the local smugglers.

'It is to me.'

The landlord straightened. 'I shall see what I can do. Although it might be a little risky to go tonight. You will need to cross a stretch of open moorland to reach Lesser Peeving,' he said, coming closer so that he could point out the moorland in question on the map, 'and it will be going dark soon.'

'A fair point. Tomorrow morning then. If I set out at first light, I can reach his house by…?'

'Oh, it isn't all that far. An hour at most. But he does come in regularly to read the papers and to allow his granddaughter to use our library, so perhaps...'

'Lizzie comes here regularly? I mean,' he corrected himself, as though in chagrin, 'Miss Hutton.'

'Ah, Miss Hutton,' said the landlord with a knowing gleam in his eye. 'It is Miss Hutton upon whom you wish to call, rather than the Colonel. You met her while in Bath, I take it? That would account for...no, no,' he said with a chuckle. 'I must not be indiscreet.'

Why not? Why could the fellow not finish what he'd been about to say about Lizzie?

Still, the landlord had put two and two together and reached the conclusion Harry wanted him to reach. That there was a budding romance in the air. If it had been a real romance, if he'd truly been pursuing Miss Hutton with a view to marriage, he would have kept his intentions completely private.

But he and Dawkins had agreed that the opportunity to have a look round the very hotel where Archie had stayed while he'd been down here had been too good to waste. And if he wanted answers from Jeavons, then he had to appear approachable. To the point of indiscretion.

'I wish to call upon the Colonel,' he said firmly.

Which was also the truth. He needed to ask his permission to court Miss Hutton in form.

Jeavons made no reply to that, though there was a knowing smirk playing about his lips when he bowed himself out of the room. The moment the door closed behind him, he turned to face Dawkins.

'I think it safe to say,' said Harry, 'that the man was alarmed to hear of my intention to visit Colonel Hutton.'

'Don't necessarily mean he is in cahoots with the smugglers His Lordship warned us of.'

'Can you think of another reason to explain his reaction?'

'No, but...' He finished with an eloquent shrug.

'Nevertheless, it means we won't be able to speak freely, even in here.'

'Perhaps you'd best start taking walks along that there promenade he spoke of. For your health.'

'Yes, and you'd better come with me.'

Dawkins gave a curt nod.

'You will come with me when I go to visit Colonel Hutton, too. And see what you can glean from his staff.'

He nodded again.

'In the meantime, we had better study this map.'

Dawkins came to stand beside him and they

stood in silence for a few moments, marvelling at the extraordinary detail in which the little bay of Peacombe, and the surrounding district, had been depicted. Someone had produced a watercolour which not only showed the main features of the coast and topography, but also a few of the more prominent buildings and what he had to assume were local places of interest. There was the Three Tuns, in the market square of Peacombe, and there was the road to Lesser Peeving, to the north, running up a steep hill before crossing an expanse of clearly rugged terrain. The spring that Jeavons had mentioned was shown gushing forth, in a most improbable manner, from some cliffs to the east of Peacombe bay.

'Ah, now that is very interesting,' he said, with a wry smile.

'What is?'

'The fact that whoever painted this map left out an entire village. Which should be just about here,' he said, pointing to a section of coastline to the east of the improbable spring. 'That is about where Peeving Cove lies, at the head of this inlet, here, see it? And is where our main suspect lives.'

'The Reverend Cottam?'

'Indeed.' Lady Rawcliffe had been close to tears

as she'd explained how they'd reached that conclusion about her brother.

'When he was sent to Lesser Peeving as curate,' she'd told him, 'instead of taking up residence in the house provided by the diocese, he moved into Peeving Cove.'

'Which is where the local smugglers have their stronghold,' Rawcliffe had explained while she'd paused to blow her nose.

'His excuse, naturally, is that he is sent to *seek that which is lost*,' she'd said, wrinkling up her reddened nose in disgust. 'Though he has never, to my knowledge, ever been responsible for reforming any of the sinners he likes to consort with. On the contrary, he seems to take great pride in organising them to make the most of whatever dubious talents they possess.'

'Which is another reason for suspecting he's the ringleader of the criminal gang that has been stealing jewels from members of the *ton* and replacing them with fakes so that the thefts went unnoticed for some considerable time. But what convinced us was his behaviour, when we visited him earlier this year.'

'He practically boasted about how clever he'd been, disposing of Archie's body the way he had.'

'Not in so many words, my dear,' Rawcliffe had pointed out.

'You've got to find proof, Atlas,' Lady Rawcliffe had sobbed. 'Solid evidence that he can't wriggle his way round, or he will keep on getting away with the most awful things...'

Lord Rawcliffe had gone to his wife's chair and rested his hands on her shoulders.

'So far, all we have is a series of what he can explain away as perfectly innocent coincidences to link him to any aspect of the crime.'

'Yes, like the way he *says* he is finding fallen women respectable employment. When, really, he is getting criminals positions in households he plans to rob.'

'I remember you all talking about what kind of person could have such unrestricted access to the houses which were later robbed,' Harry had put in at that point. 'And it struck me that posing as a clergyman—'

'Or actually being one,' Lady Rawcliffe had offered cynically.

'Yes, well, it is a perfect cover for someone intent on committing crimes. Wherever one goes, there is always a clergyman hovering on the fringes. House parties, dinners at embassies and such like. Like younger sons of noble houses, they are permitted to run tame just about anywhere.'

'Yes, we think that is probably how he managed to discover the weaknesses of the people he later robbed. But to return to the few facts of which I am certain,' said Rawcliffe. 'I did manage to pick up the scent of a girl who fit the description of someone who could have been responsible for two robberies. The trail went cold in Peeving Cove. The girl, whatever her real name was, definitely went there. And drowned.'

'Just like Archie.'

'But Cottam has also laid a trail that leads to another resident of that area. One Lady Buntingford. She is the person who provided references for the girls in question—'

'Or girl in question,' put in Lady Rawcliffe. 'We think she might have gained work in various places under different aliases. But we couldn't get in to see her—Lady Buntingford, I mean—because of her being a recluse. We did think Archie might have got in to speak to her, because she is his great-godmother, and that could be why he was killed…' She made use of her handkerchief again. 'But even when it comes to Lady Buntingford, it could be my brother.'

'What my wife means,' put in Lord Rawcliffe, giving his wife's shoulders a little squeeze, 'is that Cottam is, apparently, one of the very few people who is ever allowed in to see Lady Buntingford. And he actually told Clare that he deals with her correspondence. So he could have forged references from her. Easily.'

'I know. It was me who suggested those references were forgeries in the first place.' During one of his more lucid moments. When he was making a bit of an attempt to try to repay the kindness Rawcliffe was showing him, in offering him house room, by pretending to be interested in the affair in which they were all becoming embroiled.

'Yes, but she could just as easily be playing a part. And Cottam could be innocent.'

Lady Rawcliffe had snorted at the suggestion. 'You need to talk to Miss Hutton about Lady Buntingford,' she'd said. 'That is one reason we have decided to send you down there after her. Miss Hutton, you see, is the only other person who regularly visits her. Once a week, she goes to spend an afternoon reading to her. She will know what kind of person Lady Buntingford is. And whether she could be involved in all this crime. Or perhaps even be able to prove that she could not have anything to do with it.'

'You are not to take any foolish risks, though,' Rawcliffe had said with some vehemence. 'I know we need proof, but it is not worth you losing your life over, as well.'

What was worth losing his life over, though? Fighting for his country? Besides, what kind of life did Rawcliffe think he'd been living, since he'd gone into the navy as a snivelling young midshipman? Life was all about taking risks. And if he'd learned anything, it was that only the boldest risks resulted in success.

They could result in failure, too. As he'd learned to his cost. But he wasn't going to dwell on that, just now.

'I will do whatever it takes to find the proof you need to bring Archie's killer to justice,' he'd vowed. 'And to hell with the consequences.'

He turned away from the map and strode to the fire, holding out his hands as though needing to get warm. And truthfully, there was a bit of a chill curdling the contents of his stomach. Though not because of the atmospheric conditions. It was the prospect of interrogating Miss Hutton about Lady Buntingford that was doing it. And using his courtship as a smokescreen to conceal his prime motive for being in the area.

Though it wasn't as if she could possibly be completely ignorant of what had been going on in her neighbourhood. She spent a lot of time with this Lady Buntingford, whose name had come up time and time again in connection with the girls who'd got into the houses of vulnerable older ladies. What if it was no coincidence that Lizzie kept visiting an elderly lady who was writing references for thieves? What if *she* was the one who had been... what...filching Lady Buntingford's headed notepaper and actually forging them? What if Rawcliffe's suspicions about Cottam were all based on years of dislike and prejudice? What did Harry know about her, really? Except that she was unmarried and lonely, and poor. All good motives for turning to crime...

Stealing rubies, that was.

Not murder though. Not Miss Hutton. She was too...hapless.

Unless that was a very, very clever disguise.

But, no. She'd responded too openly, too eagerly to be any good at the arts of deception. And blushed at the drop of a hat.

When the landlord came bustling back in with

a tray bearing a couple of silver pots, some plates bearing slices of cake and two cups, Harry was still standing with his back to the room, his hands extended to the fire. Though Dawkins was still studying the map.

Jeavons set out the plates and cups upon a small table set handily near the fireside chairs, yammering on about various amenities of Peacombe, and the surrounding district. All of which Harry already knew about, courtesy of Lord and Lady Rawcliffe.

While Harry went to the table and sat down to drink his coffee, Dawkins drew Jeavons into a discussion about the accuracy of the map, in regard to distances.

'Is the cake not to your liking? Would you prefer some sandwiches instead?' Jeavons, Harry suddenly noticed, was looking rather perturbed. And at about the same time he realised that instead of eating the slice of cake he'd absentmindedly picked up, he'd crushed it, so that sodden crumbs were oozing between his fingers and dripping on to his lap.

'I find that I am not hungry, after all,' he said curtly. He got to his feet. 'Perhaps I will take a walk about the town, to clear my head.'

Jeavons leapt aside as he strode out of the room. Out of the corner of his eye he noted Dawkins snatching up his coat, before trotting out behind him, like an obedient little terrier.

Which was apt, since they were on the hunt for a rat.

Chapter Nine

The suite might have been the most luxurious accommodation The Three Tuns had to offer, but Harry got very little sleep that first night. There were too many things preying on his mind.

To start with, Jeavons had lied about having a marquess stay under his roof.

And Archie had definitely stayed in the hotel. That didn't necessarily mean that the landlord had played any part in the murder, though. He could just be one of those men who was too scared of the local smugglers to stand up to them. Most such gangs flourished in an atmosphere brewed of two-parts intimidation and one-part reward, after all. But he'd definitely been alarmed to hear Harry intended to visit the local magistrate.

Until he'd brought Miss Hutton into the equation.

And that was another thing. He should be glad

she was already providing him with an effectual smokescreen. But the more he thought about her, the more troubled he became. When he'd tried to justify his presence in her life by telling himself she could be a possible suspect, it had turned his stomach. Because he'd started to like her, he'd hated the notion of her being involved in anything nefarious so much that he'd been unable to eat anything until he'd taken a long walk. Even then his thoughts about her remained in turmoil. For, if she was involved, in even the slightest way, then she had Archie's blood on her hands. Which he didn't want to believe.

On the other hand, could she possibly be in complete ignorance of what was going on in this neck of the woods? That was equally hard to swallow.

Round and round went his thoughts, with no respite until the first glimmerings of dawn gave him the excuse to abandon even the pretence of trying to get any sleep. He rolled off the mattress that felt as if it had been trying to smother him all night and went to draw the curtains. The sun wasn't yet managing to make much headway, particularly since a squally wind was flinging handfuls of rain at his window.

So he'd have to rely on Jeavons finding him a carriage to drive across the moors to Lesser Peeving. He didn't want to arrive dripping wet and windswept, which he would if he were to walk, which was something he'd considered. For, although the road wound round the contours suitable for horses and carriages, his study of the map last night showed he could take a much more direct route if he went on foot. However, a man intent on impressing the guardian of the woman he wished to court was not going to do it by trudging across the moors like a beggar. He needed to arrive in style.

Which ambition Jeavons appeared to be determined to stifle at birth.

'I'm afraid,' he said after breakfast, when Harry asked him when he might expect to have use of a carriage, 'that the only vehicle I was able to procure at such short notice is an open gig. Which is not, I'm sure you will agree, suitable for travelling in this sort of weather.'

Harry's hackles rose. It was as if the man was deliberately attempting to keep him from visiting Colonel Hutton.

'It's only a bit of rain,' he said, shrugging himself into his greatcoat. 'Nothing compared to an Atlantic gale,' he added, clapping his hat on his head. If Jeavons was so determined to keep him away from Lesser Peeving, all the more reason to get there as soon as possible.

'But, your health…' Jeavons trotted behind as Harry strode along the passage he'd already ascertained led to the stable yard.

'I'll take my chances… Good God,' he couldn't help exclaiming the moment he saw the vehicle Dawkins was standing next to, which he had to assume was the one Jeavons had said that was all he could procure. It was the kind of thing an elderly farmer's wife might use to transport her goods to market.

Well, there went his chance of impressing Colonel Hutton by bowling up his drive in a smart, closed carriage. He might as well trudge across the moors and save the cost of hiring this ridiculous little trap.

But…no…

Even though he'd expressed indifference to the state of his health, it wouldn't do to let Jeavons, and by extension anyone else he might choose to inform, know that he was, actually, fit enough to do so.

The springs creaked in protest as Harry set his foot on the step and the entire vessel listed to port when he settled on to the bench seat. It didn't right itself when Dawkins climbed in and took the reins, either. And when he flicked them over the raw-boned horse's rump, all that happened was that the creature turned and looked at them over its shoulder as if to ask if they could possibly be serious.

Dawkins flicked the reins a bit harder and clucked his tongue for good measure. The horse took the strain with a snort of indignation. Dawkins proved to be a skilful driver well before they'd left the town. He managed to keep the vehicle from mounting the pavement, in spite of its tendency to veer to portside, by adopting a manoeuvre that at sea Harry would have described as tacking.

And then, once they'd left the confines of the town and begun the steep ascent to moors, he allowed the horse to set a pace that meant it could keep going, with only the occasional pause to get its breath back. All Harry had to do was rein in his own impatience, cross his arms across his chest and watch the scenery dawdle past while he rehearsed what he would say to Colonel Hutton.

Before long, only gorse and heather flourished on either side of the road as far as the eye could see, although he did spy a few intrepid sheep pushing their way through the undergrowth in search of sustenance.

* * *

It felt as if several hours had gone by before they eventually crested a rise that gave a view down on to a row of buildings, strung out along a section of road huddling just beneath the brow of the next ridge, as though trying to shelter from the wind.

Lesser Peeving.

From this vantage point he could see that most of the houses were small. There was only a handful of larger buildings, one of which was a church. Hard by it was the house that had to be the one Lady Rawcliffe's brother had been offered. It looked fairly substantial from up here. Harry certainly wouldn't have turned his nose up at it. Nor would most members of the clergy, he would wager. But then the Reverend Cottam wasn't like most members of the clergy. From what Lord Rawcliffe had told him—though not in front of his wife—the man wanted more than he could get from eking out the tithes and benefices which were his due. He'd been sent to this tiny hamlet, from his last church, after all, because of a complaint made by the bank into which he'd had the responsibility of depositing the collection. They would ignore a certain amount of counterfeit coin, because it had come from a church. But not the percentage which was coming to them through Cottam's hands.

As they began the descent down the last curve into Lesser Peeving, Harry paid close attention to the other two notable properties, which stood at either end of the town, like bookends.

The nearest one, which was surrounded by high walls, belonged to the infamous Lady Buntingford, the woman who might be responsible for introducing thieves into the houses of her acquaintances so that they could switch family heirlooms for cheap fakes. From up here he could see neat gardens surrounding a house that looked to be of Tudor origins. Just inside the main gates, which were high and topped with spikes, stood a small cottage. In which, he guessed, the gatekeeper lived. The person who prevented anyone except Miss Hutton, or the Reverend Cottam, from getting in to see Lady Buntingford.

Once he drew nearer, he could see that the buildings on the main street looked as though both they, and their inhabitants, had seen better days. As he drove by, he saw that the paintwork on the greengrocer's sign was flaking so badly it was barely legible, several panes of the bakery windows were broken and stuffed with rags and weeds were growing from the butcher's chimney stack.

The gates to Colonel Hutton's manor, which was a short distance beyond the last house in Lesser Peeving proper, stood open. In contrast to those of Lady Buntingford. But then they were also hanging slightly askew from rusting hinges, and the gravel drive which bisected a rather shaggy lawn was liberally sprinkled with weeds.

Dawkins drew the gig to a halt at the steps by the front door, causing the horse to heave a sigh of relief. The plan was for him to wait until they were certain Harry was going to be admitted. At which point he would drive round to the back and play the part of dutiful servant awaiting further instructions.

Harry climbed down and went to knock on the front door. It wasn't long before a man of distinctly military bearing opened it and asked his business.

'I've come to speak to Colonel Hutton,' Harry replied, handing over his card. 'And you may as well tell him I'm not going to take no for an answer,' he added, stepping forward into the hall.

The butler didn't bat an eyelid. He simply did an about face and marched off into the interior of the house. But then, since the Colonel was the local magistrate, he was probably used to all sorts of people turning up and demanding admittance.

Harry took off his hat and tucked it under his arm. So, this was where Lizzie lived. He looked round the wainscoted hall as he drew off his gloves, noting the mullioned windows on the landing at the top of the oak staircase, the series of portraits of men who all looked remarkably like her grandfather hanging from every available space.

'The Colonel will receive you in the study,' said the butler on his return. 'If you would follow me?'

Harry first took a moment to take off his soaked overcoat, which he handed to the butler along with his hat and gloves, so that at least the top half of him would look respectable.

Even so, the moment he set foot in an overheated, book-lined room to the rear of the house, the Colonel banged his cane on the floor. 'Damn jackanapes,' he snarled. 'What do you mean by coming down here, eh? The impudence!'

'I have come,' said Harry, walking over to the man and taking up a stand directly before him, 'to ask your permission to court your granddaughter, Miss Hutton.'

'Well, I shan't give it. Not to a damn sneak like you, that's already tried to worm his way into

Lizzie's affections. I know all about the kind of scoundrels who infest Bath hoping to seduce heiresses. Turning silly girls' heads with all sorts of promises they've no intention of keeping.'

'I have made Miss Hutton no promises.'

'No, too clever for that, weren't you? Thought you could turn her up sweet before making your play.'

Since that was precisely what Harry had intended to do, it took an immense effort not to wince.

'But I've got news for you,' Colonel Hutton continued. 'You've wasted your time coming here. Lizzie has no money to speak of. Hah!' He banged on the floor with his cane again. 'What do you think of that?'

'I think,' said Harry on a surge of indignation, 'that you are doing your granddaughter an injustice.'

'What? What do you mean?'

'You are assuming that no man would wish to marry her unless she was wealthy. Implying you believe she is lacking in some way.'

'Are we talking about the same gel? Most men can't look at her without sniggering.'

What? But Miss Hutton was beautiful. 'Most men,' Harry growled, 'are idiots.'

'Shan't argue with you on that score, but I still don't see why you would want to marry her. What do you see in her that other men don't, eh, that's what I'd like to know?'

'She's witty,' he promptly replied, almost as much to his own surprise as the Colonel's. He'd rehearsed all sorts of things to say, in response to any question the Colonel might ask, but this had not been one of them.

'Witty? Lizzie?'

'Yes. The first morning we met, when I bumped into her in the Pump Room…'

'You bumped into her? Other way round, more likely…'

'And that is another thing. Most women make me feel like a lumbering great oaf. They are such tiny, frail-seeming things I'm afraid I'm going to accidentally snap them in half. And I get backache just *thinking* about kissing them. But Miss Hutton and I…we match, sir. When we danced together, it was as if we were…well, a matched pair.' And no cleverly conceived answer could have carried so much conviction, he quickly saw. For the Colonel was looking at him in a new, more assessing manner. But then that answer had sprung from his heart. If he ever did seriously start considering marriage, he couldn't imagine anyone suiting him better than Miss Hutton.

'Hmmm,' said the Colonel. 'Well, I still don't like it. Don't like it at all.'

'I realise that if she does marry me, it will cause you a great deal of inconvenience,' he said, deciding it was time to deploy one of the weapons he'd already decided he could turn on the Colonel. 'You will have to actually employ somebody to fill her function as…what is it? Nurse? Companion? Drudge?'

The Colonel's knuckles went white. 'Are you daring to accuse me of being selfish?'

'Well, have you ever thought about what will become of her after you have gone? You say she has no dowry. No money. Would you not rather know that she has a secure roof over her head and a man to care for her? Even if it does mean your latter years may be slightly less comfortable than if you were to keep her chained to your side.'

The Colonel's face went puce. 'Knew you were a damned jackanapes the minute I set eyes on you.'

'For speaking the truth? For offering to provide Miss Hutton with a secure future when you are no longer able to do so?'

The Colonel growled. Worked his gnarled knuckles over the head of his cane. All the while glaring at Captain Bretherton in a way that probably had most men quaking in their shoes.

It had no effect upon him whatever. For the Colonel couldn't shoot him, or clap him in irons, or flog him, or court-martial him. Nor could he force him to leave the district to prevent him from paying court to Lizzie, with or without his permission.

'And what are your prospects, pray? Nothing but a half-pay officer from what I can see,' he said, giving Harry's scuffed boots a scornful look.

And yet Harry's pulse sped up. If the Colonel was asking about his prospects, it meant he was actually considering his proposal. So now it was time to wheel out the big guns.

'I may currently be serving as a captain in His Majesty's navy, but I am also the eighth Earl of Inverseigg. If Miss Hutton were to marry me she would become my Countess.'

The Colonel sucked in a good deal of air through his teeth. Looked him up and down.

'Estates mortgaged, are they?'

'Yes.' There was no point in lying about this. 'But not because they are not profitable.'

'Your father was a gambler, was he? Or merely incompetent?'

Harry did not rise to the bait. 'A mixture of both,' he confessed frankly.

'Then you ought to be hanging out for an heiress.'

Yes. If he'd been genuinely on the hunt for a wife.

'Yes. If I'd been thinking in terms of leaving the navy and returning to my estates,' he hedged.

The Colonel's brows drew down. 'If you mean to marry Lizzie and then go back to sea I don't see how that will be of any benefit to her at all.'

'Obviously, I would not do that.'

'What the devil are you driving at then?'

'Well, sir, I hadn't been thinking of ever marrying, before I met your granddaughter.' Actually, not before Rawcliffe and Becconsall had persuaded him to pose as her suitor. 'But since I have, I have been thinking of ways to make marriage possible.' Because he'd known he couldn't approach the Colonel without convincing credentials. So he'd looked at all the ways he might be able to convince the old man that he could provide for a wife. And had pretty soon realised that if he was the kind of man to accept the reward money that Rawcliffe, Becconsall and Archie's family had put up as a reward, he could lift the mortgages.

'I expect to come into a substantial sum of money, in the near future,' he therefore said. 'It will enable me to get back on an even keel. As I've already mentioned, the estates are profitable and should provide enough income to keep both myself and a wife in some comfort.' Theoretically.

The Colonel tapped his cane repeatedly on the floor as he turned this over. Looked at him as though he were a person, rather than something he wanted to scrape off the bottom of his shoe. That was the thing with titles. Men assessed you on a different scale entirely. Simply because of an accident of birth. Which was why he so rarely told anyone about it. And if he hadn't vowed to do whatever it took to succeed on this mission, he wouldn't have done so now.

Only, having a title *did* make guardians look upon prospective suitors with less hostility.

'And what were you doing in Bath, then? Drinking the waters? Got some tropical disease, have you?'

'I have been ill, it is true. But mostly it was the effect of being held prisoner by the French for the past year. I swam every day, while in Bath, in the hope of regaining my vigour, as well as drinking the waters.'

'Badly treated, were you? Don't surprise me. Vicious sorts, those Frenchies.'

'No, not exactly. It was…but that is beside the point. I am not yet at full strength, as you can probably tell from the cut of my clothes.' He tugged at the front of his jacket, which he was still not filling out fully. He supposed he should have bought a new suit of clothes to go courting. Only, before he'd met Lizzie it had felt more important to stress his illness, rather than his suitability as a husband. 'But I can assure you that I am recovering and that Miss Hutton is very unlikely to have to spend the rest of her life nursing me. *I* fully intend to take care of *her.*'

'I must admit,' growled the Colonel after a short, ruminative pause, 'I have been troubled about her future. This property is entailed, you see, and I doubt very much whether my successor will have the patience with her that I've—' He bit off whatever he'd been about to say. 'She won't be exactly penniless, when I'm gone. I have made some provision for her in my will. But it won't be the same as having her own husband and family. Not by a long chalk.'

'Then…you will give me your blessing? I may pay my addresses to L— I mean, Miss Hutton?'

'I can't see her getting a better offer,' he said grudgingly. 'And it's better for her to marry than

dwindling into an old maid, or being a poor relation in someone else's home. But I'm not going to
hand her straight over to you. Until the moment
this money you spoke of is actually safe in your
bank and you give me proof of its existence, I will
not countenance an official betrothal.'

Which couldn't have suited Harry better. He
would only qualify for that money once he'd un-
masked Archie's killer. At which time, everyone
would know what he'd really been doing in Dorset.
And Miss Hutton would be so angry with him she
wouldn't touch him with a ten-foot pole.

'The final decision must rest with her, though,'
the Colonel said sternly. 'So you'd better get to it.'

'Get to it?'

'Yes, the courting. She's at Lady Buntingford's
today, ye see? Big house at the far end of the village. If you set off now, you will be in plenty of
time to escort her home. You'll have to wait outside
the gates, though. They don't let anyone in to see
the old girl these days. Damn nonsense, of course,
but there it is.'

'Thank you, sir.' He grabbed one of the Colonel's
hands and shook it with such enthusiasm that the
old man winced. 'Beg pardon, sir, but you've just
made me a very happy man.'

'Yes,' said the Colonel, massaging his fingers, 'I can see that I have. Never thought I'd see the day,' he added, shaking his head. 'Young chap like you head over heels for my Lizzie.'

Head over heels? He was no such thing. He was just glad that he was laying down his cover so convincingly.

That was all.

Chapter Ten

'And then we held hands, all the way through the concert until the interval,' Lizzie sighed. 'Of course, me being as I am, I ruined it all before the evening was out. I started up like a pheasant breaking cover and knocked over my chair. And then as I bent to pick it up, he did the same, which meant that we bumped our heads together.'

'Oh, dear,' said Lady Buntingford.

'Quite,' said Lizzie rather drily. 'You don't need to say it. I *deserved* to have someone knock some sense into me.'

'Dear, dear, dear…'

'Oh, no, my lady. You must not sympathise with me. I have, after all, had a little romance of my own. Nothing like the kind I read to you about from your books, of course.' She smoothed the pages of the book that lay open in her lap. 'He did not ask me to elope with him, or attempt to snatch a kiss in a secluded arbour and tell me that his heart beat only for me. I doubt that any man, outside the pages of a novel, ever tells a woman that his heart beats only for her. But we did hold hands. And of course, it did end with Grandfather going all tyrannical when he heard about it, which is rather like the kind of behaviour of guardians in books, isn't it? Though who on earth saw us and told Grandfather all about it, I cannot think because Captain Bretherton took great care that we were sitting at the back of the room where nobody could possibly have seen exactly what we were doing.'

'Dear, dear...'

'I know. *"There is nothing hid that shall not be shouted from the rooftops",*' she paraphrased. 'Well, anyway, Grandfather shouted a lot and ended up by ordering me to pack our bags and he brought us home. Furious, I may add, that I had done something to cut short his pleasure.'

'Oh, dear...'

'Though I wasn't the least bit repentant,' said Lizzie, leaning forward to apply her handkerchief to the trail of moisture spreading across Lady Buntingford's chin. 'It felt like a triumph, rather than disgrace. I am *always* glad to come home to Lesser

Peeving. I detest Bath, as you know. All I do is hang round the Pump Room while Grandfather gossips with his cronies, or listen to others gossip while he plays at cards. But here, this little part of Dorset, has become my home. I know the hills and paths, the caves and coves, and can wander freely, safely, all on my own, whenever Grandfather does not have need of me. And of course I do enjoy our afternoons together,' she put in hastily, lest she hurt Lady Buntingford's feelings. 'And, yes, it *was* a bit of a disappointment to be wrenched away from Captain Bretherton before he had the chance to do anything really shocking. But at least now I have had my very own admirer. Nothing like the kinds of beaux you used to have when you were younger, I shouldn't think. But he was tall. And he was handsome. And he did have the darkest hair and the bluest eyes you've ever seen. My only regret is that he didn't kiss me. I suspect it would have been...' She ended on a sigh.

'Oh, dear...'

'Yes, I know, isn't it wicked of me? And also, it is rather galling to have to admit it, but I believe Grandfather was right to bring me home when he did. Because if Captain Bretherton could get me holding hands with him during a concert, who knows how it might have ended? He might have ruined me with the greatest of ease. He wouldn't have had to try very hard. And I'm not at all sure I would have regretted it, either. Because I might have ended up with a baby, if not a wedding ring.'

'Dear, dear, dear...'

'I know. Shocking of me, isn't it? Both to wish for it and to know that babies often do come to girls who get ruined. I don't suppose Grandfather would have allowed me to keep a baby, if I had one, though.' She sighed, straying a bit further into the realms of what-might-have-been. 'And not only because of propriety. Babies are such tiny, delicate little creatures that I'd be bound to drop it. Or snap off one of it's little appendages...'

'Dear, dear, dear...'

'Oh, now I have shocked *you*. I do beg your pardon. And, oh, heavens, look at the time! I have spent the whole time talking about my stay in Bath, rather than reading you the next instalment of your book.'

'Dear, dear,' said Lady Buntingford with just the hint of a smile in her faded eyes.

'You *are* a dear to be so forgiving. Well, next time, I shall read another chapter of the book, I promise you. Although I shouldn't be a bit surprised if Evangelina either swoons on to a sofa or weeps floods of tears into her delicate lace hanky.' She bent over and kissed Lady Buntingford lightly on the forehead. And then, before leaving, she took a large, practical linen square and wiped away the moisture that leaked from the old lady's eyes and the spittle that ran from the drooping right side of her mouth.

And then, once she'd shut the bedroom door softly behind her on her way out, she paused to dab at her own eyes with a fresh handkerchief. She never let Lady Buntingford see how much her condition upset her. The old lady had been so proud, and so addicted to keeping up appearances, before her seizure. It was no wonder that the only person she permitted to see her, now that she'd been robbed of her dignity, was the gawky, hopeless orphan who'd never had any grace or dignity herself.

She took her bonnet, coat, and shawl from Mrs Paul, the housekeeper, then tugged on her gloves before stepping out of the front door. It had stopped raining, thank goodness, so she hooked her umbrella over her arm and sauntered down the drive to the gate. Mr Paul, who acted as gatekeeper, was as usual ready and waiting with the key in his hand to let her out.

She thanked him and stepped out into the high road, where she noticed a man loitering on the other side of the road. She wasn't alarmed. Nobody was likely to attack her. For one thing, she wasn't worth robbing. For another, not even the smugglers who tried to instil terror into just about everyone else in the district would be stupid enough to molest her. Not if they wanted to maintain the uneasy truce they held with Grandfather.

It was a bit odd, though, for someone to lurk just outside the gates of Lady Buntingford's home. She was just wondering whether she ought to ring the bell for Mr Paul, in case the man was thinking about breaking in, when he launched himself at her.

And all her reasoning about being too unimportant to bother with fled before her instinctive need for self-preservation. With a little yelp, she swung her umbrella at the man who came looming out of her myopic mist, catching him across his upper arm.

'Miss Hutton!' He reeled back, clutching his arm. 'I did not mean to alarm you.'

'Good grief. Captain Bretherton? Is that you?' She stepped forward and peered up into the man's face. Her heart skipped a beat as his features swam into focus. The snub nose sprinkled with freckles.

Those blue, blue eyes, looking puzzled and hurt today, rather than sad. That determined chin, containing the mouth she'd just been telling Lady Buntingford she wished she'd kissed. Her head went... *fluffy*. That was the only way to describe it. And for the first time, she fully understood why so many heroines, in so many books, swooned at the sight of their hero, because right at that moment, anyone could have knocked her down with a feather.

'What,' she gasped, 'are you doing here?'

'Waiting to escort you home. If I'd thought you would object so thoroughly to my company...' he said, with a rueful grin.

'I don't object to your company. You startled me. You know you did.'

'Only once you'd bashed me with your umbrella.'

'I'm sorry. But you shouldn't have...loomed up at me the way you did.'

He took a step back and folded his arms across his chest. 'I did not loom. I simply walked up to you in a perfectly ordinary way.'

'It wasn't ordinary. You were at the very least rushing up to me.'

'Yes, because I was so pleased to see you after waiting out here for the better part of the afternoon.'

He didn't sound pleased to see her any longer. But then what man would be pleased to be struck with an umbrella after waiting all afternoon in the rain?

'Aren't you pleased to see me, Miss Hutton?'

Disappointed, that was what he sounded. She'd disappointed him. Well, sooner or later, she disappointed everybody.

'I am pleased to see you, yes. Now that I know it is you.'

'You didn't recognise me? Did our…acquaintance mean so little that you have forgotten me already?'

There it was again. Disappointment. Hurt, even. Her words had succeeded where her umbrella had failed.

She was going to have to explain.

'I haven't forgotten you. On the contrary, I've just spent the entire afternoon telling Lady Buntingford all about you. But the truth is—'

'You have? What did you tell her?'

'Never mind,' she said, blushing as she recalled admitting, out loud, not five minutes since, that she'd half-wished he'd made some attempt to ruin her. 'The point is, my eyesight is very bad.'

'What?'

'You heard me. I can barely see my hand at the end of my arm, let alone make out the features of someone's face when they are on the other side of the road.'

'But… I thought you came to visit Lady Buntingford to read to her.'

'Oh, reading is easy. I can hold a book less than an inch from my nose and the words are perfectly clear. But anything much further away…' she pulled a face '…disappears into the mist.'

'But you don't wear spectacles.'

'No. Grandfather won't allow it. He says it is bad enough that I am an ungainly long meg. He doesn't want to make matters worse by sticking spectacles on my face, the lenses of which would be so thick that they would distort my eyes and make me look like a frog.'

'You could never look like a frog. And I like the fact that you are tall. And you are not ungainly. I have never danced with a woman who was less ungainly…'

'The first time we met, I bumped into you—'

'Because you couldn't see me lurking behind you,' he said, as though seeing the light.

'And,' she continued relentlessly, 'the last time we were together, we bumped heads.'

'Again, because you did not see that I, too, was bending to pick up the chair.'

'Which I had kicked over.'

'Because I had shocked you.'

'You? Shocked me?'

'Yes. Taking your hand like that. When we'd only known each other a couple of days.'

'If you had shocked me, I would have knocked my chair over when you *first* took my hand, don't you think?'

'Then what was it? Fear of discovery? That someone would see us and your reputation would suffer?'

'No. It was—' Her face heated again. She wasn't ready to confess that she'd been almost over-whelmed by all sorts of highly improper longings.

'Miss Hutton,' he said gently. 'Will you accept my escort to your home? I am holding out my arm. All you have to do is rest your hand upon it and we can proceed. Will you?'

'I can see that you are holding out your arm,' she snapped. 'I can see general shapes, just not details.'

'But will you? Even though I loomed at you and startled you and annoyed you by not perfectly un-derstanding exactly how bad your eyesight is?' He sounded as though he was trying not to laugh.

Which was better, she supposed, than taking umbrage at her thwacking him and snapping at him.

'Will you take my arm and allow me to escort you home?'

Chapter Eleven

Allow him to escort her home? She'd just con-
fided to Lady Buntingford she'd been in serious
danger of allowing this man to do whatever he
wanted with her.

But she knew what she *ought* to do. A proper
young lady would smile coyly and thank him, and
say how kind it was of him and lay her hand upon
his sleeve demurely.

'I have no need of an escort along the High Street
of Lesser Peeving,' she snapped, instead. 'I am perfectly capable of getting myself home.'

'Armed as you are with such a terrifying umbrella,' he said with that smile in his voice. 'But
would it not be more pleasant to have someone
walk with you? To have me walk with you?'

Of course it would. But she couldn't let him suspect that all he'd have to do was ask nicely and
she'd most likely let him do whatever he wanted.

'It would.' She sighed in defeat. And laid her hand upon his sleeve in the prescribed manner. They set off, side by side.

After they'd gone a few yards in silence, he cleared his throat. 'I have not answered your question, have I? The one about what I am doing here. Because, clearly I was waiting for you. There could be no other reason for me to be loitering outside the gates of Lady Buntingford's property, could there?'

He sounded a touch nervous now. At least, he was very nearly babbling. In a manly sort of way. *Was* there a manly way to babble?

'The truth is…the truth is…well, after you left Bath, I didn't know what to do with myself. So I came down here to speak to you. Which meant speaking to your grandfather first, to get his permission.'

'His permission? To walk me home from Lady Buntingford's?'

'No. To marry you, of course.'

'Ma…? Ma…? Ma…?'

'I can see I have taken you by surprise. Had you no idea this might happen? That I might look upon you as my future bride? No, I can see you did not,' he said when she continued to try to breathe and swallow. Which was proving hard enough, without trying to form words as well.

Oh, Lord, any other woman would have received a marriage proposal with far more aplomb. They would have batted their eyelashes and smiled prettily, and said something about what an honour he was doing her. At least that was what heroines in books did. She didn't know what real women did, having no close female friends with whom to compare notes.

'It is true that we only met a few times. And, had you not left Bath, I would have spent more time getting to know you. Trying to find out if my first impressions of you were enough upon which to build a lifetime together.'

'First impressions? I soaked you with water.'

'For which I was extremely grateful. It was undrinkable.'

'But...but...'

'And then you fenced with me. Don't you remember?'

'All those dreadful puns—yes, of course, I remember.' A smile tugged at her lips in spite of herself. That had been the only time she'd ever actually enjoyed a conversation in the Pump Room. The only real conversation she'd had there, to be honest. Usually she just stood there listening without being expected to make any kind of answer.

'But, marriage? Truly? Can that really be what you want? How can you be sure?'

'This is not the kind of response,' he said with a wry smile, 'that a man hopes to hear when he proposes to a lady.'

'You haven't actually proposed. You have merely informed me that you obtained permission from Grandfather to…er…'

'Exactly,' he said cheerfully. 'He has agreed that I may spend some time getting to know you, the way I would have done had you not left Bath in such haste. After that, should I propose, you will not be able to accuse me of not knowing my own mind. And you will also have time to make up your mind about me.'

A peculiar sensation twisted her insides into a knot. When she set her mind to analysing it, she discovered that there was a good deal of panic in it. Panic that she'd put him off, when, had she not been so determined to show him she wasn't going to fall into his hands like a ripe plum, she could be betrothed to him. Right this *minute*.

And yet there was also a kernel of something else, telling her that she'd done the right thing. A man couldn't know he wanted to marry someone after ten minutes of banter and a couple of country dances. Could he?

'How long do you think it might take?'

'To persuade you that I am the man for you? Only you can decide that.'

'No, I meant…'

'Miss Hutton, do you honestly think that I would have chased you all the way to the back of beyond if I wasn't already pretty sure how I feel about you?'

'You…you…you couldn't possibly have fallen in love with me on the spot. Things like that don't really happen. Not to girls like me.'

There was a face peering out at them from the baker's, through one of the panes of windows that wasn't broken. As they went past his shop the greengrocer stepped into his doorway and placed his hands on his hips. Lizzie pretended she hadn't seen them.

'I will level with you, Miss Hutton,' said Captain Bretherton in a rather more serious tone. 'I did not fall in love with you on the spot, no. I liked you. I felt…attracted to you. But then, when we danced and we matched each other so well, it was as though…it is hard to explain. Well, I've already told you, haven't I, that I felt you were my match. And how so many women make me feel like a clumsy great gowk, they are so tiny and…fluttery,' he finished in a tone of disgust.

She reflected that she'd shared the same sort of feelings with him. She'd told him how much she'd enjoyed dancing with him. How enjoyable it was to have a partner who could cope with the length of her stride. Not to mention her weight. Had she told him about the little man she almost swung off his feet, at one of her very first dances, when she'd let caution fly to the winds?

As though he was in tune with the direction of her thoughts, he chuckled. 'Did I tell you about the woman I almost ejected through a window?'

'No.' It was uncanny. They'd both had similar experiences with members of the opposite sex. Had both felt big and ungainly and awkward, and had revelled in the feeling of having someone who… *matched*, for want of a better word.

He patted her hand where it lay on his sleeve. And all of a sudden, restraint between them ceased. For the rest of the walk home, they chatted with perfect ease, about disasters they'd had with members of the opposite sex. Incidents which had been mortifying at the time, once shared with him, now felt amusing.

All too soon they were crunching their way along the gravel drive to her front door.

She paused at the foot of the steps. Did she invite him to come in and take tea? To dine with them? Would Grandfather allow it? He'd given Captain Bretherton permission to court her, by the sound of it, but she had no idea how it had come about. And whether Grandfather had given his blessing willingly, or grudgingly. Oh, she really should have talked to the Captain about it during their walk home, rather than waste their time together trying to outdo him with tales of clumsiness and ineptitude.

'So, Miss Hutton, here you are, safe and sound at your door. And I must bid you good day. May I see you again?'

Oh, thank goodness. He'd taken control of what happened next. While at the same time letting her choose what happened after that.

'I am putting up at the Three Tuns, in Peacombe. It takes no time at all to get up here.'

'I know. I go down to use the library regularly. And Grandfather likes to go into the coffee room and read the London papers, and gossip with anyone who happens to be around.'

'When will you next be visiting the library, might I enquire?'

If she said *tomorrow*, would that sound too eager? It wasn't even as if Lady Buntingford needed a new book, since she hadn't read any of the current story today.

'It depends…' she said, when he shifted his feet, as if growing impatient to hear her answer.

'On when your grandfather can spare you,' he said. 'Of course. It…' He looked up at the sky, which was threatening rain again. 'I would call upon you and ask you if you would agree to come for a drive, or a walk with me, if the weather was a bit more promising.'

Something in the tone of his voice made up her mind for her.

'That was exactly what I meant. I mean, I wouldn't be walking all the way down to Peacombe if it was raining hard. And I never know if Grandfather is going to take it into his head to get out the carriage and drive down himself…'

The set of his shoulders altered.

'Then that settles it. I shall procure a smart carriage and come up to collect you, tomorrow, and drive you into Peacombe, where we can take coffee in the reading room after you have browsed the library, if it is raining. Or leave it in your stables so that we can go walking if it is fine.' His shoulders rose again. 'If that is agreeable to you. I am sorry. I am so used to giving orders and having them instantly obeyed I forget that with you, I should be asking what you would like.'

She got that feeling again. That feeling of having come across a kindred spirit. 'It is agreeable to me.' Very agreeable that he sounded so keen to start courting her. 'And I can always tell you, can I not, if you are growing too dictatorial? Don't forget I am used to dealing with officers.'

'Your grandfather.'

'Yes. But my brother was starting to rise through the ranks before he…' She sucked in a sharp breath as a pang of loss pierced her sharply. She shook it off. 'Though even before he got promoted he was always the leader of the two of us.'

'You had a brother?' He gentled his voice in a way that imparted the necessary sympathy and understanding without him having to put it in words. 'Was he older than you?'

'Yes. By several years. And after our parents died, he took to trying to provide for me…' She shook her head. She really didn't want to talk about Sam, not now.

As though he understood her feelings perfectly, he leaned forward and pressed her hand.

'Do you know, I think I can understand why your grandfather dislikes the thought of you wearing spectacles. It would be a shame to hide your eyes behind thick lenses. They are so very lovely. The colour reminds me of the sea, in parts of the Bay of Naples. A blue I thought I'd never see anywhere else…'

He was looming in closer. So close she could see the blue of his own eyes. And the intensity of his regard. It was as though he was looking at her with his entire face. Then his gaze went to her mouth. He parted his lips. And then blinked and suddenly withdrew.

'I look forward to seeing you tomorrow then,' he said. And with that he was gone. Leaving Lizzie standing on the front step, watching his outline growing steadily smaller and more blurred as he strode down the gravel path to the front gate.

He paused, just after going through it, giving Lizzie the impression he was looking back. That impression was confirmed when he raised his hat and waved it to her. Blushing, she darted into the house. Oh, Lord, he'd caught her staring after him like a...like a...like one of those lovesick heroines from the ridiculous novels she read to Lady Buntingford.

And yet, did it really matter? He'd turned back, too, to have one last look at her. And he'd been thinking about kissing her. She was almost sure he had.

Her lips lifted in a dreamy smile.

She had a suitor. A genuine, proper, handsome suitor. Who wanted to marry her. Her. Lizzie Hutton.

She sighed and drifted through the hall, up the stairs and into her room. When normally, she would have reported straight to Grandfather upon her return from Lady Buntingford's.

Actually, that was what she should do. She turned on her heel and marched straight back downstairs again. She needed to find out what had caused Grandfather to change his mind about Captain Bretherton. He'd removed her from Bath because he'd said she was making a fool of herself over a practised seducer of women. In no uncertain terms.

What on earth could Captain Bretherton have said to cause such an about-face?

Chapter Twelve

Lizzie wasn't sure whether to be glad or sorry when she looked out of the window first thing the next morning to see that the skies were overcast. It meant he was likely to come and collect her in his carriage, if he'd really meant what he'd said about them getting to know each other. Which he might not. Now he'd had a night to sleep on it, he might have woken up in a cold sweat, wondering what on earth had possessed him to follow her all the way down here.

Because he was an earl. That was why Grandfather had changed his mind about letting him *dangle* after her, as he put it. And he had estates somewhere in Scotland.

She took off her spectacles—the ones she wasn't allowed to wear outside the privacy of her own room—went to the washbasin and poured warm water into the basin. If Captain Bretherton, or Captain Lord Bretherton as she ought to properly call him, hadn't changed his mind, she would much rather walk out with him somewhere. Because then they could talk to each other freely. If they went up on to the moors, for instance, there would be nobody else about to overhear them.

And he might, if she was very, very lucky, go further than merely *thinking* about kissing her.

She splashed cool water on to her overheated face. And then imagined what people would say if they did spy her luring him up to a deserted spot so she could somehow get him to kiss her.

Poor Miss Hutton, they'd say, *so desperate for a man she latches on to the first one to show any interest.* And then they'd snigger.

Perhaps Captain Bretherton had been wise to suggest they spend some time getting to know each other so they could decide if they would suit, rather than just plunging headlong into matrimony after a few minutes flirting and a couple of country dances. People *would* mock her if she appeared too desperate.

Hah! They mocked her anyway.

She dried her face, flung the towel down on the wash stand and went to her armoire. And frowned at the selection of gowns hanging there. Why, oh, why hadn't she taken the opportunity, while she'd been in Bath, to do some shopping, as Lady Mainwaring was always urging her to do?

Because then she'd have had to have the bills sent to Grandfather, that was why. And while he'd never yet complained about the expense of keeping her, she knew he wasn't exactly rolling in money. He'd told her that he had made sure she would not be destitute, if anything were to happen to him. But in the meantime she'd have to get used to living frugally.

So she pushed aside any resentment about having to button herself up into the same gown she'd worn the day before. And would wear again tomorrow, like as not. She reminded herself to be grateful that she had a roof over her head and plentiful food. And that Captain Bretherton had said he was interested in her because she *wasn't* a little, feminine, dainty creature, dressed up in the height of fashion. At least, he hadn't said anything about fashion, but then what kind of man did? Not the kind she'd ever be interested in, that was certain.

She put on her spectacles and glowered at her reflection. No chance of anyone describing her as dainty, or fashionable. She had to either bend her knees to see her head as well as her toes when look-ing in the mirror, or step far enough away that she dissolved into a blur.

She took off her spectacles and flung them on to her dressing table. She never liked examining her-self too closely. It was too depressing. Though he had said he liked her eyes. She leaned closer into the mirror, so that she could see them. They were nothing out of the ordinary. Her eyelashes were rather pale. She'd always thought they were a bit bland. But he'd said they reminded her of the sea. The sea in an exotic place. And he hadn't needed to say that.

Unless he thought he ought to pay her some com-pliments, if he was going to persuade her to marry him.

And it had taken him the entire walk home to come up with that one. Her stomach clenched. And once she got downstairs she found she could only pick at her breakfast.

'What's got into you this morning, girl?' Grand-father lowered his brows and glared at her when her cup slipped through her fingers and landed with a clatter in its saucer, causing most of what tea that remained to slop over the rim.

'You startled me.'

'By sitting here?'

'No, by barking at me like that. You don't usually talk much at table.' Especially not in the morning.

'Well, you don't usually fidget and sigh, and keep gazing out of the window rather than tuck into your food, young lady. If this is the effect having a suitor is going to have upon you, I might have to send him packing.'

Her stomach plunged. She didn't think she'd made any outward show of how she felt, but she must have done, because Grandfather gave a bark of laughter.

'So, that's the way the land lies, is it? Taken a fancy to him, have you?'

'I…well, I…'

'Seems to be a sound sort of chap.'

'That wasn't what you said when you brought me home from Bath,' she said, resentment making her speak out when normally she would have held her tongue.

'That was before I knew he was in earnest.'

And before he'd discovered he was an earl.

'Devil take it, girl, what was I to think when I heard you'd been holding hands with a man you'd only just met and without him coming to ask me for permission to try to fix his interest with you?'

'Yes, well…'

'Hanging around the Pump Room in a shabby uniform two sizes too big for him, looking like a stray mongrel on the lookout for a juicy bone. But if it's a wedding ring he has in mind, that's a different matter. Particularly now he knows you ain't an heiress.'

'I… Oh!' Grandfather had thought the only reason any man could be dangling after her was if he was a fortune hunter, mistakenly believing she had one. Well, he'd as good as said so before.

'No need to look at me like that. *I* know what a good girl you are, but you have to admit you ain't the kind that draws a lot of attention from eligible men. Not in all the years you've lived under my roof, you haven't.'

'No.' Well, there was no arguing with that. But before she could grow too despondent over her acknowledged lack of feminine allure, Sergeant Hewitt came in and cleared his throat.

'There is a visitor for Miss Hutton. Captain Lord Bretherton.'

What, now? While they were still sitting down to breakfast?

'Well, show him in, man, show him in.'

Lizzie looked wildly round the table. For a moment she had the almost overwhelming urge to run to the mirror to check that her hair was tidy. Goodness, she couldn't recall brushing it. She lifted her hand to her head and found that she had, at some point, braided it and coiled it round her head the way she always did.

And then he was filling the doorway and ducking his head to come into the room, and striding round the table to shake Grandfather's hand.

'I hope you don't regard my arrival as unpardonably early,' he said. 'I wanted to catch Miss Hutton before she set out walking. The weather is fine at the moment, but—'

'No need to use the weather as an excuse,' Grandfather interrupted, sounding highly amused. 'It is clear you are eager to spend as much time as you can with my granddaughter.'

'Indeed, sir, you have found me out.'

When, she wondered, would either of them acknowledge that she was in the room, listening to every word?

'I have managed to hire a better rig than the one the landlord of the Three Tuns provided last time I came out here,' Captain Bretherton informed Grandfather. 'It has a hood which I can draw up should it come on to rain.'

'Another two-seater, though?'

Captain Bretherton shifted his weight. 'My man will stand up behind. I can assure you, your grand-daughter will not be entirely unchaperoned.'

'A bit late for sticking to decorum after what the pair of you got up to in Bath.'

'I...yes, sir, but you see—'

Grandfather slapped the palm of his hand on the table and laughed. 'Get along with you. The pair of you,' he said, turning his head in Lizzie's direction. 'Go and put on your best bonnet so you don't keep your ardent young Captain waiting one minute longer than he has to. Don't want to see him trying to steal a kiss over the breakfast table, what?'

As if he would do anything of the sort. But Lizzie got to her feet and hurried from the room, relieved to escape her grandfather when he was in such a jocular mood. It wasn't like him. Not at all. She was inured to the way he barked orders at her and snapped when he was in pain because of his various ailments. It all felt off kilter, somehow. As if the world had shifted so that the floor which used to be perfectly even was now tilted to one side, so that she was having to feel her way along.

Even Captain Bretherton looked different this morning, somehow. Perhaps it was because she now knew he had a title and an estate—even if it was on the verge of ruin by the sound of it. Anyway, whatever it was, he seemed far more unreachable. She could believe that a half-pay officer recovering from a long-standing illness might seek out her company. Even, almost, that he'd want to marry her.

But an earl? She shook her head. He could marry just about anyone.

So what was he doing, following her down to Dorset, after knowing her for only a few days?

It didn't make sense.

Chapter Thirteen

'So…' he said, after they'd been driving along for some time in excruciating silence. For some reason, Miss Hutton looked distinctly uncomfortable this morning. If only he could think of something to say, or do, that would put her at ease.

He cleared his throat. 'You, ah…your interests are…that is, do you enjoy reading to Lady Buntingford? I am sorry…' He shot her a sideways glance. 'You can probably tell I am not used to attempting to court a female. When we were just talking, like…friends, it seemed much easier. Now that we both know marriage is on the horizon, somewhere, ah, possibly…'

She took a deep breath. 'It isn't just that. Not on my part, anyway.'

'Oh? What is it then?'

'Well, it is just that, you are going to think this

awfully silly of me, but when I thought you were just a…a…half-pay officer, I found it far easier to… to just talk to you like a friend, as you put it. But now, I have learned that you are an *earl*.'

'I am still the same man.'

'Yes, but an *earl*. You could marry *any*one. So I don't quite see…'

'I could not marry anyone. As I told your grand-father,' he said, glad that he'd already stuck as near to the truth as possible, for if he'd started weaving too many stories he was bound to trip over one of them eventually, 'before I met you I never thought I'd get married at all.'

'But…' She wrinkled up her nose in the most endearing fashion. 'Earls need heirs, don't they? And Lady Buntingford used to say that, whenever she was teaching me about how to behave if ever I met anyone of rank, that you would expect a cer-tain *standard*…'

The way her shoulders drooped showed that she didn't believe she met that standard. What was wrong with all the people around her, that all they'd done, all her life, was make her feel as though she didn't measure up?

'I have heirs,' he said, rather more shortly than

he'd intended. 'A pair of cousins who grew up expecting to inherit my title and estates.'

'But how could they? I mean…' She wrinkled her nose in that endearingly confused way again.

'Why do you think my uncle sent me away to sea as soon as he could persuade the other trustees it was the best course? It was because,' he answered before Lizzie could even draw breath to make a conjecture, 'he knew he wouldn't get away with actually killing me.'

Miss Hutton gasped.

'I became the Earl of Inverseigg at the tender age of eight, you see, at which time my uncle became my guardian and chief trustee. He showed his true colours from the start. I have never met a more mean-spirited bully anywhere else in the world. I can't tell you how happy I was when some of my mother's family put up some money to send me to school. Those few terms at Eton College were among the happiest of my life. But I am convinced that Uncle Edgar spent that time planning the best way to dispose of me,' Harry continued by way of explanation. 'To make sure he, and then his own sons, inherited he exposed me to the harshest environment he could think of. If I did not die in action, he hoped I'd be carried off by some tropical disease.'

She reached over and placed one gloved hand on his sleeve. 'It must have been horrid for you. But I still don't see why it meant you did not wish to marry.'

'My father left the estates teetering on the verge of bankruptcy. He was a gambler.'

'Which explains,' she said thoughtfully, 'your aversion to cards.'

He'd expected her to draw the conclusion about why he hadn't been thinking of taking a wife. But Miss Hutton never acted the way he expected most women would.

'Indeed. But anyway, because I had to live on my pay, it would not have been fair to leave a wife to struggle alone while I was away at sea.'

She frowned. 'So, what changed?'

Typical of her not to think that she was what had changed his mind. How he wished he could tell her the truth. As it was, he gritted his teeth to maintain the fiction he'd already told her grandfather. It helped to keep his eyes fixed firmly between the horses' ears as though he needed to study the road and concentrate on handling the reins.

'I will soon be in a position to lift the mortgages

with which my property is encumbered. Ironically, my uncle's ambition for his own sons meant that he worked hard to bring the estates into good working order. I could, very soon, return with a bride on my arm and live there in comfort instead of enduring the privations of life at sea.'

It was true. Though it had not been his intention to do any such thing. Although he could see Miss Hutton at Inverseigg. She would fit right in with the rugged scenery. Nor would the rather Spartan grandeur of the Hall daunt her. She'd settle right in as though she was born to rule over it all.

'But,' Miss Hutton said, 'why hide the fact that you are an earl? Most men brag about their rank. And insist that everyone acknowledges it.'

'I always felt the title was a rather hollow one.' He frowned. That did not seem an adequate explanation, somehow. 'And as a boy, it had brought me nothing but danger and deprivation. If I had been just… I don't know, a crofter's son, perhaps, nobody would have tried to steal my inheritance, would they? And then again, I derived a good deal of satisfaction from rising through the ranks on my own merit, rather than trading on my connections. I suppose,' he mused, 'I needed to prove my own worth.'

Even as the words left his mouth, they struck a chord. That was why he'd found imprisonment so hard to bear. He'd been helpless. Reduced to the conditions he'd endured as a boy, at the mercy of pitiless captors.

'Which you have done, admirably,' she said, making him wince. 'I did wonder if…the way Grandfather teased us, had made you a little…' She wriggled in her seat. 'I mean, *I* was ready to sink through the floor when he started laughing at the thought you might have been thinking about attempting to snatch a kiss.' Her cheeks turned pink as she spoke. 'As though you would ever consider doing anything so improper,' she finished, with a funny little laugh which sounded almost bitter.

He kept his gaze fixed firmly on the road ahead at the sting of her words. For he *had* considered kissing her. If it would have furthered his cause, he wouldn't have balked at the impropriety of it.

'Holding hands with you during that concert was not the act of a gentleman,' he pointed out, 'was it?' Dammit, someone ought to warn her about the kind of men who took advantage of lonely, largely unsupervised young females. 'No wonder he removed you from Bath the moment he found out about it.' But the Colonel had been too late. The damage was already done. Miss Hutton had looked at him, yesterday, as though she would be all too willing to let him kiss her. In those few encounters they'd had in Bath, he'd clearly made inroads into her heart.

Which was a good thing—for the investigation. It meant that he had a plausible reason to be here. Miss Hutton's reaction to him would convince everyone he was here because of her, and her alone. The way she'd looked up at him, as he'd escorted her home the day before, must have already convinced the shopkeepers and other villagers they'd passed by that she was receptive to his advances.

Receptive? Her face had positively been glowing. And she'd kept looking into his face with a sort of wonder.

It had given him another sleepless night. It was a deuced uncomfortable feeling, having another person's happiness in his hands. His only consolation was that she would come to less harm with him than she would have done at the hands of those other three rogues Rawcliffe had considered hiring. He would at least leave her virtue intact. No matter how adoringly she gazed up into his eyes.

'He's…very protective…' she began hesitantly.

'Protective? He let you go to Lady Buntingford's yesterday, completely *un*protected.'

'Well, there is really no need for me to have anyone escort me the length of the High Street...'

'I frightened you,' he pointed out grimly, 'by approaching you outside her gate. You cannot deny it. Else why would you have hit me with your umbrella?'

'You *startled* me,' she corrected him gently. 'Most people know that my eyesight is poor and don't leap out of the bushes at me the way you did.'

'What is he doing, forbidding you to wear spectacles which would enable you to see any dangers that might be lurking?'

'That wasn't what you said yesterday,' she said, rather sadly.

'Eh?' Oh, yes, he'd said he'd thought it would be a shame to hide those lovely eyes of hers behind lenses which would distort them.

Which reminded him, he was supposed to be *making up* to her, not criticising the lax way her grandfather let her wander about, unsupervised, leaving her prey to every unscrupulous scoundrel that set his sights on her.

And it could have been a scoundrel like Lieutenant Nateby, if he hadn't drawn the long straw. He imagined the officer, who derived such pleasure from flogging the men, holding these reins, driving her into Peacombe, and shuddered with revulsion.

It made it very hard to say anything further.

'Anyway, I have been in the habit of walking up to Lady Buntingford's ever since I was quite a small girl,' she said, before he could think of something that Lieutenant Nateby would never have dreamed of saying. 'Well, a young girl, anyway. I've always been tall. Or so it seems,' she finished on a frown.

'You have lived here all your life?' At least it didn't feel like a gross impertinence to probe into her background now that he'd shared some of his own.

'Oh, no. We only came to live with Grandfather, Sam and I, after my parents died. I…' she began shyly, 'I know what it is like to suddenly feel as though you've lost everything. My father, too, left nothing but debts behind, which Grandfather was obliged to settle. He was not being unkind when he warned us we'd all have to get used to living frugally. In fact, I'd say he has been very kind, in his own, rather gruff way. And he would have preferred to put Sam in the army, like himself, only Sam was so keen to go to sea. Because, you see, when we first came here, those days were…

Sam and I—well, nobody bothered us at all. And we found the area a marvellous playground. We'd swim and explore all the tunnels along the cliffs, hide pretend contraband in secret caves, row out to sea to dive for kegs and fight mock battles with revenue men on the beaches.'

His stomach lurched to hear she'd played at being a smuggler, since he'd already spent several sleepless hours wondering what he'd do if he were to discover she was in league with the local ones. But he didn't follow up on his misgivings. His mission demanded he play the part of adoring swain, no matter what she revealed about her past, or her sympathies.

'What happened,' he prompted her, 'to change that?'

She sighed and twisted her hands into the strings of the large and lumpy reticule he was beginning to recognise as her one and only accessory.

'Lady Buntingford came across me and Sam fighting a mock battle in the churchyard. She went to Grandfather and complained about the way he was bringing me up. Or failing to bring me up. Quite a lecture, she gave him, about letting us run amok among the tombstones, instead of ensuring I learned how to be a proper young lady. And shortly after that, I began my tutoring, at her hands. She tried to teach me to embroider and curtsy, and talk about nothing more controversial than fashion, and insisted I wear dresses *all* the time, which effectively hampered most of my more adventurous pursuits. Although, without Sam there as my playmate, there didn't seem much point in them anyway.'

'He went away at about the same time, did he?'

She nodded. And bit down on her lower lip. 'I missed him terribly, but at least he wrote to me regularly. So that I knew exactly what…oh,' she said, half-turning in her seat. 'You must have gone through similar horrors when you first became a midshipman.'

'He surely didn't tell you…'

'Enough to make my toes curl,' she said with a shudder.

'What kind of brother tells his little sister that sort of thing? Surely, he would have wanted to protect you by making light of…'

'Oh, he did! Truly, he tried to make it all sound as though he was having a grand adventure.'

'Hmmph.' That was exactly what he'd done in letters to his school friends.

'But, I could read between the lines…'

Which was more than they'd done. They'd devoured his tall tales with great enthusiasm. So that when he'd finally met up with Becconsall in Naples, Major Jack Hesketh, as he'd then become, had looked upon him as though he were some sort of hero out of Greek mythology.

As though he really were Atlas.

'And it made me stop feeling sorry for myself, I can tell you. Whenever I felt like complaining about the treatment Lady Buntingford was meting out, I only had to think of the things Sam was having to do, like…like climbing rigging on a ship that was pitching and tossing in a gale, or keeping watch all night. And that at least she wasn't making me eat hard tack with weevils in it. But, oh, how I resented poor Lady Buntingford in those days,' Miss Hutton continued with a shake of her head.

'And yet you devote your afternoons to reading to her now? That is very kind of you, considering.'

'Oh, no, not at all.' She half-turned to him, her brow creased in an earnest expression which made her look totally adorable. 'It was my fault she had that seizure. At least, I always felt it was, because I was with her when she had it and we had been arguing, as usual…'

'She had a seizure?'

Miss Hutton bit down on her lower lip. 'I am

not supposed to say. Oh, dear, how upset she will be with me. You see, she doesn't want anyone to know how very helpless she has become. Well, when you know how proud she was, what a stickler for etiquette and appearance and so forth, it is completely understandable, now that she can barely move. Or speak.'

'She must be able to speak a bit, surely?' Or how did she manage to let everyone know she didn't want visitors?

'No. That's the terrible thing. After the second day, all she has ever been able to say is *oh, dear.* Or sometimes *dear, dear.*'

His pulse sped up.

'So how does she make her wishes known? By writing notes?'

'No, she is unable to write. She is completely paralysed all down her right side and can only move her left hand just a little bit. She lays in bed all day and has to be fed with a spoon.'

'How long ago did this seizure occur?'

'About five years ago.' Her brow furrowed in concentration. 'Yes, that's right. Not long after Reverend Cottam came to take up his place as curate of Lesser Peeving.'

So, shortly after Cottam came to the area, he'd

stumbled across an elderly lady who was almost completely helpless. He'd have to check with Rawcliffe, but he wouldn't be a bit surprised to learn that it was at about that time that the first of the jewel thefts took place. Lady Rawcliffe had told him that Cottam *saw to* all Lady Buntingford's correspondence. Aye, he would wager he did! He'd help himself to her headed notepaper and either forge, or have a skilled forger write, a reference in a likeness of her hand, and other ladies who'd been corresponding with her for most of their lives would trust what she had to say. They'd take in a girl upon her recommendation and trust her, never dreaming she'd be busy switching family heirlooms for cheap replicas.

'So, naturally,' Miss Hutton continued, in complete oblivion to the dark direction of his thoughts, 'I don't mind giving up one afternoon a week to read to her, even though the kinds of stories she likes are not really to my taste.'

'How do you know she likes them? How does she make her wishes known, if all she can say is *oh, dear*?'

'It is the way she says *oh, dear.* And also, she gets a sparkle in her eye when she is enjoying the story.'

'Yes, but if all she can say is *oh, dear*, how did she let people know she didn't want visitors?'

'Well, that was the fortunate thing. She did manage to speak a bit, just at first. Reverend Cottam reached her before the doctor did and apparently she told him that she didn't want anyone to see her like that, apart from myself and the Reverend of course, since we'd already witnessed her condition, just before she suffered another seizure which left her...well, the way she is now.'

How convenient. For Cottam, that was. If Lady Buntingford actually *did* have a second seizure. He clenched his jaw. By the sound of it, in either case, he'd effectively turned Lady Buntingford into a prisoner in her own home. So that he could use her name, and her stationery, to further his own ends.

Chapter Fourteen

Lizzie shivered as they crested the last dip in the moors and Peacombe came into sight, spread out below them as though hugging the semi-circular bay.

Things had been going so well. They'd fallen into an easy way of talking again as they chatted about their childhoods, then all of a sudden it was as though he'd retreated into a dark place and pulled up the drawbridge behind him.

Why had her last remark done that to him? Or had his reaction been coming on for some time and she just hadn't noticed it as she'd been prattling on? He'd certainly looked a little thoughtful when she'd told him about how she'd played at being a smuggler. She supposed she could understand him disapproving of anyone who appeared to sympathise with smugglers. Sam had certainly changed his attitude about them, after he'd joined the navy.

But was it just her attitude towards smugglers he hadn't liked to hear about, or the fact that she'd admitted to being happier playing boys' games than learning deportment and embroidery? And as for complaining about her not wearing spectacles, and walking along a High Street on her own...well...

She heaved a sigh. It was beginning to look as if it was going to be much harder to sustain a relationship with a man than it had been to look back wistfully over one she'd thought had failed before it even started. Especially if they were going to react in completely contrary ways to sharing experiences. For while he had gone all stiff and withdrawn once the conversation petered out, all she wanted to do was snuggle up against his body, link her arm through his and rub her cheek against his shoulder in the manner of an adoring kitten. And at the same time, to hug the poor, lonely, frightened little boy he must once have been and tell him... Though what did she need to tell him? He'd survived all that his wicked uncle, or the elements, could throw at him and grown into a fine, upstanding man. A man who appeared to regret having admitted to being a helpless little boy at all. Was that it? Was that why he'd withdrawn and adopted the kind of face she'd expect an earl would wear when obliged to drive a rather dowdy country miss through the streets of a little town where everyone's heads turned as they went past, no doubt in amazement that a man like him could bear being seen with the likes of her?

It was a bit of a relief when Captain Bretherton turned the gig into the passage that led to the stable yard. She was ready for a drink. How she wished she were a man and could ask for a glass of brandy. Though, if she were a man, she wouldn't be flummoxed by the unpredictable moods of the man who'd driven her into town. They would just be talking about…sport of some kind. Or horses, or something similar. Not their childhoods, or their hopes and dreams for the future.

She eyed him thoughtfully as his servant jumped down and ran round to hold the horses' heads. For the first time since she'd met him, she tried to imagine him standing on the deck of a ship, barking orders to his crew who would jump to it. That was where he was probably most comfortable. He wasn't used to spending much time with women. He'd admitted it, almost the moment they'd set out that morning.

And he had said, hadn't he, that they needed to spend some time getting to know each other?

And now he was climbing down and coming round to her side of the carriage, and holding out his hand to help her down, like a true gentleman. In short, doing his best.

As she placed her hand in his, she couldn't help smiling at him. Even when he was being a bit, well, grumpy, he hadn't made her feel as if it was her fault for being a lumbering, great, unattractive old maid, the way most men did. On the contrary, he was treating her with all the gallantry she could wish for.

'Do you wish to go to the library first?' he asked her rather stiffly. Which she found rather endearing. For nobody else ever asked what she preferred. Grandfather just told her what he wanted her to do and expected her immediate compliance. 'Or the coffee room?'

'I should like to go to the coffee room,' she said. 'It's always lovely and warm in there. Mr Jeavons will be able to tell me if the books I have requested have come in yet. And probably bring them to me while we are taking refreshments.'

'Ah, Captain Bretherton, Miss Hutton,' cried the landlord, the moment they stepped across the threshold. 'What a pleasure to see you both. Together.' He rubbed his hands in that oily way which always made her feel slightly queasy. Not that she'd ever let him know, of course.

She felt Captain Bretherton's arm stiffen slightly beneath the hand she'd laid upon his sleeve. She could tell, just from that tiny change in him, that he felt the same as she did. Which was the wonderful thing about him. They saw eye to eye over so many things.

'We have called in to take coffee,' said Captain Bretherton in a clipped voice.

'And to collect the latest novel for Miss Hutton to read to Lady Buntingford,' put in Mr Jeavons with a tone in his voice that put her in mind of a dish of lard. 'Only just in this morning, and the talk of London, by all accounts. And Miss Hutton could not wait to get her hands on it.'

And that was another thing. He was always talking about her as if she wasn't right there in the room. As though she had no substance.

'We will wait in the coffee room,' she said, removing her hand from Captain Bretherton's sleeve. 'You may fetch Lady Buntingford's order to us there,' she informed Mr Jeavons imperiously, before stalking down the corridor, yanking off her gloves. Which wasn't easy when the strings of her reticule seemed determined to wind themselves round her fingers.

Captain Bretherton still managed to reach the room before her, darting round her and opening the door before she had to perform the menial task for herself.

'Lady Buntingford's order?' He leaned close and murmured into her ear as they passed through the doorway together. 'Didn't you tell me she could only say a couple of words?'

'Well, yes, and it's true…' she said on a little sigh. He was standing so close to her that she could feel the heat from his body. Which did something peculiar to her knees. And her stomach. It created a sort of wonder…and yearning.

'Then that means that you have deliberately ordered a racy novel, under the pretext of doing an elderly invalid a good turn.' He shook his head in mock reproof.

'Racy? Who said anything about it being racy?'

'If it is the talk of London, then it must be.'

'Must it?' She could feel her cheeks heating. 'No, probably not… I mean, most of the stories that promise scandal turn out to have heroines who do little more than sit about waiting for some hero to come and rescue them from whichever villain is currently oppressing them. Weeping copiously while they're at it,' she said with scorn.

'You don't approve of females weeping?'

'I would much rather they did something to the purpose. Like…get up and…fight. Or at the very least struggle. Of what use is sitting about weeping?'

'Well,' he said after a short reflection, 'if there was a fire, they could wring their hankies over it and put it out.'

She sucked in a sharp breath. There he was again—that man she'd met in the Pump Room. The one who joked with her. Who made her want to laugh.

'It sounds,' she said after only the slightest pause, 'as though you have read some of those books where the girls do nothing but weep for chapter after chapter, if you can imagine them putting out fires that way.'

'What are you trying to imply?' he said in a low growl.

'What were you?' she answered pertly.

'Touché,' he said, tapping the tip of her nose with one forefinger. 'However, it is blatantly obvious that you are not the kind of female who would sit

down and weep when life throws adversities in your way, are you?'

'Absolutely not.' With a toss of her head, she eased her way fully through the door and made for the nearest table. And since they were supposed to be getting to know one another, she might as well confess how very unfeminine she really was. 'My brother taught me to defend myself, when he knew he was going to have to go away to sea and leave me on my own. We didn't just pretend to fight on the beach. He made sure I can really fence and box, and shoot a gun. And when he came back on leave, he also taught me how to fight in close quarters with a knife.' A knife which he'd given her and told her to keep upon her person at all times. She still wore it to this day, buckled round the upper part of her boot, in the sheath he'd also had made for her. Perhaps, if she told Captain Bretherton that she carried it at all times, and knew how to defend herself with it, he might stop complaining about her going about *unprotected*.

Or perhaps not. He might think it was disgraceful for her to carry a sharp weapon and forbid her to do so any more. People had funny ideas about what was proper for a female to do. She had only to think how shocked Lady Buntingford had been over many things Lizzie had thought perfectly acceptable. And if he disapproved, then she'd have to make a choice—whether to stay true to Sam's memory by keeping her promise to him to keep his gift to her on her person at all times, or to try to please the man she was hoping to marry, by leaving it off.

She was going to have to feel her way carefully.

'Do…do you disapprove?'

'I cannot approve of you pretending to kill revenue men,' he growled.

'Oh, but that was only a childish game, Captain Bretherton. Sometimes Sam played the part of a revenue man and I was a smuggler, and sometimes the reverse. He went into the navy himself, don't forget.'

'Beg pardon. It's just that so many people seem to have more sympathy for the kind of men who are, after all, criminals of the worst sort…'

He gave her a long, considering look. And then stepped even closer.

'Don't you think you ought to remove your coat? So that you will feel the benefit of the fire?'

'Oh. Oh, yes, I suppose…' she began as she drew off her gloves. As she slipped the buttons from their holes, Captain Bretherton went round behind her to help her off with it. He was standing so close that she could swear she could feel his breath, hot on the back of her neck. And suddenly it was not only her coat, but also her bonnet she needed to remove. The strings were far too tight round her neck. It was getting hard to breathe.

'I take it,' he said, 'that you did not weep when your grandfather removed you from Bath?'

What? Bath? They'd been talking about smugglers. And how on earth was she supposed to be able to follow the thread of a conversation with his large, capable hands sliding down her arms as he removed her coat?

'I have always detested Bath,' she admitted, though how exactly they'd got back to that, she couldn't imagine. 'I was glad to come home.'

'Did you not feel even the slightest bit sad?'

When she turned round to look at him, she saw that he was taking off his own hat and tucking it under his arm. 'I know you did not shed any tears, but did you not miss…anything, or any*one* you left behind in Bath?'

'Are you…?' She sat down rather suddenly, in the nearest chair. 'You are, you are fishing for compliments!'

He sighed, mournfully, as he took the chair on

the other side of the table. 'I fear I would be wasting my time. You are clearly a hard case.'

'That is what most people believe,' she said sadly. 'That I have not a shred of feminine softness about me.'

'I did not mean to offend you,' he said, running his fingers through his hair as though vexed with himself. 'This is what comes of trying to flirt with you when I have so little experience.'

He stretched out his legs and stuck his hands in his pockets. She couldn't see his face, but she could imagine, from that pose, that it bore a glum expression.

'Then don't flirt with me again,' she said. 'I don't expect it. And to be honest, since I'm not used to it, I don't really know how to deal with it anyway. Could we not just…?'

'What? Just what?' He sat up straight, as though straining towards her.

'Just be ourselves. Be honest with each other.'

He slumped back down again. 'Honest.' He shook his head. 'Miss Hutton,' he began. 'If I were to be completely honest with you…'

And then the door opened to admit Mr Jeavons himself with a couple of books tucked under his arm, closely followed by a waiter bearing their re-freshments.

And whatever Captain Bretherton had been about to tell her remained frustratingly unsaid.

Chapter Fifteen

Oh, why did Mr Jeavons have to come in at this precise moment? Harry had been about to tell her something. Something she wasn't going to like, judging by the tone of his voice. What could it be? Had he decided he didn't want to marry her, after all? Or had he lied about being an earl to try and impress Grandfather? No, that couldn't be it. He surely wouldn't have fabricated the wicked uncle and the grasping cousins, and the debts and all the rest of it.

Perhaps it was that he'd heard he needed to go back to sea in a week's time?

And why wouldn't Jeavons just put the books down and go away? Surely, the way Captain Bretherton was glowering up at him—at least she was pretty sure he was glowering from the tilt of his head and the set of his shoulders—and her own fidgety manner must be telling him they wanted to be alone?

And why was he going on and on about all the lovely walks to be had in the area? She'd lived here for most of her life and knew all about the fossils littering the beach round the headland they could reach along the newly constructed promenade. And the gardens created on a series of terraces on that same headland. And had played in the tunnels where the waterfall had its source and had marvelled at the way ice brought down from the moors could stay frozen all year round in certain alcoves in those tunnels.

Had he no sensitivity? Couldn't he imagine that she might have wanted to tell Captain Bretherton about all those places of interest herself? And show them to him herself?

'One enters the promenade by the harbour and, for the fee of one penny, visitors can stroll the entire length of bay and gain entrance to the gardens...'

'Or,' she said, finally losing patience with the hotel manager, 'one can go over the moors and reach the headland entirely for free.'

Mr Jeavons drew himself up to his full height. 'Only by means of a path that is overgrown by gorse bushes, which comes perilously close to the cliff edge, in places. It is a treacherous path, Captain Bretherton,' he said, turning his shoulder to her. 'Not at all suitable for a lady.'

'I know those paths,' she retorted, 'like the back of my hand.'

'Perhaps Miss Hutton does,' he said to Captain Bretherton, stoking her irritation up to the point of clenching those hands into fists, 'but it is not advisable to encourage visitors to the area to take risks. There have already been two unfortunate accidents...' He faltered.

'Accidents?' Captain Bretherton sat up straight. 'What do you mean?'

'Ah...' Mr Jeavons finally set down Lizzie's books on a table by her elbow. 'It was nothing. Nothing for you to worry about, that is, Captain, I'm sure. One mustn't dwell on...that is, we don't want the area to get a reputation for... Jones!' He suddenly whirled round and snapped his fingers at the waiter, who was still fiddling with the cups and plates. 'Come along now. Back to the kitchen. There is work to be done.' He bowed briefly to Lizzie, then Captain Bretherton, and slunk out of the room.

'What,' said Captain Bretherton, 'was that all about?'

'That,' Lizzie said with a sigh, 'was Mr Jeavons letting his tongue running away for a good while before suddenly coming to his senses.'

'What do you mean?'

'Besides, they weren't accidents. Not the two cases he mentioned, if that was what he was talking about, and I can't imagine he meant anything else.'

'Now you have really confused me.' He got up and came to stand by her chair.

'Do we really have to talk about them? They were both terribly upsetting...'

'Hmm...' he said. Then went to the table on which the waiter had set out the refreshments and picked up the coffee pot. 'Sometimes, it helps, you know, to talk about incidents which otherwise have a tendency to prey on the mind.'

He slammed the coffee pot down suddenly, walked across to the window and ran his fingers through his hair. 'No, forget I said anything. I shouldn't press you to talk about things which upset you. It is just—'

'Just that the little hints Mr Jeavons dropped have roused your curiosity. And my reluctance to enlighten you has fanned that curiosity to a flame.' And she should know, because the way he'd hinted at having something to confess had just had pretty much the same effect on her.

Perhaps, if she satisfied his curiosity, he might return the favour.

'I didn't know either of them that well. The people Mr Jeavons mentioned,' she began. 'So I didn't exactly grieve their loss. Though any sudden, accidental death is unpleasant. To be honest, it was the gossip that followed that I found so upsetting. Especially since so much of it was wildly inaccurate. And so I refused to join in when anyone speaks of either death, you see. If he was a different sort of man, I suppose you might think that was why he stopped talking about them when he did. Out of respect for my feelings,' she finished glumly, since respect was the last thing Jeavons had ever accorded her. Not real respect for her as a person.

Captain Bretherton turned round. Squared his shoulders. 'Point taken. If you dislike indulging in gossip I shall not press you to repeat it. Indeed, I admire you for your attitude.'

His words made her brief dip into the gloom disperse like mist before a stiff sea breeze. And, strangely, also made her want to confide in him.

'I would not mind giving you a factual account of what happened,' she said, going to the table and picking up the coffee pot he'd abandoned moments earlier. 'Shall I pour?'

'Please.' He came to her side as she poured the coffee. And though she was concentrating on her task, she could feel him watching her intently.

'The first person who drowned along this part of the coast earlier this year,' she said as she handed him his cup, 'was a maidservant. A girl called Jenny. A Londoner, from her accent, who'd had some dealings with the Reverend Cottam. Which was why she came down here when she got into trouble. To seek his advice, or perhaps to ask for refuge.' She frowned down into her cup as she poured her own coffee. 'That is where it gets a bit confusing. Depending upon whom you speak to about her.' Lizzie couldn't help giving a shudder. 'Poor girl. To begin with, people thought her drowning was just an accident. Until another visitor to the area, a young man this time, went the same way. Although...'

'Although, what?'

'Well, after Mr Kellet—that was the young man I mentioned—after he drowned, people started saying he'd been responsible for Jenny's trouble. That there had been some sort of doomed love affair. They even started to call the headland where they were supposed to have thrown themselves into the sea, Lover's Leap.'

'But you don't believe it?'

'Absolutely not. There was no mention of any sort of lover until Mr Kellet drowned as well. I think people put that story about to stop holiday makers thinking this part of the coast was dangerous, to tell you the truth. Better some wild tale of star-crossed lovers than the prosaic truth about the currents just offshore being too dangerous for anyone to go sea bathing. Besides…'

'Besides?'

'Well, I spoke to Jenny, a couple of times. I found her up on the headland—the one they started to call Lover's Leap, it's true, but I'm pretty certain it wasn't unrequited love that made her jump. Because she didn't say anything about a man being at the root of her unhappiness at all.'

'Didn't she?'

'No. She was just upset about an elderly lady she'd been working for. The lady had died while she was in the house and she felt responsible, because she was the one to administer her medicine. Which, at the time, I thought sounded a bit silly.

I mean, why should she feel guilty if an elderly lady, who must have been under a doctor if there was medicine being given, died? Especially since it had never done anyone else any harm.'

'What do you mean, never done anyone else any harm?'

'Oh, just that she said she'd given it to other old ladies, without them…er…*kicking the bucket* was the expression she used. Which was why I didn't perfectly understand what she meant until some time later.'

'No,' he said faintly. 'Why would you?'

'And what's more, Mr Kellet never spoke about being in love, either. He just wanted to know why he couldn't go and visit his great-godmother. Lady Buntingford, that is. And he spoke to me about her several times, because I am the only one, just about, who ever visits her. And I cannot believe a young man who could barely stammer out a complete sentence without going beetroot red could have possibly treated Jenny the way people said he must have done. Why, he couldn't have seduced anyone. Let alone abandon them. He was far too… well, he just wasn't smooth enough. If you know what I mean?'

'I know exactly what you mean.'

'Besides, it was only after he'd drowned, as well, that a tale began to circulate about him having broken Jenny's heart and flinging himself into the sea in a fit of remorse. When there'd been no mention of a broken heart at the time of her death. Not even a whisper. So, after a bit, I decided that someone deliberately started that rumour to make the tragedies more interesting to holiday makers. And less off-putting to people considering coming here. It's the only explanation that makes sense.'

'So you don't think there's an ounce of truth in the lovers story?'

'No. And I don't want you believing in the rumours, either.'

'Why is that?'

'Well, Mr Kellet was such a nice young man. It doesn't seem fair that his memory should be tainted by tales of that sort.'

He reached out and gently squeezed her hand.

'You are a remarkable girl.'

Something inside her turned over. 'I am not the slightest bit remarkable. I just don't like people making up tales about people. Especially when they have no means of refuting those tales. It's almost like bullying them.' She shook her head. 'And I cannot stand bullies.'

'No,' he said sombrely. 'No more can I.'

'Have some cake,' she said, picking up the plate and holding it out. 'Mr Jeavons might be a most annoying and rather unscrupulous person, but his cook does make the most delicious cakes and pastries.'

'What do you mean, unscrupulous?'

'Oh, well, just that he doesn't seen all that bothered about things like telling the truth if it will get in the way of making a profit. That kind of thing.'

He hesitated, his face turned to hers for several moments before he lowered his gaze to look at the plate and selecting one of the slices.

'Now,' she said, setting the plate back on the table as he threw the fruit cake into his mouth and began to chew, 'that I have satisfied your curiosity, perhaps you can satisfy mine.'

He swallowed. 'In what way?'

'Well, just before Mr Jeavons came in and interrupted, you were about to confess something. And I have to admit that I cannot stop wondering what it might have been. Will you tell me what it was? Please?'

Chapter Sixteen

Thank goodness he managed to swallow what was left of the cake swiftly, rather than spitting it out, or choking on it.

'Confess?' He managed to wheeze the word with relative clarity, before walking away to the window and running his fingers through his hair. He could not confess what had been on his mind *now*. Admittedly, for one crazy moment, back there, he'd been on the brink of taking her into his confidence. Confessing that he had an ulterior motive for making her acquaintance and following her down here.

But that would have hurt her. What woman wouldn't be hurt, when she discovered that a man supposedly engaged in courting her was actually doing his utmost to prise information out of her? Not that he'd had to work all that hard on her. She was so open, so trusting, that she was revealing all sorts of crucial information without having the least idea of its importance.

But if he did anything to damage that trust, she might never tell him anything of relevance again. Perhaps never even *speak* to him again.

What was more, had he yielded to the temptation to let his regard for her override his need for secrecy, at that precise moment, she would not have told him what she knew about Jenny and Archie's death. And what else might she know, without even knowing its importance?

What harm might he do to the investigation by easing his conscience over the way their acquaintance had been stage-managed? He might well feel a weight roll off his shoulders, but he would hurt her…and he found himself wanting desperately not to do so. It was time, well past time, that he acted up to his namesake. The punishment of Atlas was to bear the weight of the world on his shoulders. Not to make confessions and hope that people would understand him. If only he'd been able to remember that when he'd first returned to England, none of this would have happened. If he hadn't been…wallowing in some sort of… Slough of Despond over the fate that had befallen his crew when they'd been ambushed on that beach…been stuck in the mindset he'd sunk into while being held prisoner. A sort of creeping lassitude. He should never have tried to seek solace over his physical and mental deterioration in the bottom of a bottle. Then he would never have sat back and let Archie try to take on the task of investigating what had started out as a jewel theft. Even though he'd had so little sympathy for the rich old women who'd been robbed.

'Captain Bretherton?'

He whirled round. While he'd been drowning in a morass of bitter recriminations, Miss Hutton had come up behind him and was now laying her hand, tentatively, on his upper arm. He realised he'd curled his fingers into a fist. Had struck the window upright.

'I don't deserve your regard,' he ground out. 'I am...' He lowered his head. 'I have failed to act honourably.'

'Oh, no, I'm sure not.'

Her voice was soft. Laced with concern. And stung worse than the lash of a cat-o'-nine-tails.

'Yes,' he hissed. And because he could not, at present, confess what was uppermost in his mind, regarding her and the false courtship upon which he was engaged, he decided he'd better tell her something else instead. Something that had, indeed, been troubling him for some time. 'We were speaking about being honest with each other, weren't we?' he said. 'Of getting to know each other, rather than flirting. And I thought I might tell you...confide...how I felt when I failed my men. So miserably. I was imprisoned, you know? By the French? Because I made a complete c—a complete mess of planning the operation. I didn't check the terrain thoroughly enough—'

'Terrain? You mean, you were on land? But you are a captain in the navy...'

'Yes, but we were responsible for getting troops ashore many times. This time, I led everyone straight into an ambush a schoolboy should have seen. The entire operation ended in failure. I should have been court-martialled.'

'Why were you not, then?'

'Oh, some nonsense about unreliable intelligence. But I'd believed it. Completely. When I should not have done. I should, at the very least, have sent a small party ashore to double-check the details. And then the crew from the other ship, who managed to get away while my men held back the French, put in a report about us sacrificing ourselves so that they, and the infantry, could escape. They even tried to make out I'd been some kind of hero.' He shuddered in disgust.

'But…weren't you? To stand and fight while others escaped?'

'The infantry might have got away. And the crew of the other ship. But my men all either died, or were captured. And the conditions they suffered, at the hands of our captors, were brutal. And there was nothing I could do about it. Nothing. I…you see…as an officer, they offered me parole. Which meant that as long as I promised not to try to escape, I had relative freedom. I tried to use it to do what I could for the men, but…' He bowed his head. The food he'd managed to get to them, from time to time, had been a mere drop in the ocean. Though he'd gone without, time and time again, until the flesh melted from his frame, it made little difference to them. One by one they'd died. The injured first and then the stronger ones.

'When I was released, I failed to act like an honourable officer of His Majesty's navy, too.' He'd let his former schoolfriend, Rawcliffe, take him into his house and feed him, and had gone along with whatever he'd suggested, because it hadn't seemed to matter what he did. 'I failed even to uphold my own standards. For so long…'

He'd been drifting. Without a compass. He hadn't really set his hand to the tiller again until he'd heard that Archie had died, doing a job he'd been so ill equipped for. *He* was the one who should have come down to Dorset. And, yes, been the one to die. Nobody, then, would have cared a rap. He was worthless. Spent. Whereas Archie was such a brilliant man. Had so much promise. Archie had been destined to make discoveries that would improve the lot of mankind.

All Harry could do was train men in the arts of destruction. He'd spent his entire adult life blowing things up and tearing things down.

Well, now, he vowed again, grinding his teeth, he was going to put those murderous skills to good use. He would tear down whatever organisation was behind sending servant girls to steal jewels from wealthy families. And bring those responsible for Archie's death to justice. And he wouldn't let anyone or anything stop him.

Not even soft words from a girl he liked and admired, and felt such a strong kinship with. For it wasn't as if he could really marry her. He wasn't yet so deeply into the role that he believed they could really have a future. He was here to do a job.

And part of that job was to pass on whatever information he gleaned to Rawcliffe and Becconsall.

That was one mistake Archie had made that he would not repeat. Whatever Archie had discovered while he'd been here, whatever it was that had caused the criminals to kill him, nobody would ever know. Because he hadn't passed that information on. That was one thing his training, as well as his mistakes, had taught him. Information was the key. Every day, officers kept logs of everything that happened, so that there was always a written record against which to compare the fading impressions of memory.

So, before this day ended, he would have to write down all that he'd learned so far. So that even if he did meet the same fate as Archie, at least his death wouldn't be completely in vain.

'Miss Hutton, I have suddenly recalled that there are things I should be doing. Things I have neglected. I will escort you home and then apply myself to…some long-overdue letters I should write.'

Her face fell. Poor Lizzie. He wished…but no. He *had* to pass on the knowledge he'd gleaned so far.

Rawcliffe and Becconsall needed to know the exact date when Lady Buntingford had suffered that seizure. And how, from that point on, she could not write. If the references purporting to have come from her had been issued after that event, then she couldn't possibly have written them. Couldn't even have ordered them to be written on her behalf. Far from being the brains behind the series of jewel thefts, she must surely have become Cottam's puppet. Lady Rawcliffe had already found out that he was using her address as a sort of secret post office. Cottam himself had told her that if she wanted to get in touch with him without her husband's knowledge, she could do so by addressing her letter to Lady Buntingford, because, as her trusted advisor, he dealt with all her post.

Trusted advisor? Hah! He was no such thing. On the contrary, he was practically her jailer. Harry couldn't believe that story about her telling him she didn't want anyone seeing her in such a helpless condition, just before suffering a second seizure. It was all just a little bit too convenient. For Cottam, that was.

Harry also had to let Rawcliffe know what Miss Hutton had just told him about Jenny. That could be another coincidence, he supposed, that a girl called Jenny had drowned shortly after coming down here to Cottam for help. And that she'd been mixed up in the death of an elderly lady for whom she'd been working. But Rawcliffe had certainly been hunting for a girl known as Jenny, who'd been working for Archie's great-grandmother, and who had mysteriously vanished immediately after her death. There had also been a Jenny working for Lady Rawcliffe's aunt. And in both households, jewels had been replaced by fakes. And in both cases, the 'Jenny' in question had been hired on the strength of references supposed to have been written by Lady Buntingford.

Rawcliffe was already convinced that Cottam was behind all of it. The jewel thefts and forged references, as well as Archie's death. And the more Harry found out, the more inclined he was to agree. The way Cottam had so callously treated Lady Buntingford made it all too easy to see him working behind the scenes, like some big fat spider, crouching at the centre of a web whose strands reached as far as London itself.

Once Harry had written his report, he'd have to take steps to make sure it reached Rawcliffe safely. From what he could tell, the locals were all either scared of, or in the pay of, the smugglers with whom Cottam was so closely connected. So it wouldn't be a straightforward matter to get information out of the area. But that was where Dawkins was going to come in handy. He could act as a courier, taking letters to somewhere near enough so that he'd be there and back within a day, so that they could relay any new information they discovered on a daily basis, if necessary.

They'd decided on Bath. The postmaster there could surely not be in the pay of a gang of Dorset smugglers. And they could also drop hints about consulting a medical man there, or fetching medicine, or some such thing. In fact, he promptly decided as he looked down into Miss Hutton's troubled face, he would have Dawkins consult an oculist on her behalf.

He took hold of her hands and squeezed them.

'I am sorry, Miss Hutton. But…'

'No. No need to be sorry,' she said, lifting her chin as she returned his grip. 'You came down here on the spur of the moment. Now that you have… now that we are…that is, I am sure there is all sorts of business you need to attend to. My brother was in the navy, don't forget. And though he was the dearest, kindest brother a girl could ever have, sending me part of his pay so that I could have a little pin money, or put it away for a rainy day,' she said, squeezing her reticule as though it contained some sort of talisman, 'when he was on furlough, he often had to spend hours and hours doing…well, all sorts of things that didn't include me. Important things, to him. So you mustn't think I will ever be the kind of female who will demand that you are constantly dancing attendance upon me.'

What she clearly meant was that she didn't believe she was the kind of female who *deserved* much attention. Ah, Lizzie! He hadn't wanted to join the ranks of all those people who made her feel second rate.

'I have plenty to be doing,' she continued with determined brightness. 'Especially now that I have these new books. But…' She chewed on her lower lip, clutching on to her reticule even tighter, as though steeling herself to address something unpleasant.

'Yes? Miss Hutton, you surely know you can tell me anything.' He winced. For most of what she'd told him so far was about to be written up into a report he was going to send to Rawcliffe.

'Well, I hope you don't think I am being…insensitive, but it is just that, because Sam was also an officer in the navy, I know a little bit about the service. And the action you described…well, it doesn't sound to me like a failure. It sounds as though you fought bravely to ensure that most of the men who landed got off safely again. Sam was always telling me how circumstances can change rapidly during battle, or even just when a storm blows up. And that losses cannot be helped sometimes during war. And that a good officer is one who thinks on his feet and snatches victory from what should have been catastrophe.'

She was sweet to say that. But she didn't really know…couldn't really know…

'Was? You said your brother was an officer in the navy?'

'Yes. I thought I told you, at some point, that he…' She bit her lip and lowered her head to her reticule.

'When was it?'

'Just after Trafalgar, when a storm blew up as he was trying to take one of the prize ships to port. I got the letter from him, jubilant at the amount of prize money he was going to send me. And I commissioned…this,' she said, undoing the drawstrings of her reticule and drawing out a small brass telescope. 'I had it engraved. But never got to give it to him. By the time it was ready, we'd heard…'

Poor Lizzie. Her life had been one tragedy after another. And now she was stuck with him. A man who was only pretending to court her in order to romance information out of her.

'Lizzie...' he began, and faltered. For what could he say? He couldn't promise her that she'd never be alone again, that she could depend upon him, for she couldn't.

But she was looking up at him holding that telescope representing her loneliness, her eyes brimming with tears.

Right after making a valiant attempt to offer him comfort. When he didn't deserve it. Didn't deserve her. Would *never* deserve her.

But, oh, how he wanted her. Wanted the comfort she offered. Wanted to be the man she needed.

He found himself drawing her into his arms and cradling her to his chest.

'Lizzie,' he groaned into the crown of her head. 'Lizzie...' She was so sweet, so trusting. So womanly and yielding.

She slid her arms about his waist and, for a moment, nothing else seemed to matter. She was here, in his arms, wanting him, trusting him. And there might never come another opportunity like this.

Would it be so wrong to taste her lips, just the once?

He slid one hand under her chin, and raised her

face to his. And she parted her lips. Gazed up at him as though he was the sun, the moon and the stars.

Just once, he vowed.

And proceeded to break just about every code by which he'd ever lived.

Chapter Seventeen

He'd kissed her. Oh, my word, he'd kissed her! And held her tight.

And yes, admittedly, it had all been over in a flash. And then he'd set her away from him, and said he shouldn't have done it, that in fact they should not have stayed in the coffee room when he'd seen there was nobody else there to act as chaperon.

But the point was, he *had* done it.

She couldn't have told anyone later exactly how she'd got home. His servant might have taken her in the little carriage, or she might have walked, it made no difference. Because she felt as if she'd floated there, the way the seeds of a dandelion clock soared on the current after someone plucks them and blows upon them.

Now, finally, she could believe that he really had

followed her here, after the brief time they'd shared in Bath, because he wanted her. He hadn't been able to resist kissing her, had he?

And he'd been avoiding her, ever since. As though he daren't be alone with her any more, or who knew what might happen?

It made her giggle, as she lay in bed at night, to think of herself as irresistible. Sometimes she'd press her fingers to her lips in wonder, recalling the way her heart had pounded and her blood had surged when he'd pulled her, so suddenly and almost roughly, into his arms.

It was Sunday before she saw him again. Standing under the shelter of the lych gate, clearly waiting for her. For the moment Grandfather's carriage came to a standstill he darted forward, an umbrella at the ready, to shelter them as they made their way through the graveyard.

As she placed her hand upon his sleeve she could picture herself as a bride, walking along this same path, she really could. With him at her side. Because he'd really meant all those things he'd said about her eyes and her hair, and so on. For some strange reason, he really did find her attractive.

And what was more, she felt attractive when she

was with him. No longer an awkward, burdensome creature who never fit in anywhere.

She'd drifted right up to the church door in a cloud of imaginary orange blossom before she noticed he wasn't in the same frame of mind. On the contrary, as he folded up his umbrella and leant it against the porch wall, she caught an expression on his face that was positively grim.

Could he still be feeling guilty over behaving improperly, as he'd put it, after kissing her? Or was that stern expression, that tightly clenched jaw due to him struggling to behave properly *now*?

She almost giggled at the thought of him wrestling with the urge to snatch a kiss as they ducked under the low arch of the church door.

No, she mustn't indulge in such flights of fancy. Not in church. She bent her own head in penitence as soon as she took her place in Grandfather's pew, determined to adopt a more proper frame of mind. And as she stood, and kneeled, and made her responses mechanically, it gradually dawned on her that his mood today might have nothing to do with her at all. Captain Bretherton had troubles a-plenty. Why, the very first moment they'd met, she'd noticed a haunted look in his eyes. And the other day he'd begun to tell her what had put it there. Guilt.

Just before he'd kissed her, in fact, he'd told her what it had felt like to be defeated and taken prisoner, and be helpless to do anything for the men under his command. Only, that kiss had driven all else from her mind.

She darted his stern profile a swift glance. He'd probably done nothing but brood about his men, and what he perceived as his failure, all the while he'd been a prisoner. In fact, she wouldn't be a bit surprised if all that brooding was what had done the damage. Because terrible things happened all the time during war. And if he'd gone straight back into action, it would have just been one more skirmish, no worse than any of the other horrors he'd been through.

Oh, how she wished she could talk to him about it. But there was no point in even trying. Men didn't like to speak of such things. She was sure Sam had seen some terrible sights, but all he would write to her about were the funny things that happened. The characters of the men he served with. The exotic locations he'd visited. And when he did come home, he clammed up every time she tried to get him to unburden himself. Even when he couldn't sleep at night, he would accuse her of prying if she so much as asked him what his nightmares had been about.

So she wouldn't pry into Captain Bretherton's past, either. She would simply be understanding if ever he did want to unburden himself.

'The sermon this morning,' said Reverend Cottam, 'is taken from Matthew, Chapter Eleven.'

She wrestled her mind away from Captain Bretherton as she found the passage in her bible, determined to give the sermon her full attention. But as Reverend Cottam started to expound the text, it felt as if he was speaking directly to her. Because it was all about weary, troubled souls letting Jesus take their burdens from them and finding rest. And she saw that was what this big, brave officer at her side needed. Someone who wouldn't expect him to bear his own and everyone else's burdens, simply because his shoulders were broader than everyone else's. Someone to just love him.

She came out of church, as she so often did since the Reverend Cottam had come to the area, feeling all fired up with determination to be a better, less selfish person. And also certain that even if she couldn't be, that the God Reverend Cottam preached was so full of forgiveness that He would understand.

No wonder he was so popular with the villagers. Especially the ones who so often strayed on to the wrong side of the law. He made everyone feel as if God was within reach. That he wasn't just waiting in the wings somewhere, ready to rain down fire and brimstone on the heads of sinners. And as if to reinforce that image, he made a point of waiting in the porch, after the service, so that he could shake the hand of everyone who'd attended. From the greatest to the least.

'Good morning, Miss Hutton,' he said, when it was her turn for a handshake, though his head swiftly turned in the direction of Captain Bretherton. 'Won't you introduce me to your...friend?'

'Yes, of course, Reverend Cottam,' she said, feeling somehow as though it was an introduction she should have performed much sooner. 'This is Captain Bretherton.'

'Indeed. You served in the navy with Samuel Hutton, perchance? You are paying a long-overdue visit to his family?'

She blushed. 'No. Captain Bretherton and I... that is, we are...'

'We met in Bath,' said Captain Bretherton, fiddling with his umbrella rather than take the Reverend's outstretched hand.

'They will need to be calling on you soon, I shouldn't wonder,' said Grandfather from behind them. 'To talk about reading the banns.'

'Banns? Oh! Like that, is it?'

Captain Bretherton tensed. Drew in a breath. Turned back to the curate.

'Perhaps I *should* call on you. When would be convenient?'

'Oh, no need for that. I shall call upon you. You are staying at the Three Tuns in Peacombe, I believe? Rather than with the family?'

Just a minute.

Why were they excluding her from the visit that people considering marriage normally paid to the clergy?

'Yes. Wasn't sure of my welcome when I followed Miss Hutton down here...'

'Sent him to the rightabouts, if you must know,' put in Grandfather, with a chuckle. 'Can't be too careful with the kind of chaps you meet hovering round the gels in Bath.'

'I see,' said Reverend Cottam. 'Well, then, perhaps tomorrow? I have some business to attend to in town. Shall I call in and take coffee with you?'

'I will look forward to it,' said Captain Bretherton, grimly, before marching out of the church.

'What is wrong?' he said, before they'd gone three paces. 'What have I said to offend you?'

'What,' she said with resignation, 'could you possibly have said to offend me?' Just because he'd been paying her more attention than any man ever had before, she ought not to take offence because, for a moment or two, he'd left her out of a conversation.

'I don't know, but I clearly have. You have gone as stiff as a poker.'

She sighed. It seemed that all her resolutions to not be troublesome had come to nothing. Already. The effect of Reverend Cottam's sermon had worn off before she'd even reached the edge of the church yard. 'I beg your pardon. I don't mean to be a shrew.'

'You are not being a shrew! It is I who have been clumsy, in some way. And you had better tell me what I've done, so that I don't repeat my error.'

He sounded so full of remorse that she felt she just had to explain the way she'd reacted. Even thought it had been rather silly of her.

'It wasn't your fault. It was…well, I feel a bit petty even saying it, but I was a bit…hurt, I suppose, by the way the Reverend excluded me from the meeting he seems so keen to have with you. I mean, is it not my marriage, too?'

He appeared to consider this for a moment or two. 'I dare say he wants to make sure I am worthy of you,' he said. 'You must admit, even your grandfather had his suspicions about me. And he said as much, just now.'

'But surely the fact that Grandfather approves of you now should be enough?'

'Perhaps…he thinks that I have somehow pulled the wool over his eyes, too.'

'That's outrageous! If I wish to marry you and Grandfather approves…'

'Oh, you have decided you are going to marry me, have you?'

She felt her cheeks heat. 'If you ever do get round to proposing to me, properly, I have to admit that I am more inclined to accept than when you first came down to Lesser Peeving, yes.' Even though she no longer thought of him as some impossibly perfect hero out of a book. He was far from perfect. He was a touch unsure about how to converse with a female. He was overshadowed by feelings of guilt and remorse, largely, she believed, because he had set himself such high standards. In fact, the more she learned of him, the more flaws she discovered, the easier it was to see herself living alongside him. After all, how uncomfortable would it be to marry a total paragon? Only think how inferior to him she would always feel.

He pulled open the lych gate for her and stood still, waiting for her to pass. 'Miss Hutton, I…' He faltered to a halt, taking up a position that meant she would have to brush right past his body to get by.

'That's enough of that!' From behind them Grandfather's voice boomed out. And Captain Bretherton took a step back, putting a more decorous distance between them. 'In the churchyard,' said Grandfather with a shake of his head. 'Have you no respect?'

'Beg pardon…' Captain Bretherton began.

But Grandfather suddenly gave a bark of laughter and clapped him on the shoulder. 'Better get the banns read sharpish, eh? Good job you're going to be meeting with the Reverend tomorrow. Settle a date, what?'

And just like that, the irritation Lizzie had worked so hard to stifle sprang back to life. They were talking about her, about her future, as though it was all settled. As though she had no say in it. It made no difference that she *did* want to marry

Captain Bretherton. More than she'd ever wanted anything. It was the way first Reverend Cottam, and now Grandfather, were attempting to organise her life without even consulting her.

The only man in her life who would never do such a thing was Captain Bretherton.

Harry gritted his teeth as he strode along the corridor to the coffee room of the Three Tuns the next morning. This meeting with Cottam was going to be in the nature of a skirmish with a very clever enemy, who outnumbered and surrounded him. He was going to need to employ every weapon in his arsenal, both to escape exposure as the spy that he was, while doing his utmost to obtain solid proof of Cottam's guilt.

He knew Cottam was the puppeteer, now. Knew it in his bones. The moment he'd seen him climbing up into his pulpit, he'd recognised him for a villain. It made no difference that he looked so very much like Lady Rawcliffe, his sister. Lady Rawcliffe was different inside. And it shone through her eyes. From her attitude. Cottam was like…a wax effigy of a good man. Scrape the surface and there would be nothing inside that was true. He'd had men like that serve under him. All respectful attitude and willing smiles when officers were around. But the minute they thought nobody was looking, they'd be watering down the rum and fiddling the dockets so they could sell the proceeds, leaving the crew short of provisions. Or run any other rig by which they might enrich themselves at the expense of others.

And the devil of it was, because they had such good reputations, nobody would believe they were the culprits unless they were caught in the act.

Even he might have fallen for Cottam's act of piety and bonhomie, if Rawcliffe hadn't warned him about the theft of the takings from one of his former parishes. If there hadn't been so many links between him, and the girl who'd been hired in not just one, but two of the houses where jewels had gone missing.

But he *had* been forewarned. And, unlike Archie, he was practised in the art of warfare. He'd sailed under false colours more than once, in order to outwit the enemy.

'Ah, good morning, good morning!' The Reverend Cottam came striding across the room to him, his hand outstretched as if in friendship. Harry had no option but to take his hand, and shake it today. And disguise the fact that he wanted to take out a handkerchief to wipe off the coating of imaginary slime that handshake left behind.

'I trust you enjoyed the service yesterday? Though I dare say my sermon was not to your taste. I have ordered coffee, by the way. And told Jeavons to bring it as soon as you arrived.'

In short, attempting to act as host, thereby putting Harry in an inferior position from the outset.

'What makes you think that? About the sermon, I mean?'

Cottam hitched up his coat tails before sitting down and indicating Harry should take the chair on the other side of the fireplace. Harry sat.

'Well, you are a navy man, are you not? You do not believe in easing the burdens of men serving under you, but in flogging them until they scurry to obey every order you give.'

'Not true. There are times when only a flogging will suffice, but I have always regarded it as a last resort. Generally, I prefer to instil self-respect into my men, with a combination of training and leading a good example.'

He frowned. Dammit, but Cottam had managed to get him into a defensive position, not two seconds after their encounter began.

'Leading by example? Yes, yes, I am a great believer in that myself. Which is why I have chosen to live among the most desperate members of my flock. I dare say you have heard talk?'

Ah, now that was more like it. Cottam felt the need to explain *himself*, now. To give a plausible excuse for living cheek by jowl with a group of people known to be the most cut-throat band of smugglers along this part of the coast.

'Colonel Hutton has mentioned that you have been holding prayer meetings, and so forth, encouraging the worst of the vicinity's miscreants to attend. With a view to reforming their way of living.'

'Just so! One only has to look at the success that the Methodist ministers have with simple folk, to see that there is something in their, ah, method.' He laughed at his own pun. 'Though I have no intention of ever leaving the Anglican fold. But still, I cannot forget that there is more joy in heaven over one sinner who repents, and so on and so forth.'

'And have you caused many sinners to repent?'

Cottam's face closed up. 'I believe in the absolute sanctity of the confessional,' he said in a manner that Harry considered positively pompous. 'I could not possibly disclose any of the confidences reposed in my care.'

In other words, no, he had not turned anyone from their lives of crime. Or not according to Lady Rawcliffe, his sister. And she should know.

'But that is not what I came here to discuss,' he said with a smile, as the door opened and Jeavons came in bearing a tray.

'We have the fruit cake you like so much today, Reverend,' said Jeavons, setting the plate on the table at Cottam's elbow. 'And hot milk to go with your coffee.'

'Ah! Just the way I like it. What a good fellow you are, Jeavons.'

Something about the interchange put Harry in mind of a pair of otters, oiling their way round each other. It wouldn't have surprised him if they'd started grooming each other's whiskers.

'Jeavons tells me,' said Cottam, the moment the man had left them to their own devices, 'that you have been spending almost every waking hour with Miss Hutton.'

Apart from the time he'd spent writing reports of his progress with the investigation. How right he'd been to send Dawkins to Bath to post them. It looked as though Cottam had just about everyone in this town, and possibly the surrounding district, in his pocket.

'I have,' he said curtly.

'Really?' Cottam crumbled a piece from his slice of cake and shot him an amused glance. 'Miss Hutton? Do you really expect me to believe that after only a few brief meetings in Bath, you became so smitten that you pursued her down here with a view to marrying her?'

'Why should you not believe it?'

'Well…' he laughed again '… I mean. Miss *Hutton.*'

'Why do you say Miss Hutton in that fashion? What do you mean by it?' He got to his feet and leaned over Cottam's chair. 'If you were not a man of the cloth, I'd have you by the throat and shake an explanation from you.'

The curate's eyes widened fractionally. And then narrowed. 'What a show of indignation.'

'Of course I am indignant. I resent the implication that Miss Hutton is lacking in any way.'

'You wish me to believe you find her perfect, do you?'

'She *is* perfect,' he said with complete honesty. 'For me. She is…the woman I have been seeking all my life, without even knowing it. The moment I met her…'

It was true. What he'd just said. He had been

searching for someone like her, all his life, without even knowing it. Which was why, not long after he'd approached her, he'd been able to say they were a perfect match. They *were* a perfect match. Or could have been, if he'd met her under different circumstances.

He glared down into Cottam's sneering features, wishing he could simply wring the fellow's scrawny neck and have done with it. How dare he imply that nobody in their right mind could possibly fall in love with Lizzie? She was utterly adorable. Beautiful. And highly desirable. Ever since he'd given in to his baser instincts and kissed her, it had been damned hard not to seek opportunities to do it again. And at night, he'd lie in bed imagining how those long, supple limbs of hers would match his. How her hair would ripple across his chest like liquid moonlight.

He sat down. Raked his fingers through his hair in a desperate attempt to wipe such impure, inappropriate thoughts about Miss Hutton from his mind. He needed to focus on this skirmish with Cottam, not sheer off into salacious daydreams about a woman who could never be his.

'Are you quite well?' Cottam was peering at him intently.

His first instinct was to tell him that of course he was well, that he was just regrouping in readiness for the next skirmish, when he realised that he could actually use this moment of weakness to his own advantage. After all, he was supposed to be making sure that Cottam didn't see him as a threat.

So he smiled, weakly.

'I am stronger than I was,' he said, choosing once again to stick to the literal truth. 'Though I have not regained my full health.'

'You have been ill?'

The man *knew* he'd been ill. That he'd been in Bath to take the waters, which nobody would do unless some doctor had convinced them they were medicinal.

'Yes. A result of, well, I was taken prisoner of war. And suffered a recurrent fever.' And had been drinking too much, for far too long. 'It was thought that drinking the waters at Bath—' instead of all that grog '—would help to revive my weakened constitution. Instead, I met Miss Hutton. And found…healing of a different sort.' He gave the curate a self-deprecating smile. And saw the man take note. Rawcliffe had told him, before he set out on this quest, that Cottam liked to think of himself as a father confessor. That he encouraged people to confide in him. And so he continued, 'Balm for my loneliness, if you like.'

'Loneliness?' Cottam pounced on the word Harry had tossed him.

'Yes. You cannot imagine,' he said, leaning forward and clasping his hands over his knees, 'what it is like, being held captive in a foreign country. Or even what it is like to return to the land of your birth with a feeling that a sort of glass wall still separates you from everyone else. Nobody really understood me. Until I met Miss Hutton, and she…' He gave what he hoped was an eloquent shrug.

'She is something of an outsider, too,' said Cottam, pensively. 'She understands what it is to be lonely.'

'Well, it isn't just that. She is a splendid girl.'

'Splendid?'

'Yes. Well, I don't expect you will understand, but most females are so…little. And frilly. They make me feel like a great, lumbering fool. And I get clumsy round them, trying not to trip over their dainty little feet. Miss Hutton, on the other hand…' He spread his hands wide.

'No. Nothing dainty about her, is there?'

He didn't like the way Cottam smiled. With just

a hint of mockery beneath the apparent under-standing.

But he decided to let it go. Better for the man to think him feeble and a bit slow. That he was the kind of lovelorn sap who would confide in a total stranger simply because he was a man of the cloth.

So that he would not see him as a threat.

Chapter Eighteen

Lizzie pressed her nose to the window and peered up in the direction of the sky. And sighed at the fullness of the moon which gazed serenely back at her.

A whole week had passed since he'd had that meeting with Reverend Cottam. A meeting which he'd refused to discuss. The only thing she knew for certain about it was that they hadn't arranged to call the banns.

Which was just as well. Imagine how shocking it would have been if he'd gone ahead with that, without even informing her. Without even having proposed come to that. She would have…she would have…well, she would have gone along with it, probably. Even if she'd been hurt that he hadn't consulted her. At least it would have been proof that he was truly keen to marry her.

As it was, she was simply a bit confused. She fiddled with the end of her plait, wondering why Captain Bretherton had been so unwilling to talk about his meeting with Reverend Cottam. Whenever she'd tried to broach the topic he'd distracted her by paying her compliments, instead. Which was wonderful, in a way. She didn't think she'd ever tire of hearing him tell her how lovely he thought she was. But if he thought she was so lovely, why hadn't he proposed? What was he waiting for? She'd have thought, after that day he'd appeared unable to resist kissing her, he would have wanted to get her to the altar as soon as possible.

For once, she wished she had a female friend in whom she could confide. Because surely most females knew ways of getting a man to propose. Since she'd made it as clear as she could that when he did, she was going to accept.

If only Lady Buntingford hadn't had that seizure. Lady Buntingford had kept dozens of beaus dangling, when she'd been young. She would know exactly how to bring him up to scratch.

She drew the curtains shut and went to her bed. Day after day went by and he'd call at the house, and they'd go for a walk, or a drive, always in a different direction, and he'd get her to tell him all about the local landmarks and they'd talk nonsense to each other by the hour. Although, strangely, it felt as if they had talked about everything. He'd told her, only yesterday, that it was as if he'd come to know her better than he'd ever known anyone. And she felt the same about him.

Which was all very enjoyable, she thought as she pulled back the covers and climbed into the bed.

But they still were not officially betrothed.

She pulled the sheets and blankets up to her waist, leaned over and blew out her candle. It only took a second or two for her eyes to grow accustomed to the gloom. Especially since the moon was bright enough to make its presence felt through her rather moth-eaten curtains. She rolled over and shut her eyes. And as usual, wondered what he was doing, right at that moment. Was he in bed? Lying there, thinking of her? No, probably not. Men didn't seem to go to bed as early as women. Even Grandfather, at his advanced age, seemed to be able to sit up, with a bottle of port and a newspaper, for hours and hours past the time he sent her to her bed. Although she often lay there reading a book, rather than sleeping. So that when she heard his tread on the stairs, she'd have to extinguish her candle quickly and stuff the offending novel under her pillow for good measure. He didn't approve of novels. The only reason he permitted them in the

house was because he believed that Lady Buntingford was choosing them.

She stifled a feeling of guilt at using Lady Buntingford as an excuse for reading books that were
not the slightest bit *improving*. Though at least Captain Bretherton did not disapprove of her reading
novels. He'd even admitted to having read a couple
of the same ones as her. And had agreed with her
that the heroines were the most stupid creatures
ever to be invented and the plots so full of holes
they wouldn't hold water. And also that in spite of
their failings, they were tremendous fun to read.
And Lady Buntingford *did* enjoy listening to them.
Lizzie could tell. Even though the poor old lady
could only say two words, she could still smile
with her eyes and nod encouragement to go on. She
liked hearing about how she and Captain Bretherton were getting on, too. Although she wasn't able
to offer the advice she would no doubt have given,
were she able to speak.

When she visited Lady Buntingford tomorrow,
Lizzie decided, she would tell her how frustrated
she was becoming with Captain Bretherton's style
of courtship. Even though her mentor wouldn't
be able to share the wisdom she'd gleaned in her
youth during a series of brilliant Seasons, at least

she would understand Lizzie's frustration. And confusion.

Afterwards, Captain Bretherton would be waiting for her, outside Lady Buntingford's gate, and he would escort her home. And perhaps Grandfather would ask him to stay to dine. And then...

A cold fist gripped her stomach. And then he would make his way home, late at night. And it was a full moon.

Oh, dear. The Gentlemen would, like as not, be landing a catch. Not that anybody ever told Grandfather when there was going to be a run, because as a justice of the peace, he would be honour bound to inform. And the same went for her. But both of them usually had a pretty good idea. For one thing, it always coincided with a full moon. For another, there was a sort of suppressed excitement in the air of the village. Shops tended to close a bit earlier. People didn't loiter in the streets, chatting.

She'd have to watch out for those signs on her walk home tomorrow, and if it seemed likely, then she'd have to warn Captain Bretherton to take care.

Lizzie was growing impatient. And he could hardly blame her. He'd spent all day every day acting the part of a besotted suitor and had jumped at the chance of having a private interview with her curate. Any woman would expect a proposal, in such circumstances. Once or twice since then, she'd even made a clumsy attempt to turn their conversation in the direction of marriage and he'd swiftly had to turn it elsewhere.

He wasn't sure how much longer he could keep her dangling. He folded his arms and leaned against one of the gateposts of Lady Buntingford's park.

It had been a good week since he'd had that interview with Cottam and, though Lizzie had shown him all over the area and told him all about the lives of all the locals, he still hadn't managed to find one scrap of real proof that the man was responsible for Archie's death. He really didn't think Lizzie was going to be able to provide him with anything more.

What was worse, he couldn't wander around and try to discover anything on his own. Because he was being followed. Whenever he went anywhere, but especially when Lizzie wasn't on his arm, there was always a couple of men, or boys, shadowing his every move.

He ground his teeth as he shifted his weight. It was a message from Cottam. He might have pretended to take Harry's explanation for being here at face value, but he wasn't taking any chances.

Harry was pretending to be unaware of his shadows. If he'd been an innocent man, completely besotted by Lizzie, then he probably wouldn't have noticed them. Especially since it was rarely the same two on any occasion. But he'd noticed them all right. He'd even begun to recognise them. One of them was pretty hard to miss. He was as tall as Harry himself and as broad. And walked with an aggressive swagger that had everyone else darting out of his way. He wasn't the one tailing Harry today. Instead it was a bandy-legged ruffian with a face like a weasel and the youth with a mop of fair hair that was always falling into his eyes.

At last he saw the gatekeeper come forward with his bunch of keys, which meant Lizzie was on her way down the path. He stepped forward and eyed the gatekeeper thoughtfully. The man eyed him back, jutting his jaw out for good measure. It didn't matter how big and tall Harry was, that jaw seemed to indicate he wouldn't be getting in to pester Lady Buntingford. However, Harry was starting to think he was going to have to do something other than courting Lizzie. Something to provoke a reaction. Something to smoke Cottam out of his nest. If he forced entry to Lady Buntingford's home, perhaps, and saw for himself that she could neither write, nor make her wishes known...

'Captain Bretherton!' Lizzie's face lit up when she saw him. It made him want to grab her round the waist and swing her round, before setting her on her feet and smothering her dear face in kisses. How he wished he had the right. But what kind of rogue would take advantage of a trusting young woman in such a way? She was going to be upset enough when they parted as it was. Though not heartbroken, not she. Lizzie was not the kind of woman who'd sit about weeping over a man. Or anything. She despised such weakness. She'd told him so. It was the one consolation he could cling to, whenever he thought about the inevitable result his duplicity must have upon her. That she would survive him, as she'd bravely survived so much else.

'Miss Hutton,' was his measured response instead. Though he couldn't help smiling at her. 'How did you find Lady Buntingford today?'

Lizzie lay her hand on his sleeve, the light dying from her eyes. 'Much the same as ever. It is such a shame.'

'Don't you think,' he said, as they set off in the direction of the High Street, 'it might cheer her up to have more visitors? I am sure, since she has taken such a keen interest in your education, she would at least want to meet the man who is court-ing you.'

'I would have thought so, too, but—'

'Besides, I don't see how she managed to tell any-one that she didn't want to have any visitors. Not when she can barely speak.'

'I told you, the Reverend Cottam got there be-fore she had the second seizure that rendered her so helpless…'

'Yes, but if she wasn't helpless when she had her first seizure, why would she have forbidden anyone to visit her? I can understand it if she'd somehow made her wishes for complete solitude, or almost complete solitude,' he said, pressing her hand where it lay on his sleeve, 'after that sec-ond seizure which robbed her of so much dignity. But…'

'Well, the first one was pretty severe. To be hon-est, I was surprised she managed to say anything to Mr Cottam. Because she certainly couldn't say anything to me.' Lizzie frowned. He waited for her to reach the same conclusion he'd drawn. Because if she once started to suspect the Reverend Cot-tam wasn't as honest as he would have everyone believe, then, perhaps, he'd be able to start to tell her about the rest of it.

Her face cleared. 'She must have rallied, for a moment or two.'

His heart sank. It was as if Lizzie had turned her back on him. But then people always wanted to trust a man of the cloth. Cottam had laughingly spoken of this advantage he had, in a meeting with Lady Rawcliffe. Never mind being a wolf in sheep's clothing. He was a villain in clerical robes.

'Oh,' said Lizzie, suddenly stiffening. He followed the direction of her gaze, to see the baker pulling down the blind on his window. In the shop next door, the greengrocer was taking all his wares inside.

'Is it early closing day?'

'Um, yes, it must be.'

He glanced at her troubled face. 'The shops did not close early last time I walked you home from Lady Buntingford's.'

'It…er…wasn't a full moon last week.'

Was she implying there was going to be a run?

'Captain Bretherton, I can tell that you understand what that means.'

'Indeed.' If he'd been a huntsman, he would have lifted a horn to his lips and blown it. This could be the chance he'd been hoping for. Because if he could catch Cottam taking part, then he'd have him. If not for the other crimes, then for this one. And surely, if he could get him on one charge, the other ones would be more likely to stick.

She sighed. 'I also know that as a navy man, your natural instinct would be to…lay information. Or even try to catch some of them in the act.'

'You know me well.'

She sighed again. Her steps slowed. Finally, she stopped walking altogether and turned a beseeching face up to him.

'Please, Captain, please don't try to do anything.'

He flinched. 'What are you saying? Do your sympathies lie with those men?'

'Not at all. But you don't understand how…vicious they are. I expect you must have heard how much less trouble there is in these parts since Reverend Cottam got involved with Bolsover's gang. But obviously even he cannot stop them from landing contraband altogether, not when it is such a lucrative business. And they…if you tried to interfere…they would…' Tears welled in her eyes. 'And I could not bear it if anything were to happen to you. I don't want to lose you.'

'Lizzie, I mean, Miss Hutton…'

'Please. If I mean anything to you, anything at all, promise me that you will stay within doors to-night. That you won't go after those men.'

Chapter Nineteen

'Lizzie…' He watched her gulp in an effort to check the tears that were forming in her eyes. Because she was worried about him.

Because she cared.

It struck him with the force of an Atlantic gale that if he died, she would miss him. For the first time in his life, he actually mattered to someone.

Or at least, since he'd been too young to remember. He was certain that if he'd mattered to his father, he wouldn't have played fast and loose with his inheritance. Wouldn't have left him at the mercy of an uncle notorious for being mean-spirited and cruel. It had only been because his mother's family insisted he get a good education that he'd been able to escape the brute. Even then, Uncle Edgar hadn't let up. He'd somehow eventually managed to persuade everyone concerned that it made more sense to get Harry into the navy where he might carve out a career for himself. Solely in order to dispose of him permanently.

He'd battled his way up through the ranks, alone. Then endured captivity at the hands of the French, alone. He might have kept in touch with Zeus and Ulysses, and Archie by letters, but they'd all treated him with a sort of lingering hero-worship for the way he'd stood up to the school bullies. Which he'd only done because he knew how it had felt to be alone and helpless, and at the mercy of someone bigger and more powerful, and utterly without mercy, and couldn't stand seeing anyone else suffer what he'd gone through at the hands of Uncle Edgar.

They didn't really know the man he was now. Not like Lizzie did.

'Lizzie…' He took hold of her upper arms, his mind spinning. If he did as she asked, he'd be wasting a golden opportunity to catch Cottam red-handed.

And yet this was the first thing she'd ever asked of him. And she was only asking him to be careful, that was all. She had no idea that if he did as she asked, he would be throwing away the first chance he'd had, since coming down here, of apprehending the villain.

Or would he?

Did he really stand much chance against who knew how many smugglers might be involved in tonight's run? He'd be alone, apart from Dawkins. Facing what was, by all accounts, a gang of ruthless men. All of whom knew the terrain far better, having lived here all their lives.

And who was to say Cottam would actually be taking part in this run? Wasn't it more his style to sit at home, organising crimes which he sent others out to commit, so that they would run all the risks?

Might it even be a trap? Everyone in the area seemed to be aware there was going to be a run tonight. Cottam must know that he'd get wind of it. And be almost unable to resist the urge to lay information, at the very least.

Whichever way he looked at it, the chances of catching Cottam doing anything at all tonight were pretty slim.

His conscience writhing like an eel, he drew Lizzie fully into his arms. So that she couldn't see his face as he gave her his answer.

'I will do as you ask, Lizzie. I won't go after those men. I won't even lay any information against them.' Because if he did that, Cottam would know he was on to him. 'I will stay in my room. Playing whist with Dawkins, if you like, so that you cannot even accuse me of bending my vow by sending him out to do the job.'

She slid her arms round his waist. 'Thank you. Oh, thank you!'

He put her from him guiltily. 'We mustn't. Lizzie, I know the street is not as busy as usual, but people mustn't see us embracing in broad daylight.'

She cocked her head as she looked up at him. 'Does that mean you have nothing against embracing at night?'

'You...' She surprised a bark of laughter from him. 'What am I to do with you?'

She blushed. Lowered her head. Shot him a coy look from under her eyelashes. And he knew what she was thinking. She hoped he would marry her.

It was like being hit in the face by a bucket of cold water. Would she still want to marry him if she was privy to his train of thought, just now? She clearly thought he'd made the promise because he cared about her. And, to be honest, that had been part of it.

But not all. Not by a long way.

'Come on,' he said, tucking her hand into the

crook of his arm and setting them both in motion again. 'I had best get you home. Before you put any other outrageous ideas in my head.'

She'd given him the perfect opening to propose. She'd even been in his arms. And *still* he'd drawn back.

What was the matter with him?

Or was it that there was something the matter with her? Was he changing his mind about courting her?

No, no, that couldn't be it. If he was really having second thoughts, then he could simply pack up and leave. He wouldn't even have to stay to give her an explanation. The fact that he'd gone would tell her everything.

Except, he hadn't gone. He was walking her home. Deep in thought. Probably fuming that she'd extracted a promise not to go after Bolsover's men tonight.

Though he needn't have promised her anything. If he didn't care, he could have simply said that his duty took precedence, or something like that.

Only he hadn't.

He'd given her the assurance she'd sought. Even if he didn't look at all happy about it.

Perhaps he thought that if he went ahead and married her, she would always be trying to stop him acting according to his conscience. Perhaps…

Oh, bother all these perhapses! She was sick of not knowing what he was thinking. Of what was going to happen to them.

'Will I see you tomorrow?' His voice was gruff.

'You are not stopping to dine with us? Grandfather said…'

'No. Not tonight. I…' He shuffled his feet, looking away over his shoulder. 'I don't think I would be very good company. Not knowing, or at least suspecting, that there is a run going on, under my very nose as it were, and me not doing anything to prevent it. Nor could I…at least, I think I would struggle to be affable with your grandfather. Because it strikes me that he makes a habit of looking the other way, rather than rousing himself to root out the nest of brigands he knows live right on his doorstep.'

'It isn't that simple,' she retorted. 'There has been little work for common folk round here since the quarries shut down. And the Gentlemen, as the locals call the smugglers, bring in a lot of money. Surely, running the odd keg of brandy, or bolt of lace, to avoid paying revenue isn't all that dreadful, is it?'

'If only that were all,' he growled, thinking of the jewel thefts taking place in London, the death of, to his knowledge, at least Jenny and Archie. 'You have told me that the local men are vicious. That people dare not cross them. Which *is* dreadful, is it not?'

'Well, yes, but there are other factors you know nothing of.'

'Such as?'

'Well, even if Grandfather wanted to arrest them all, it would take a small army. The place where they live, Peeving Cove, is tucked deep into an inlet in the cliffs, which nobody can sail into, except at high tide, because the entrance to the inlet is so rocky below the waterline. You can't get into the village at all from the landward side. Not...' She shook her head. 'Well, there are tunnels that lead from the old marble quarries. But it is such a maze, and the tunnels are so narrow, that they are easily defended, too.'

'They don't stay in that stronghold the entire time, though, do they?'

'No, but you cannot just arrest a man without evidence. And naturally they don't walk about

Lesser Peeving with barrels of brandy tucked under their arms.'

'Except during nights like tonight.'

'What do you mean?'

'I would wager that a barrel of brandy will appear under your grandfather's window, tonight. Or at the gatepost.' He waved his hand in that direction.

'Yes, I suppose Grandfather could arrest who-ever left...'

'His bribe?'

She sucked in a short, shocked breath. 'Grand-father does not take bribes.'

'What do you call it when a man knowingly lets a criminal escape when he has stolen goods about his person? Worse, receives said goods in return for looking the other way?'

'You don't understand...' The person they always used to drop Grandfather's gifts at their gate was a boy. A mere boy. The son of their cook. Naturally Grandfather was not going to turn the lad over to the authorities. Cook would be heartbroken if the lad went to the gallows. Or got sent into the army.

And might retaliate by leaving his service. Which Grandfather would hate, because she knew exactly how Grandfather liked his meals.

'I understand only too well,' he said grimly, after

she'd been continuing with that train of thought, in silence, for more than a moment.

'It's all very well for you, coming down here and thinking you are better than everyone else,' she blurted, in her frustration.

'Is that what you really think of me?' He took a step back. Taking his face out of range of her eyesight. 'Then there is nothing further to be said. I bid you good day.'

'No, wait! I didn't mean it like that…'

But it was too late. He'd gone marching back down the drive and had disappeared thought the gates before it occurred to her to run after him.

Lord! They'd had their first quarrel.

Chapter Twenty

Lizzie dragged herself out of bed the next morning as soon as she heard a scullery maid raking coals across a hearth somewhere below stairs.

As she rubbed her gritty eyes she wondered why poets and novelists went into such raptures about falling in love. So far, in her case, all it seemed to do was rob her of sleep.

Though to be fair to Captain Bretherton, it wasn't *entirely* his fault she'd scarcely slept a wink all night. Yes, she'd gone over and over their argument far too many times, but she hadn't been able to stop wondering what was going on out at sea, either. And later, as daggers of moonlight pierced her elderly curtains, whether there was activity going on across the moors above her house as well. Many of the local men would get involved once the kegs, or packages, or whatever was being landed, had been brought ashore. Or would turn a blind eye when their horses and carts went missing for a day or so, knowing that Bolsover's gang would leave them some kind of reward. And, more importantly, that if they protested, or reported the *borrowing* to the parish constable as theft, they would face the consequences.

She'd heard tales about what happened to people who tried crossing Bolsover. First, he'd give them a warning. Something in the nature of smashing a few of their windows. At night, when they and their family were asleep in their beds. Only once or twice had anyone tested his determination beyond that and he'd promptly set fire to some of their property. They'd got out alive, then left the area altogether. The blackened remains of their cottage still stood as a testimony to the whole affair.

She'd tried flipping on to her back, but there had been no getting away from the fact that Captain Bretherton had a point. It would be better if Bolsover's gang stopped behaving that way. But what could anyone do? Round them all up and arrest them? Even if that were possible, which it wasn't considering how impregnable Peeving Cove was, then what would become of their wives and children? And the economy of the whole district, come to that. Those men had money to spend, which they spent locally. They supported the grocers and the drapers, and the bakers and butchers...

She poured water into her basin, hoping a wash would help clear her head before going down to breakfast.

But when she reached the dining room it was to find Grandfather appeared to have woken up on the wrong side of the bed as well.

'My egg is runny,' he said as he flung his spoon on to the table in disgust. He then bellowed some extremely unpleasant words at Sergeant Hewitt, as though he was responsible for the condition of the egg when all he'd done was serve it.

She sighed. Were all men so prone to anger? She was beginning to think they must be, given the way Captain Bretherton had reacted yesterday, merely because she'd expressed some opinions that ran counter to his own.

Well, and made him agree to act counter to his conscience, she reminded herself.

Yes, but what should she have done? Kept her opinion to herself? Meekly bowed her head and said *Of course you must be right, dearest*, instead of telling him what she really thought? Perhaps if she had they wouldn't have quarrelled, though, and he wouldn't have stalked off in high dudgeon. And she might have had a decent night's sleep.

'I will go and see if Cook can do you another egg,' she said to Grandfather, since there was no point in sitting down and having her own breakfast. He would be impossible until his own needs were met. 'You drink your coffee,' she said, whisking his plate away before he could throw it, too, across the room. 'I am sure it won't take a minute to do you another egg.'

'It should take *four* minutes,' he snapped. 'Not one.'

Yes, and since Cook knew Grandfather could not abide a runny egg and normally prided herself on serving everything up precisely as he liked it, that meant there must be some kind of trouble brewing below stairs.

Just as she'd suspected, when she got to the kitchen it was to find the cook sitting at the table with her head in her hands, a pan boiling over on the stove and the scullery maid hopping from one foot to the other, and twisting her hands in her apron.

'I am sorry to have to trouble you,' said Lizzie, handing Grandfather's plate to the scullery maid, thus giving her something useful to do. 'But Grand-father cannot eat his egg.'

Cook said something rather rude about the egg. 'What does eggs matter,' she then wailed, 'when our Billy has gone and got himself tangled up with that Bolsover's lot? What do they want with the likes of him? What good can he be to them, that's what I want to know? More skin and bone, he is, than muscle. And not a lick of sense in his head.'

So there *had* been a run last night.

'Oh, dear. No wonder you are too distracted to think about such mundane things as eggs.' Lizzie went to sit next to Cook. Gingerly, she patted the woman's hunched shoulder.

'He ain't a-coming back,' sobbed Cook. 'Prom-ised him riches, that's what they did, I shouldn't wonder. And excitement. And the silly sod is prob-ably lying drownded somewhere with a knife in his back. Just wait till I get my hands on him. I'll give him what-for, so I will, for running off and scaring his mother like this...'

'Yes, well...' Lizzie began, with no real idea of what to say. And as she glanced round for inspira-tion she noted the pan sputtering water all over the hotplate. 'Perhaps it would help if I were to see to Grandfather's breakfast this morning?'

'You? No, miss, don't you dare!' Cook shot to her feet, scurried across the kitchen and took up a defensive position in front of her stove. 'You'd end up burning the house down like as not and then I'd be out of a job and a home as well as losing my boy.'

'Well,' said Lizzie, drawing on all the years of experience in dealing with such slights, so as not to reveal how hurtful that remark had been. And reminding herself that at least her suggestion had prodded Cook into action. 'What could I do to help, then?'

'Nothing,' said Cook, reaching for a fresh egg and tossing it into the boiling water. 'There's nothing anyone can do about the likes of Bolsover. A law unto hisself, he is.'

'Oh. But then I wasn't thinking of actually going to see him and demanding an explanation.'

Cook whirled round, her spoon dripping water on to the flags. 'If anyone *could* find out where my Billy is, it would be you.'

'Me?'

'Yes. Stands to reason. He wouldn't look on you as a threat for a start, would he, miss?' Cook eyed her in a way that made her feel like a slab of meat on the butcher's block, being judged for her tenderness on roasting. 'Everyone knows how gentle and harmless you are,' except when it came to eggs, stoves and fires, apparently. 'And you would only be asking after the welfare of one of the staff from your own house, wouldn't you?'

But then, abruptly, her shoulders sagged. 'No, no, I couldn't ask it of you.'

But Lizzie's heart was pounding. For a moment there, Cook had really thought that she might be able to deal with a man like Bolsover. A man Lizzie knew by sight, and by reputation, but to whom she'd never spoken.

'He wouldn't really dare do anything very dreadful to me, either, would he,' she mused aloud. 'Not with Grandfather being who he is…'

The smugglers and the local law enforcement existed in an uneasy state of truce. Grandfather did not interfere in Bolsover's business, as a rule. But if anything were to happen to Lizzie, that state of affairs would soon change. And Bolsover was not a stupid man. He wasn't the ringleader merely because he was taller and stronger than everyone else, but because he could think clearly. All of which gave Lizzie a kind of immunity.

'You'd really do that for me? You'd really go and find out what's become of my boy?'

Lizzie had never had anyone really believe she

could accomplish anything before. So the sound of hope and faith in Cook's voice acted on her like a shot of rather strong spirits.

'Yes,' she vowed. 'I would. I will.'

There was no sense in returning to the breakfast table after that. If Grandfather got wind of what she was planning he'd be bound to put a stop to it. Besides, her courage might evaporate as swiftly as Cook had roused it. So Lizzie went straight upstairs to her room.

And it wouldn't just be Grandfather who would disapprove, she reflected as she bent down to strap on the knife that Sam had made her promise to wear every time she left the house. She and Captain Bretherton had already quarrelled about their differing outlook with regard to the smugglers. He'd be furious if he knew she intended to seek them out. Even if it was in a good cause.

What was worse, she thought, shoving her arms into the sleeves of her coat, she was supposed to be spending the morning with him. He'd want to know where she was if she failed to turn up. And would probably come here to ask after her. And then Grandfather would start shouting at the servants, as if Cook didn't have enough on her plate today.

So…she would have to convince him she had a good reason for cancelling their arrangement. Which posed another set of problems, because normally she would send Billy down to Peacombe with any message she wanted delivered. But Billy was missing.

One thing at a time, she decided as she tied the ribbons of her bonnet under her chin. She could easily deal with any objections Grandfather might pose, by going down the back stairs and slipping out of the kitchen door.

As for Captain Bretherton, well, she would just have to hope she came up with some clever ruse to deflect his suspicions during her walk across the moors to Peacombe.

She'd hardly left the bounds of Lesser Peeving before it occurred to her that while she was making her way through Peacombe, she could very easily pop into the Three Tuns and leave some kind of message for Captain Bretherton, which would throw him off the scent. Surely she could come up with some reason for not wishing to spend the morning with him, without having to resort to a bare-faced lie? Something that would ensure he wouldn't come up to the house asking after her, either. She didn't want him to somehow get wind of Billy's plight and become concerned, and offer to come with her, because his presence would ruin everything. Bolsover, like most of the locals, regarded her as a harmless, rather pitiful creature. He might become irritated with her for approaching him on a matter he'd think was none of her business, but he would only regard her as an irritation, not a threat.

Captain Bretherton, on the other hand…

She worried her lower lip between her teeth. She could just be deliberately vague, she supposed.

In fact, if she was going to be leaving a message with the likes of Jeavons, Captain Bretherton would not be the least bit surprised if she kept the details to a minimum.

That was that sorted then. She'd tell Jeavons to tell Captain Bretherton that she was unable to spend the morning with him, because she had a private and personal matter to deal with. And she'd say it down her nose, for good measure.

She reached that decision at just about the same time she came to the last rise of moorland, so that she could see Peacombe spread out below her around the bay.

She peered at the boats moored in the harbour, even though she had no intention of hiring one and getting someone to sail her up to the narrow inlet that most people said was the only way in or out of Lesser Peeving. Because not only was that too public, but she also had a much better idea.

During their childhood, she and Sam had explored the maze of tunnels that riddled the cliffs along this part of the coast. They'd used balls of twine to find their way out again, just as Ariadne had enabled Theseus to do in the Minotaur's labyrinth. And one day, to their utter surprise, they'd discovered that one of the tunnels emerged in the cliffs overlooking Peeving Cove. They'd run home as quickly as they could, balling up their string as they went so that nobody would know they'd ever been there. But ever since then, she'd been able to understand how it was that Bolsover seemed to be able to pop up in Peacombe when the tide indicated he shouldn't have been able to sail out of his cove.

Harry finally put his signature at the bottom of the report he'd started writing before dawn and rang for Dawkins. Perhaps, now he'd got the thing done, he could contemplate eating some breakfast.

Not that he deserved any. Not after compiling what amounted to a list of excuses for not acting on the information Lizzie had given him yesterday.

Suspecting that Rawcliff would regard his inaction as proof that Harry wasn't cut out to be a spy, that he was growing too susceptible to the charms of the woman he was supposed to be charming, he'd made a lot of analogies about the need for 'sailing under false colours' in order to get close enough to the enemy to 'fire a devastating broadside'. He shuddered to think what Lizzie would think of this report if it should ever fall into her hands.

Lizzie, who he was going to have to face in little over an hour from now. Lizzie, who was expecting a proposal, who deserved a proposal, and who was becoming increasingly confused and hurt by the way he must appear to be dragging his heels.

There was a light tap on the door and Dawkins came in. His eyes went straight to the document folded in Harry's hand.

'You have another dispatch for Their Lordships?'

Harry looked down at it with revulsion. 'Yes, take the damn thing,' he growled, thrusting the report at Dawkins. 'And this letter as well. It will need to go to my lawyer.' Although Miss Hutton wasn't actually his fiancée, nor was ever likely to be, there was nobody else to whom he could leave what savings he had. And it would go some way to atoning for the way he'd drawn her into Cottam's web, should he suffer the same fate as Archie.

Which was more than likely. For he was going to have to make some sort of move against the man soon. This stalemate between them had gone on long enough. And the longer it went on, the more deeply hurt Lizzie would be when the truth came out.

He was not sure, yet, what form his move should take, only that he would have to keep his eyes open for some opportunity. Or create one. He was growing increasingly frustrated with the state of affairs. It wasn't like really sailing under false colours in order to confuse an enemy so he could get close enough to fire a broadside into an undefended hull. Or sneaking ashore at dead of night to commit a spot of sabotage. Whatever he did, here in Dorset, meant betraying someone. If not Rawcliffe, then Lizzie. If not Lizzie, then Archie.

Once Dawkins had taken the despatches, he felt sorely in need of coffee. And since he'd been holed up in this room since dusk the night before, he decided to go downstairs to the coffee room to take it, rather than ring to have somebody bring it up to him. Even though he hadn't yet shaved. He'd order some breakfast while he was at it. There was plenty of time to spruce himself up before Lizzie was due to arrive.

Or so he'd thought. But the first thing he saw, the moment he reached the lobby, was Lizzie, coming in through the hotel door, untying the strings of her bonnet.

'Oh!' She stopped dead when she saw him, her expression a picture of guilt.

'Good morning,' he said, wondering what on earth she was doing here at this hour of the morning and why she looked so guilty.

'I wasn't expecting to s-see you,' she stammered, backing up a pace, instead of stepping toward him and smiling.

Something like a fist clenched in his gut. And he remembered the way they'd parted. After quarrelling.

'Why are you here then, if not to see me?'

'Oh. Um.' She lowered her head. Lifted it and met his gaze with more than a touch of defiance. 'I only came to leave a message for you. To say that I would be unable to spend the day with you as arranged.'

Since sometimes the best form of defence was attack, he took a step forward. 'How, then, are we to be able to patch up our quarrel?'

'Quarrel?' A look of confusion flitted across her features. 'Oh, that. Um…'

It was like the ringing of alarm bells. The woman who could forget a quarrel with a man she considered her suitor was a woman who had something far more troubling on her mind.

'Are you in some kind of trouble? Is there anything I can do to help?'

'No!' Now she really did look alarmed. 'That is, I am in no trouble. And the best thing you can do is to stay well out of it.' She flushed. Took a breath. Licked her lips. 'That is, I mean to say, I am perfectly capable…' She shook her head. 'No, that wasn't what I meant to say. Oh, dear. I had a perfectly good speech worked out before I got here…'

Dear Lizzie. She was such a terrible liar.

'Captain Bretherton, please…' she stepped closer and laid one hand on his forearm '…please will you forgive me and excuse me, but there *is* something I have to do, today. Something I have to do *alone*.'

Something that had cropped up overnight. During a night when the smugglers had been active.

This could be it. The opportunity he'd been looking for. Lizzie knew something, or was covering for someone who was involved. And was planning to…well, he had no idea, but he was damn well going to find out.

He took her by the upper arms.

'What kind of man would I be if I left you to deal with whatever it is on your own?'

'A sensible one. Because if you try to get involved, it would only make matters worse.' She shut her mouth with a snap, as though realising she might have given too much away. Which indeed she had.

'Lizzie, I—'

'Please, don't ask me any questions. I don't want to have to lie to you. Or…or quarrel with you.'

'I don't want to quarrel with you, either.'

'Can you not just trust me?'

He thought very carefully about his response before making it. In many ways he had come to trust her. She might be a bit muddled in her thinking about the smugglers, but she couldn't be involved in any of the crime going on in this area. She was too open, too honest. She'd been too upset about the rumours circulating about the deaths of Archie and the girl. What was more, she couldn't even look him in the face while she was attempting to dodge round telling him something that fell even a little bit short of the truth.

Still, he didn't want her to go dashing into what might be a dangerous situation under the naïve assumption that her gender, or her rank, would protect her.

'Are you certain you wish to go ahead with this plan of yours and act in a way you will probably be unable to relate to me, at a later date?'

'Oh.' She stepped back, breaking his hold on her, and ran one hand across her forehead. 'I knew you would be like this. That you'd try to stop me instead of…believing in me and supporting me…'

'Dammit, Lizzie, it isn't like that! I can see that you are planning to walk into a situation that may well be dangerous. You cannot suppose I will let you walk into any sort of danger alone?'

'*Let* me?' Her eyes flashed fire. She flung up her chin. 'Until such time as you take it into your head to propose, and I accept, you have no say over what I do or where I go,' she snapped, tying her bonnet ribbons into a lopsided bow. 'I bid you good day,' she finished, whirling round and storming out of the inn.

As though that was an end to it.

Chapter Twenty-One

Well, if that was what she thought, she was very much mistaken. Scarcely pausing until she'd left the Three Tuns, Harry darted out of the door after her. She was heading across the market square in the direction of the lane which led down to the harbour. Where else?

He cast one experienced eye to the skies and saw that it would be foolish to pursue her without the benefit of a hat and coat. But in the time it would take him to return to his room and fetch his own, she might get so far ahead he'd lose her trail.

Fortunately, he could see a fisherman's-type smock affair hanging on a peg just inside the tap-room. And a cap on another peg beside it. He took a moment to thrust his arms into the jacket, thankful that the loose cut meant it fit him. Where it touched, that was. Then clapped the cap on to his head and dashed after her.

There was no sign of her by the time he emerged into the square. It was just as well he'd taken note of the direction she'd been heading. He strode across the square, head down against the stiff breeze blowing in from the sea, then plunged down the lane he'd seen her take.

When he reached the harbour he first scanned the many boats dragged up on to the beach, assuming she'd hire one to take her to the smuggler's lair. But she wasn't there. His heart flipped over. Surely he couldn't have lost her? Dammit, he should have just gone straight after her and taken no notice of the rain that was going to fall later on this morning, to judge from the weight of the clouds rolling in. Or perhaps he should have insisted on going with her and made her wait until he was sufficiently protected from the elements.

Although what would he have learned, if he'd done that? This way, he could both discover exactly where Lizzie's sympathies lay, exactly how involved she might be, if at all, and be on hand to rescue her if she got out of her depth.

If he could find her, that was. Where the hell was the impossible woman?

Not on the beach. Not by the harbour wall. Not climbing the street that led back up to the moors across which she'd be going if she was heading home. But there! Marching along the promenade which led to the terraced gardens and the medicinal spring Jeavons had rhapsodised about. There she was.

Grim-faced, he set off after her. It only took a few minutes to draw near enough to be able to come to her aid if she did get into any trouble, but far enough away that she wouldn't be likely to notice him.

Though actually, he could be three feet away from her and she wouldn't be exactly sure who he was, not until he spoke to her, not with her eyesight being so bad. And, now he came to think of it, wearing a loose smock and workman's cap was also adding to his ability to evade recognition. She'd grown used to seeing him wearing his navy tailcoat and tricorne hat. Though his height gave him such a distinctive outline that even she might have recognised him if she ever took it into her head to glance over her shoulder, she never seemed to think to do so. She was striding along with her head high and her elbows pumping. A wry smile tugged at his mouth. Even when she was on her high ropes Lizzie Hutton was absolutely adorable.

Lizzie was so cross she'd got halfway along the promenade before it occurred to her that he'd taken her exit rather tamely. Which just went to show... She wrinkled her nose. She wasn't sure what it went to show. But it certainly didn't encourage her to believe that he cared about her. One moment forbidding her to go out and meet the smugglers—not that he knew that was what she was doing—and then, when she disobeyed him, simply washing his hands of her, by the looks of things. He certainly hadn't come after her. He could easily have caught up with her, if he'd wanted to. But he hadn't. Which proved he...

She sniffed. Blinked rapidly to clear her eyes. Flung back her shoulders and kept right on going. Past the end of the promenade, where she had to delve into her reticule for the entrance fee to the cliff terrace gardens, and then up along the winding paths until she reached the top.

'I don't need a guide through the caves,' she said to the startled warden, as he thrust a black-glass bottle hastily on to shelf behind his chair. 'I know my way round.'

'Sure you do, Miss Hutton,' he said with a relieved smile in his voice. He probably assumed she hadn't noticed his sleight of hand with the bottle. Just because she couldn't make out details with any clarity, people assumed she had *no* idea what they were doing.

'You'll want to take a lantern, though.'

She supposed she did. It grew dark not very far into the tunnel system, due to the fact that they went off at odd angles. Presumably following the seam of whatever it was they'd mined here in ancient times, before they'd discovered the marble. Or perhaps because the workings were from several successive enterprises.

Whichever it was, she hadn't gone far into the maze before her anger, and the determination to rescue Billy from Bolsover's clutches, began to fade under the increasing awareness that this was the first time she'd been in this deep without Sam. And that Sam had always taken the lead. And that he'd always had those balls of twine in his pockets to make sure they could find their way out again.

Also, they'd never entered the system from this point. Usually, they'd gone in via a false tomb in the churchyard in Lesser Peeving. They'd found their way *out* to the cliffs at Peeving Cove on one of their sorties. But things never looked the same when facing them from the opposite direction.

It would be hard enough for a person with keen eyesight. But for Lizzie, who could barely make out the features of her own grandfather across the table, it was rapidly becoming a nightmare. And there was also the odd sensation, caused no doubt by an echo of her footsteps, that someone was following her.

Her heart was beginning to beat very rapidly. And it was starting to feel hard to breathe. She could feel the weight of all the rock, overhead, pressing down on her. In spite of her lantern, the darkness was growing thicker. As thick as treacle.

She paused as a wave of dizziness hit her. Reached out to lean her hand on the wall to steady herself. Which was worse. The moment she stood still, she got the peculiar impression that the tunnels were holding their breath. With a sort of devilish glee. As though they knew she was lost, that she would never get out. And they were relishing the prospect of swallowing her whole.

At which point, she remembered she'd had no breakfast. *That* was why she felt dizzy, she told herself bracingly. She wasn't on the verge of having hysterics just because she might be lost.

Underground.

She took a deep breath. She'd have to keep moving, if this was what happened when she paused to try and get her bearings. At least if she was moving, she would end up getting *some*where. It was when she stood still, that was when everything started to feel as if it was pressing down on her and her heart started beating so erratically that she had to struggle for breath, and her brain began scrabbling at nothing like a mouse behind a wainscot. And…oh, did that odd streak of white slashing from floor to ceiling look familiar? Like an arthritic finger with a rumpled nail! If she was recalling it correctly, then in five or six more paces… yes…there it was. Oh, thank heaven! Another slash of white, just before a fork in the tunnels.

She'd reached a point east of Lesser Peeving. A section of the tunnels that was more familiar.

She couldn't say that she was feeling exactly confident, but at least the panic had subsided to a point where her mind was working almost rationally again. She was able to pick out the natural markers which showed her the way. And was choosing the correct fork each time with scarcely a pause.

Which was, she was to later think, where she

went wrong. The earlier spate of near panic had made her want to hurry to get out of the maze of tunnels, so she wasn't proceeding with much caution.

And so she had stumbled into one of the large chambers which were natural features of the maze, before checking to see if anyone was already there. Which she should have done, considering there had been a run the night before.

The men who were huddled round a pile of barrels and bales all looked up, the moment she stepped out of her tunnel. And made a collective, growling sound.

What she should have done, at that point, was to step forward boldly and tell them they had nothing to fear from her, because she was only looking for Billy. But, probably because she'd been on the verge of panic for such a long time already, the sight of Bolsover's gang, en masse, startled her so much that she let out a squeak of fright. And dropped her lantern. And then darted back into the tunnel from which she'd come.

They, naturally enough, set out in pursuit. They must have thought she'd stumbled on them by mistake.

But worse was to follow. It turned out that she

hadn't imagined she was being followed, after all. There, looming up ahead of her in the tunnel which was her only way of escape, was some hulking great man. So tall he had to stoop so that his head didn't strike the roof.

It could only be Bolsover himself!

But he was alone.

And behind her she could hear the sound of many pairs of booted feet, echoing off the walls like a volley of gunfire.

And she was strong.

And her reticule contained a brass telescope. All folded in on itself.

And he wouldn't expect her to put up a fight.

If she was lucky, she'd startle him enough—if she could land one really good blow in a strategic spot—that she'd be able to dart past him…

Even as the thought formed in her head, she closed her fingers round the neck of her reticule and dashed forward, swinging it in the direction of the hulking man's face.

'Lizzie? What the—?'

Captain Bretherton's voice! But it was too late to stop her wild swing. Sam's telescope caught him full on the nose and he went staggering back, striking his head on the tunnel wall before slithering down into a slumped heap on the floor.

'Captain Bretherton!'

She was just about to go down on her knees, to find out how much damage she'd done him, when several pairs of hands reached out of the darkness and dragged her away. Back down the tunnel to the chamber where all those packages lay stacked up on all sides.

Chapter Twenty-Two

'Well, well, what have we here?'

Lizzie might not be able to see very clearly, but she had no trouble recognising that voice. It was Reverend Cottam! What could he be doing here? With the smugglers? The day after what appeared to have been a highly successful run?

And more to the point, why wasn't he urging the two men who were holding her arms to let her go? Particularly since one of them was pressing what felt like a knife to her throat.

'Miss Hutton,' said Reverend Cottam, reproachfully. 'Whatever can you be doing down here in these tunnels? And with your…beau?' He added the last just as another set of smugglers emerged from the tunnel half-dragging, half-carrying the stumbling, sagging form of Captain Bretherton.

They flung him roughly to the ground, where he lay utterly still.

'I wasn't *with* Captain Bretherton,' she protested, since she'd always known these men would all regard him with hostility and didn't want them to think she'd deliberately led him down here. 'In fact, I specifically told him I did not wish to spend any time with him today.'

'That's probably true,' said one of the men who was holding her arms. 'When she saw him in the tunnel, she decked him.'

'Oh? I assumed the state of him was your work.'

The men who'd flung him to the floor made growls of dissent.

'Got him good and proper she did.'

Surely she hadn't hit him that hard? Besides, he'd leaped back as she took her wild swing at him, and...oh! He'd bashed his head while dodging her. The tunnel roof was low, and rough, and he was very tall. That might account for it.

'So, you didn't lead him down here,' said Reverend Cottam, 'so that he could catch us all red-handed?'

'No!'

'Then would you mind very much, my dear,' he said, stepping out of the shadows into a pool of light thrown by some lanterns, 'explaining exactly what you were doing?'

Lizzie swallowed nervously. *Us all.* He'd said that as though he was one of Bolsover's gang, not an evangelical cleric determined to cure them of their criminal ways.

Not that it made any difference to her reasons for coming here, which she could tell them all, with perfect honesty.

'I came to find out what has happened to Billy,' said Lizzie, lifting her chin. 'The son of our cook. She is beside herself with worry because the boy went out last night and didn't come home. She was convinced he must have become involved in Bolsover's activities and begged me to try to find out what became of him. And since I know these tunnels so well, I thought it would be the most discreet way to do so. Billy isn't hurt, is he?'

'Billy is not hurt, no.' Cottam made a signal to the men holding her arms and they let her go. He then waved an arm to a stack of packages, as though inviting her to take a seat. And in spite of pretending she wasn't scared, she found that her legs were shaking so much she was actually rather grateful for the suggestion.

'He was up way past his bedtime last night,

though,' Reverend Cottam explained. 'So we simply let him sleep in this morning. By now, he is probably back at home.'

'So,' she said, sitting down rather suddenly as her legs gave out. 'This was all a waste of time.'

'Rather more than that, Miss Hutton,' said Reverend Cottam, sitting down beside her. 'You see, although I am prepared to believe you did not mean to do it, you *have* led a navy man to the heart of our operations.' He took her hand. 'Even you cannot be so foolish as to believe he will keep quiet about this.' He waved his free hand about the cave, stashed from floor to ceiling with all manner of contraband.

'He might...' She'd persuaded him to stay indoors while the run had been taking place, after all.

He patted her hand in a consoling manner. 'I very much doubt it, Miss Hutton. But no need to worry. I shall come up with a plan to make all right.'

'Thank you, Reverend,' she said with relief. Even though he was clearly more involved with Bolsover's operations than he ought to be, he was, after all, a man of the cloth.

After patting her hand once more, he stood up and began to pace back and forth, his hands behind his back. 'It all hinges, of course, on the precise moment that you realised his courtship of you was merely a ruse.'

'A...a what?'

Cottam ignored her startled exclamation and carried on pacing. 'It must have been in the last day or so. You were seen quarrelling only last night. And this morning, you went to the Three Tuns to tell him you never wished to see him again...'

'No! I didn't, I...'

He held up his hand for silence. One of the men who'd hauled her along the tunnel came to stand over her. And she caught the glint of light reflecting off metal. He was threatening her with a knife. At the Reverend's instigation. It was shock that he could do such a thing, more than fear of the smuggler, that made her fall silent.

'Yes, you did,' Reverend Cottam continued, as he paced back and forth. 'Because you'd discovered that the only reason he had come down here was to spy on me and my little...enterprise.'

'Spy on...on *you*?'

'This...' Cottam waved his hand at the goods stashed round the cave '.is merely in the way of being my...warehouse. Goods come in here and depart again from all over the country. And beyond. Did you not know?' He stopped right in front of her. 'Ah, poor, deluded Miss Hutton. Too foolish to see what is going on right under your nose.' He stroked one finger down the length of it. Lizzie flinched back, making Cottam laugh in a horrible, cold, malevolent manner that sent shivers down her spine.

'Your Captain knew, though.' Cottam turned in his direction. 'Knew, but could prove nothing. Which was why he deliberately sought you out, in Bath, so that he could make you the excuse for poking around down here for an indefinite period.' He turned to her. 'Poor, plain, lonely Miss Hutton,' he sneered. 'So desperate for romance that you fell into his hands like a ripe plum.'

Her stomach lurched. Hadn't she known, deep down, all along, that it had been too good to be true? A man as handsome and accomplished as Captain Bretherton could never really have been so smitten with a clumsy great beanpole like her that he'd pursue her all the way to Lesser Peeving. Especially after having met her only a couple of times.

And it certainly explained why he'd been so interested in all the locals. And why he'd been asking so many questions about them all.

Yet it hurt so much to learn what a fool she'd been

that Reverend Cottam might just as well have ordered his smuggler to plunge that knife right into her. So much that she couldn't help letting out a cry that was half-protest, half-acceptance of the horrid truth.

And all humiliation.

'It wasn't like that!' she heard Captain Bretherton protest and couldn't help turning her face in his direction, hoping he might go on to say…

But it was no good. Before he could say anything at all there came the sickening thud of boot leather on flesh. And Captain Bretherton, who'd started to push himself up on one elbow, from what she could make out, collapsed into a large round heap, rather than the great long outline he'd made earlier. As though he'd curled into a ball.

'It was exactly like that,' Cottam spat out, going to stand over the groaning, curled-up mound of lying, cheating, hurtful…*liar* that was Captain Bretherton.

'Rawcliffe told you all about her, didn't he? And decided to use her, the way he'd used my own sister, to further his vendetta against me. He married her, can you believe it,' he said, suddenly swinging round to Lizzie, 'simply to have a plausible excuse for coming to this area. You met my sister, didn't you, Miss Hutton? You probably thought she was very gracious and charming.' He gave a strange, bitter laugh. 'But she is a viper! She told her husband all about you, what easy prey you'd be for a certain type of man, and then he sent this rogue,' he said, waving one hand in Captain Bretherton's direction, 'to Bath to romance you.'

'No,' Lizzie gasped instinctively, even though his words had the ring of truth about them. Perhaps *because* they had the ring of truth about them.

'Yes,' Cottam hissed. 'He didn't even bother to think up a new strategy. Because he'd already succeeded in duping one innocent, gullible young woman, he assumed one of his friends would be able to do the same thing.'

'F-friends?' Lizzie stammered. 'What do you mean?'

'It isn't how he's making it sound,' Captain Bretherton just managed to grate, before the same vicious henchman kicked him again. This time, after he curled into a ball, he made horrible retching noises that made her curl her arms about her own stomach as it, too, clenched up in protest.

'Then why were you living in Rawcliffe's London house when you first returned to England?' said Cottam sarcastically. 'Why were you one of the men standing up with him at his wedding to my sister?'

'How can you possibly know all this?' Reverend Cottam was making it all up. He had to be.

'I have people in London,' said Cottam smugly, 'who watch what is going on in the great houses during the Season and report back to me.'

Captain Bretherton groaned. And since nobody had kicked him, this time, Lizzie heard it as an admission of guilt. Because even though he'd said that it wasn't how the Reverend was making it sound, he wasn't denying that Lord Rawcliffe was his friend, or that he'd attended his wedding.

And he'd kept that fact from her. Which was such a peculiar thing to have done, if he'd had nothing to hide. For, when people first met, they always discussed mutual acquaintances. When he'd learned she lived near Peacombe, it would have been natural for him to have mentioned he knew someone who'd spent his honeymoon there and then she would have said, *Oh, yes, I remember Lord and Lady Rawcliffe.*

But he hadn't.

And that was when tears of anger and humiliation began to well up in her half-blind eyes.

'You have good reason to be furious with him,'

said Cottam, as she dashed them away with the back of her hand. His voice sounded almost sympathetic. Almost. But if he'd really felt anything for her predicament, then he would have warned her about Captain Bretherton's deception. Or have mentioned his suspicions to her grandfather.

But he hadn't done any such thing.

No—because that would have meant owning up to his own part in Bolsover's business.

'Hell hath no fury like a woman scorned and so forth. Or in this case, a woman deceived and used. No wonder you lured him down into these tunnels, then struck him down...'

'What? No? I didn't *lure* him...'

But Cottam had started pacing up and down again. 'Yes, you lured him down here and then killed him.'

'I didn't! He isn't dead!'

Cottam waved a hand as though that point was immaterial.

'You killed him and then, filled with remorse, you came to me for some reason.' He paused. 'To seek absolution,' he answered himself, then carried on pacing. 'And, because I am a man of great compassion and could not bear to see such a lovely young woman condemned for a crime that was committed in the heat of the moment, I arranged to dispose of his body in such a way that no blame could ever be laid at your door.'

'Dispose of his body?' But Captain Bretherton wasn't dead.

Though... Reverend Cottam was speaking of him as though he was.

Which could only mean... She swallowed down bile as it hit her. They were going to kill him. And put the blame on her.

'No!' She leaped to her feet. He might be a lying, cheating heartbreaker, but she didn't wish him dead. 'You cannot mean it!'

The man who'd been set to guard her put a meaty hand on one of her shoulders and pushed her back down.

'Why not? It is the cleanest solution. Your grand-father will not wish to see you go to the gallows. He will, if not exactly applaud the action I am about to take today, exonerate me. For your sake.'

'No, no, please, there must be some other way...'

'I fear not. Not unless...'

'Yes? What?'

'You may share his fate, if you wish.'

'Wh-what?' Her blood ran cold.

'Ah, dear, what a reputation this area will gain

for doomed young lovers choosing to die together, rather than live apart...'

'What?'

'I take it, from the expression of horror on your face, you do not love the man so much you would rather die with him than live your life alone?'

'You cannot mean that...' Although, could that be what had happened to Jenny? The girl who'd come here to consult the Reverend? Had he done away with her, then made up the story about Mr Kellet breaking her heart? And if he'd done away with someone once...

'Miss Hutton, think very carefully before you make your decision,' he said, while she sat there gasping in horror and disbelief. 'And if it is that you want to live, which seems to be the case, then remember that once I have...disposed of Rawcliffe's minion, I can relate the tale of his death in such a way that you will be condemned for his murder. Everyone about here will believe me, once they hear how he deceived you, how you lost your temper with him, how I found you distraught, sobbing over his battered body...'

'That isn't what happened. What is going to happen, I mean...'

'Even your grandfather will trust my version,

rather than yours. I am a man of the cloth, you see. People respect the calling so much that they don't look any deeper than the clerical robes. He will be bitterly disappointed in you, naturally...'

No, no, Lizzie wanted to say. But her throat had seized up. Because she could just picture everyone believing Cottam's version of events rather than hers. Because he would be all smooth and plausible. While she'd be either hysterical or tongue-tied.

And people did naturally trust him. Why, she could hardly believe what he was planning, what he'd clearly already been a party to, though he was standing right there admitting to it.

Without showing one shred of remorse.

'Miss Hutton,' he said with satisfaction, 'I believe you have taken my point, at last. You have seen that Captain Bretherton's fate is sealed. The only question now is, do you wish to join him in his watery grave, or do you wish to live?'

'I... I...' Lizzie gripped her reticule. Glanced just once in Captain Bretherton's direction. If she went along, meekly, with Reverend Cottam's plans, she would never get over the guilt. But if she tried to oppose him, he'd either dispose of her, too, or spread the tale that she was a murderess. Besides, how *could* she oppose him? There was only one of her and he had a whole gang of smugglers at his command.

She felt her shoulders droop as she prepared to admit defeat.

'I want to live.'

'That's a good girl,' said Cottam, patronisingly, setting her teeth on edge.

'I cannot prevent your grandfather from being bitterly disappointed in you,' he said with false sympathy. 'But I can ensure he will be grateful to me for my effort to protect your reputation. I shall tell him that I used my influence with these Gentlemen to dispose of the body and then, together, we will all spread the tale that after your quarrel yesterday, your false beau gave up his pursuit and has left the area. We may put it about that he discovered you have no money, after all. That he only set about to woo you because he mistakenly believed you were an heiress. Yes, that will account for his presence in the area. It will be nothing to do with me.'

Oh, no, it wouldn't. If Cottam told that tale, Grandfather was bound to smell a rat. Because they'd covered the issue of her lack of fortune, right at the start. It was a small glimmer of hope, but Lizzie clung to it. And took it as a sign that no matter what it looked like, now, Cottam would not win in the end.

'So, how do you want it done then, guvnor?' A huge man stepped out of the shadows, making Lizzie jump. She couldn't believe someone that big could have been concealing himself so effectively.

'The same way we disposed of the others, of course, Bolsover.'

The others?

'What others?' But even as she spoke she knew the answer. 'You mean poor Jenny, don't you? And Mr Kellet.'

Cottam rounded on her. 'What do you know of them?'

Her heart began banging against her ribcage. If she told him what she knew, it would be like signing her own death warrant.

'Explain!'

'W-well...' The hands on her shoulders gripped her painfully hard. The man gave her a little shake, as though he was growing impatient.

And Cottam bent down to peer into her face.

'Only that I could never quite swallow the tale that went round after Mr Kellet drowned. And Jenny never said anything about having her heart broken, either. And then, when you said that about me and Captain Bretherton being star-crossed lovers ending it together, I just…'

'Not so stupid as you look,' hissed Cottam into her face. 'Bolsover!'

'Yes?' The giant stepped forward.

'Prepare the necessary equipment. And bring the boat to the High Inlet. Now.'

'Now? But, it's broad daylight…'

'Don't argue with me, man. Just do it!'

Bolsover melted back into the shadows. And the man who'd been standing guard over her wandered over to where Captain Bretherton was lying.

And then, all of a sudden, Captain Bretherton shot to his feet, drew back his arm, catching one of his captors in the face with his elbow, then punched the other one. Her own guard quickened his pace, but he wasn't any more successful in subduing Captain Bretherton. Instead, the pair of them went down and before she could blink, it looked as though all four of them were rolling around in a blur of thrashing limbs.

And then he was surging up out of the melee, shaking all three smugglers off him, the way a terrier shakes off a pack of rats.

'Run, Lizzie,' he yelled. 'Run for your life!'

Chapter Twenty-Three

They were going to kill him anyway. So what did it matter if they did it here with their boots and fists and knives, or out at sea somewhere? At least this way he'd give Lizzie a chance to escape.

He'd have taken them on sooner if he hadn't seen them holding that knife to her throat, effectively holding her hostage. If he'd made one wrong move, they might have used it on her.

He hadn't let them have it all their own way, though. To start with, he'd slumped down, giving the occasional groan as though he was half-stunned, so that the next pair of ruffians to come upon them had to haul him to his feet and half-carry, half-drag his limp body back the way they'd come.

They were both strong men, for their size, the way so many tough, wiry sailors were. But by the time they'd dragged him all the way along the tunnel and out into a kind of natural cavern, they were blowing hard.

For the next little while he'd lain still, surreptitiously looking around him for anything he might be able to use as a weapon. And listened to Cottam interrogating Lizzie. It wasn't too bad at first. Indeed, he'd felt an immense surge of relief upon hearing that she'd come down here to seek out a lost boy. He might have known it would be something of the sort, rather than her having a secret link to such a cutthroat gang. That the naïve, brave, trusting girl had rushed in on someone else's behalf. She was not involved in Archie's death in any way. Not even by association.

Only then Cottam had spilled some information of his own. In such a way that his involvement with Rawcliffe sounded far worse than it was. And he'd caught a glimpse of Lizzie's anguished face and couldn't keep silent any longer, no matter what the risk.

A couple of deftly aimed kicks had put a stop to any explanation he might have given her. Indeed, for a moment or two, just breathing, and keeping the contents of his stomach in place had been all he could manage.

Besides, it served him right. He deserved the pain. For putting that look on Lizzie's face—for although Cottam had been the one to wrench the veil from her eyes, Harry had been the one who'd hurt her.

So when Cottam had offered her a way out he'd gritted his teeth and prayed she'd take it. Prayed that she hated him enough to actually want him dead. Because if she showed any sign of resistance, they'd kill her, too. They'd already killed one woman. Admittedly, Jenny had been one of the gang and far from innocent, but if they'd killed one woman, they could certainly kill any other who might pose a risk to their organisation.

But his prayers were in vain. The moment Lizzie blurted out what she suspected about Jenny and Archie's death, it changed everything. Cottam was never going to let her go now.

The only way she might ever get out of this alive would be if he created a diversion, giving her a chance to slip away through the tunnels she'd said she knew so well.

So he staked everything on one last throw of the dice.

Maybe, in years to come, she would remember this last, sacrificial act and find it in her heart to forgive him for exposing her to such danger in the first place. She'd pleaded for his life, after all, just when he'd started to think he was beyond forgiveness.

Or perhaps he *was* beyond forgiveness. Perhaps it was just that Lizzie could not face the thought of becoming party to murder. Even if she did despise the intended victim.

'Run, Lizzie,' he yelled as the smugglers came rushing to him from all sides. 'Run for your life!'

She stood up. Out of the corner of his eye he saw that much.

But then pain exploded in the back of his head. And darkness closed in.

The next thing he knew, someone was dragging him along yet another tunnel. He could hear the sound of waves breaking somewhere up ahead. And Reverend Cottam's voice, from behind.

'Careful, lads,' he said.

'They know the drill,' came a voice he was beginning to recognise as that of Bolsover, from somewhere further back. 'As few marks on him as possible.'

He supposed he ought to be thankful for small mercies. Since they were being careful not to leave any tell-tale injuries, they were dragging him by the arms, rather than his feet which would have ended with his skull being bashed in. His head did throb and there would probably be a lump like a goose egg where they'd hit him, but it didn't feel as if they'd done him any permanent damage.

'Come along, Miss Hutton,' said Reverend Cottam, in a wheedling tone. 'If you walk a little faster, it will warm you up. And then again, you know, you will feel much better when we get out of these nasty, dark tunnels.'

Good Lord, he was talking to her as if she was a simpleton. Her blood must be boiling. No wonder she didn't bother answering him, though he knew she was there. He could sense her. Could almost feel her misery and despair reaching out to him like tendrils of a vigorously growing plant.

Though why she hadn't run when he'd given her the chance, he shuddered to think. What means might they have employed to prevent her? He hoped she wasn't hurt. He strained all his senses in her direction and heard the light, firm tread of her footsteps through the heavier trudging of the men.

Though all the sounds were altering slightly as they grew nearer to the exit from the tunnel system. From hard-packed floor to crunching shingle.

Upon which they dropped him, face down, before trudging on ahead. He half-opened one eye and noted that it wasn't much lighter outside than it had been underground. It felt like early evening. Had he really been unconscious that long?

He imagined poor Lizzie, sitting all alone in that cave, waiting with no hope, and wanted to groan. He gritted his teeth. He must not give any sign he was coming round, or they'd tie him up, he was sure. And he'd stand a far better chance of doing something to ensure Lizzie could get away, if they left his arms and legs free.

It cost him dearly to keep to that vow when a couple of the men returned, dragged him across a bank of rough shingle, and then manhandled him over fairly steep gunwales into their craft.

'Gently, lads, gently,' said Reverend Cottam.

'I've told you, my men know their business,' said Bolsover in a rather surly tone, as Harry landed face down on a pile of netting. The smugglers did indeed know their business, he concluded, for the netting, though extremely pungent, had cushioned his fall very effectively.

'Come along, my dear,' said Reverend Cottam from the beach. Lizzie must have demonstrated some reluctance to get into the boat, because he continued, 'In you get. And we'll give you a ride back. I'm sure you don't want to go back into those nasty, cold, dark tunnels on your own again, to try and make your way home, do you? Especially not without a lamp.'

The boat rocked as Lizzie gave in and did as she was told. He hoped it was a good sign that she chose the bench closest to where he lay sprawled. His heart leapt when, under cover of another person clambering in, which made the boat rock again, she bent down and laid one hand swiftly against the exposed nape of his neck. Was she checking to see if he was still alive? Even after everything she'd heard about him? Glorious girl. No wonder he loved her.

Loved her?

The boat rocked again as someone else clambered in. Or was it only his head reeling at the momentous discovery he'd just made? Why hadn't he noticed the feeling creeping up on him? Though at least he now understood why he'd just decided he would rather die for her, so she might have some fond memories of him. In a sort of attempt to atone for any hurt he might have caused her.

What a time to discover the state of his heart. When he couldn't tell her. When she wouldn't want to hear it, either.

It was Reverend Cottam who'd climbed aboard. Harry recognised his shoes on the planking close to Lizzie's feet. So, he was sitting next to her. Though not as close as he'd intended, for she shifted away at once. And then there was a lurch and the distinctive sound of planking dragging across shingle as somebody launched them into the sea. And more rocking. And the rattle of oars. Since this was a time when everyone would be concentrating on getting the craft underway, Harry took the chance to open his eyes and take a swift glance round.

Under the bench, between Lizzie's feet and Cottam's, he could see two more sets of sea boots in the forward thwarts. By letting his head roll as the craft got under way, he noted two more men sitting at the stern, wielding an oar apiece. Before he shut his eyes again he also spied a central mast, from which hung a tightly furled sail. But what was best, over the splash of the oars and slapping of the waves against the hull, he could hear the sound of the rest of the gang crunching their way across the shingle.

Two smugglers in the bow, two at the stern and the Reverend Cottam, that was all he had to overcome.

The odds against him had drastically reduced.

* * *

Lizzie had no idea what she could accomplish against a gang of smugglers armed with knives. There were so many of them. And all able bodied. And all with eyes that worked properly.

She only knew she couldn't abandon Captain Bretherton, not while he was still alive. No matter what he'd done, she couldn't bear the thought of leaving him alone, in the hands of these merciless men, not while he was unconscious.

And anyway, who was to say that if he came round, there might not be some way to escape?

From the middle of the ocean?

Actually, the odds improved considerably once they got into the boat. Most of the gang went back into the caves after loading Captain Bretherton into it and shoving it into the water.

If only he'd wake up.

The boat pitched as the men rowed it beyond the shelter of the inlet and his body rolled nearer her feet, his hand flopping against her foot.

And then, under the cover of her skirts, she felt him squeeze her foot. Her heart sped up. He was awake! He'd been shamming it! Though why should she be surprised? Shamming was what he was best at. But never mind resenting him for that now. Whatever he'd done, he didn't deserve to be drowned for it.

Did he have some kind of plan? He must have, or why let them put him in this boat while pretending to be unconscious?

Whatever it was, she hoped it resulted in Reverend Cottam going to trial. He was a disgrace to his calling. She was so disillusioned with him, she... well, she could actually see why Captain Bretherton might have gone to such lengths to expose him. Every now and then, that was, when she wasn't writhing with chagrin and misery, and the conviction she must be the most stupid female ever to draw breath. Both of them had fooled her. Both the Captain and the Curate.

But at least Captain Bretherton was trying to break up a gang that was steeped in all sorts of wickedness.

So she had to do what little she could to help.

The only thing she could think of, right now, was to draw attention away from Captain Bretherton, lest somebody notice he was starting to come round. Or they'd hit him on the head again, and he wouldn't be able to put his plan into action.

If he even had a plan.

'I don't understand,' she said aloud, drawing attention to herself, lest anyone should take it into their heads to examine their captive too closely. 'This makes no sense.'

'What, disposing of one man, so that the rest of us may carry on living in peace?'

She shook her head, resenting Cottam's jocular manner. Good heavens, he was talking about murder.

'No. I mean the others. Why kill Jenny? Or Mr Kellet? Oh—I suppose he wasn't down here just to visit Lady Buntingford, then, was he?'

'Congratulations, Miss Hutton. Or may I call you Lizzie? I feel that we are going to grow very close over the next little while.'

She shifted further along the wooden thwarts. Not that she could move all that far. The boat was narrow. Even so, she had to do something to show that she had no intention of letting the man close. Even metaphorically.

Besides, as she moved, she managed to flick a bit more of her skirts across Captain Bretherton's arm.

He might be a lot of things, but he wasn't a fool. He kept a firm hold on the heel of her boot. And then, as though his fingers wondered what the strap could be, began to explore the holster which kept her knife in place.

Oh, good heavens, Sam's knife! If she could work it out of its holster, without anyone noticing, then…

Sam had shown her how to defend herself with it. And had made her practise stabbing pretend smugglers made out of sacks of meal. She gulped. Could she actually use it against a real, living, breathing smuggler? She didn't think so.

Nevertheless, she might as well get it in her hand. She could pass it to Captain Bretherton.

She was sure, she reflected bitterly, *he* would have no qualms about plunging it right into someone's heart. And twisting it.

'Jenny had to go,' Reverend Cottam was saying. 'She was a danger to our whole fraternity. Had an attack of guilty conscience when one of her marks died.'

'Marks? I don't quite follow. Although she did mention an old lady she was working for…and some medicine…'

Reverend Cottam clapped his hands. 'Now you are beginning to use your brain. Yes, the old lady she was working for had an unexpected reaction to the, er, medicine Jenny gave her. And died. Though I fail to see why that should have upset her so much. Old ladies die all the time. If only she'd kept her head…' He shook his own.

'Instead, she came down here, to you.' Lizzie encouraged him to keep talking so that he wouldn't notice the way she was slumping down, so that her hands could reach her ankles. For once she was glad that Lady Buntingford had never been able to completely cure her of the habit of slumping her shoulders. And that all of them had seen her doing it, during what had felt like the hours she'd been sitting in the smugglers 'warehouse', shivering with cold and loneliness, and humiliation.

'Yes. The stupid girl,' Reverend Cottam sneered. 'She might have led the authorities straight to me. So of course, she had to go. I could see she would be of no further use to me.'

'But...why was she...no, I don't understand what she was doing giving old ladies medicine.'

'It was only to make them sleep. On the occasions she was either lifting or replacing, their jewels.'

'Jewels?'

'Yes.' Reverend Cottam sighed. 'It all started with a lucrative little sideline I got going with the help of my...exporters.' He waved one hand in the direction of Bolsover and his men, who were pulling on the oars with some vigour. Taking them further and further out to sea.

'I come across all sorts of men, in my professional capacity. Visit everyone from condemned men in their prison cells to great families with more money than they know what to do with. The men in their prison cells impart all kinds of information about their lives of crime. And the great families demonstrate such carelessness with their goods that, really, they deserve to have them removed.'

'You…you started stealing jewels from wealthy families?'

'Yes. It was when…an elderly lady with leanings to the high church had me in to hear her final confession. And there was this jewellery box just lying there, on the dressing table. Well, I couldn't help opening it, to see what might be inside. And there was this necklace. Diamonds.' He sighed. 'Well, what would you have done? I was all on my own, with those sparklers just winking up at me.' He chuckled. 'They went into my pocket. And I went straight to a fence I'd met not long before. Only…' he shook his head '…it turned out that they were worthless copies, not the real thing. Can you believe it?' He sounded affronted.

'Many of the great families,' he continued, in that indignant tone, 'are not as wealthy as they would like the rest of us to believe. They pawn jewels and silks, and furs. Or, in the case of the females, have their jewels copied so that their foolish, fat husbands won't find out about their gambling debts.'

The men were glancing over their shoulders from time to time, as though looking out for some sort of marker. And Reverend Cottam was in full spate. For once, she was glad that she was the kind of girl people didn't pay much attention to. It meant she could reach down as though she was scratching her ankle and get her fingers round the hilt of the knife. All she had to do was ease it from its holster without anyone noticing.

She could do it. She *could*. It was growing darker by the second. The moon was on the rise. And Reverend Cottam's voice was coming to her from the shadows, though he was only a few feet away from her. It was actually rather sinister, hearing him relate his descent into crime with such glee when she couldn't see his face. She shivered again.

And under cover of that shiver, freed the knife from its holster, sat up straight and wrapped her arms about her waist again, concealing the knife under her reticule.

'Which gave me the idea for an almost undetectable crime,' Reverend Cottam was boasting. 'I'd get a nice-looking young pickpocket into the house of one of those stupid old women who leave jewels lying about all over the place. She would lift them, take them to be copied, then return the fakes to the old woman and send the genuine article to me. Before long, I was taking orders. Can you imagine? And with my good friend Mr Bolsover's connections across the water, I developed a most lucrative business. Until one old lady died and my best jewellery thief grew a conscience. Even then, we might have got away with it, had not some jealous, suspicious husband had all his wife's jewellery examined and noted some of them were paste.'

'So… Jenny was…'

'My light-fingered young protégée, yes. A shame I had to get rid of her, really. Although the planning that went into the disposing of her will certainly come in handy, today.'

'What…what do you mean?'

'Well, we didn't want her death to point back to us, did we? Had to make it look as though she did away with herself. Which meant there had to be no marks of violence on her body, or as few as possible. It would have been easy enough to hit her over the head, to stun her, then throw her into the sea and hope she drowned. But there was no guarantee. The shock of the cold water may have roused her. She may have been a strong swimmer, do you see?'

'Ye-es.' She gulped. For what she could see was that Reverend Cottam had planned out a chilling murder without suffering as much as a ripple of conscience. His only concern had been to ensure that nobody could trace the crime back to him.

'We ruled out tying her hands behind her back, or any such clumsy ploy to ensure she drowned, since it would have been obvious that it was a case of foul play once her body washed up. But in the end, the solution I came up with was rather brilliant.' He leaned close to her, jabbing his fingers in the direction of Captain Bretherton. 'What we needed was to connect a sack filled with rocks to the body, so that it would submerge her long enough to ensure she drowned, but in such a way that the ropes would slip away from her before she was in the water too long. And, you know, men of the sea are fantastically clever at creating knots and fashioning contraptions from netting. But it was my own notion of employing ice which ensured our success.'

'Ice?' Her horrified eyes flew to the blocks which lay beneath the thwarts.

The *two* blocks of ice. And then she realised that the couple of bulky sacks, which she'd taken no notice of before, must be full of rocks. She gave an involuntary shiver.

'Yes. We hoped that it would melt, so that the ropes would loosen enough to part company from the body. And then the body would rise to the surface and drift ashore on the next tide. Which proved to be the case. Nobody saw anything amiss in the small amount of netting tangled round either Jenny, or Mr Kellet, since such things get left behind at the tide mark all the time.'

Lizzie gripped her knife hard, her stomach churning. He wouldn't be telling her all this, in such detail, if he had any concern whatever that she would ever be able to tell anyone else. He was simply gloating. Crowing over the way he planned to dispose not only of Captain Bretherton…but also of her.

At her feet, she felt Captain Bretherton tense, as though he, too, had reached the same dreadful conclusion.

'Almost there, guvnor,' said Bolsover, suddenly. 'Want me to get him ready?'

'Yes, yes, you may as well.'

Bolsover and the man next to him stowed their

oars, while the two sitting behind her and Reverend Cottam kept on rowing. But only one of the smugglers bent to the piles of rope lying in coils in the bottom of the boat. Bolsover, instead, inched closer to her.

'May as well hand that over,' he said, reaching for her.

For one awful moment she thought he'd noticed she had the knife in her hand. But it was her reticule he snatched from her hand. He had the strings open and Sam's telescope in his hand before she had time to blink.

'This'll come in handy,' he said, admiring the gift she'd scrimped and saved to buy her brother, in recognition of his heroism.

And Lizzie saw red.

'Give that back,' she cried.

'You won't be needing it no more,' sneered Bolsover.

She lunged for it anyway. And Bolsover struck her across the face with the back of his hand. She landed with a thump on the coils of rope lying in the bottom of the boat at the exact same moment Captain Bretherton suddenly surged up out of them, yelling like a fiend.

He appeared to have his hands round Bolsover's

throat. And Bolsover was reaching for something, something that flashed silver in the moonlight.

'No,' she screamed and flung herself at the struggling men.

'Sit down, you damn fools,' shouted Reverend Cottam, as the boat rocked wildly. 'Or you'll have us all o—'

But before he could even finish it, Reverend Cottam's prophecy was fulfilled.

The boat tipped over.

Launching all seven of them into the sea.

Chapter Twenty-Four

Lizzie and Bolsover, and Captain Bretherton and the smuggler who'd been in the process of deploying Reverend Cottam's patent drowning device, all went over together in a tangle of flailing limbs and trailing rope.

A tangle that was going straight down, as if some unseen force had them in its grip. Which, of course, it had. Somewhere in the mass of nets and rope was one of those sacks of rocks.

Thank goodness she'd already got the knife in her hand.

Making sure she had a fistful of Captain Bretherton's jacket in her free hand, Lizzie sawed at the rope which felt as if it was under the most tension. It parted swiftly and Bolsover and his accomplice vanished in a swirl of bubbles.

Even though she and Captain Bretherton were

no longer plummeting down as fast as they'd been going before, for some reason they weren't immediately heading in the opposite direction, either. And since she could move all her limbs freely she had to assume that Captain Bretherton was still being pulled down by something.

She felt her way frantically down his body, making sure she always held tight to some part of his clothing so that they wouldn't be parted, somehow certain that if she let go, he'd keep on going down, while she'd go up. And he'd drown.

And there, round his knees, she found it. A tangle of netting and one of the blocks of ice. It took a few moments to hack away the netting where it was wound tightly round his leg. And when it parted, their descent into the depths slowed, considerably.

But they didn't immediately start to ascend, either.

So she began to kick her legs. At almost exactly the same moment that he did. As though they'd shared the same thought, the same instinct for self-preservation.

It felt like a long way to the surface and took far longer to fight their way back up to the air, than it had taken to go the same distance in the opposite direction. Her lungs felt as if they were on fire and it was all she could do to fight the instinct to take in a breath.

Not yet, not yet, she said to herself, over and over again.

But at last, just as she'd begun to despair of ever reaching the surface, a gust of blessedly fresh air slapped her in the face. She sucked in a breath. Then another. And then, oh, no! She sank beneath the surface again.

This time it was his hands pulling her back up. She gasped in just one breath, as he yelled, 'Your clothes. Your boots. They're dragging you—'

He didn't manage to finish his warning before she went under again. But it had been enough to let her know what she needed to do. First she got the knife under the lowest button of her spencer, and yanked it upward, then slashed the ribbons of her bonnet.

It made little difference. Her spencer just flapped round her shoulders like a pair of wings. How the heck was she going to get her arms free? Let alone get her boots off? Oh, God, she was going to drown after all. Her sodden clothing was almost as effective as Cottam's sack of rocks in pulling a body down to the depths.

And then she felt strong hands grabbing for her.

Captain Bretherton got one arm round her waist and she found herself clawing at him, though how he was going to stop her from drowning she couldn't think. In her panic, she almost let go of the knife, somehow feeling that his big, solid presence represented safety. And he used that panic to take the knife from her. For a moment she was stunned by the theft. Until she felt a slight twinge in her back, just before her spencer split all the way up. And then he was pulling it from her.

For some reason, at that moment, their heads broke the surface once more and she gasped in a couple of breaths.

'I'm going to cut your clothes off,' he yelled above the roaring of the waves.

She had just time to notice that he was already only in his shirtsleeves and wondered how he'd been able to get rid of the rough jacket he'd had on, before she went back under again.

This time, he felt his way down her body until he was at her feet, hacking away at her boot laces, then he worked his way back up her body, pausing only to sever the waistband of her skirt. She half-toed, half-kicked off her boots and sort of floated her way out of the lower half of her gown on her way to the surface.

This time, when her face broke into clear air, there was next to nothing pulling her back down. But…where was Captain Bretherton?

She circled wildly, staring in every direction. The waves which now lifted or lowered her made it hard to make out more than short glimpses in any direction. She spied the upturned hull of the boat, several yards away, and a couple of oars floating nearby. But no sign of any people.

The loss of Sam's telescope was as nothing to the feeling she got then.

'Harry,' she screamed. Never mind Lady Buntingford's lessons. This was no time to stick to the rigid rules of etiquette that demanded a single lady should never use a single man's given name.

'Harry,' she yelled again. Oh, what did it matter that he had played her false? Her feelings had been true, right from the start. He was the man she loved. And if she lost him now…like this…

There was a whoosh, not far to her left, and his head and shoulders shot free from the crest of the wave.

In two swift kicks she was beside him, had looped her arms round his neck and was holding tight. 'I thought you'd drowned,' she sobbed.

'No, you saved me,' he said, pushing a hank of

her hair from her face. 'Thank God for that knife.' He pressed it into her hand. Though she had nowhere to stash it, not now she'd kicked off her boots. All she was wearing now were her shift, stays and stockings, which were sodden.

'Just a moment,' she said. Then let go of him, rolled on to her back and tucked her feet up one by one to peel her stockings off. Then, as she trod water, she pulled the busk from her stays and stuffed the knife into the pocket left behind.

'I think you must be part-mermaid,' he said, once she'd finished her manoeuvre. 'I have never seen anyone so at home in the water.'

'You were tremendously agile yourself,' she replied in an effort to deflect the compliment.

'The boat,' he said with some urgency, indicating the upturned hull. 'Come on.'

He began to swim in its direction and Lizzie caught up with him after only a few strokes, though what good it was going to be Lizzie had no idea. It was too big for them to overturn it and use it to sail home. Still, they both grabbed hold of it and rested against it for a moment or two, panting for breath.

At which point the moon came out from behind a cloud and she caught the distinctive sheen of bare skin.

'Where is your shirt?'

'Gone. Along with my boots and breeches, I'm afraid.'

He was naked?

'I thought I'd better give us the best possible chance of surviving. Clothes were dragging us down, over and over again. And it is some way to shore.'

He was naked? Beneath the waterline, he had not a stitch covering his body?

'Do you think you can make it?' He turned and looked landward. 'Damn, it seems to be getting further and further away.'

That was because of the current.

'Come on, the sooner we get started, the sooner we will get to shore.'

The current!

'No! You must not try to fight the current. It is too strong.'

'What?'

'You will exhaust yourself if you try to fight it. Besides, this part of the coast is so rocky we would be more likely to get dashed to pieces than find one of the few tiny coves. And then we'd be too exhausted to climb the cliffs to safety before the tide turned. Our only hope is to just stay afloat as long as we can and let the current carry us—'

'But it's carrying us straight out to sea.'

'No. Well, it might appear so, but believe me, it only flows so strongly, in this direction, for a while and then it curves in again just past the headland they've started calling Lover's Leap. Anything that goes in the sea round about here washes up in Whitesands Bay, eventually.'

'Eventually? That doesn't sound promising.'

'No. Well, perhaps we could speed up the process by swimming *with* the current. If we turn on to our backs and let it get a hold of us…'

He started wrestling with the boat. 'If only we could overturn it and sail it to safety. But I can't get any purchase,' he said, resting his forehead for a moment against the planking.

'Could we not just cling to it, as it drifts with the current?'

'No, Lizzie, I'm afraid not. The water is too cold for us to survive in it for very long. That was why I wanted to get you out of it as swiftly as possible.'

'We could use it as a kind of flotation device? Hold it and kick our legs…'

'No, that won't do either. The mast and sail will act like a drogue. A kind of anchor used to slow a craft down,' he swiftly explained when she wrinkled her nose at the technical term. 'I saw the sail had come unfurled on one of my, uh, forays beneath the surface.'

'Did you see…anything else? Anyone else, that is?' She'd seen Bolsover and one other man plummet to the depths in a swirl of bubbles. But of Cottam, and the other two smugglers, there was no sign. 'Are we the only survivors?'

'I'm afraid so, Lizzie.' His voice sounded grim. 'When the boat overturned, the ropes and what have you spilled out on top of us all. Only you had a knife at the ready and the presence of mind to use it to such purpose that we escaped the tangle.'

He paused for a moment as Lizzie let that awful truth sink in. Nevertheless, she strained her ears for some telltale clue that there were other people nearby, over the sounds of the ocean.

There was nothing. No splashing. No cries for help. And even though she'd wanted to escape those horrible men, the thought of them all going to the bottom in a tangle of netting and ropes and rocks was so nasty she couldn't help shuddering.

'We'd better start swimming,' said Harry. 'The cold is getting to you already.'

It wasn't the cold. But she didn't argue. A keen

sense of revulsion had her pushing herself away from the boat, and all it represented, with a mighty shove.

She heard another splash and interpreted it as Harry doing the same. Then realised that, in the dark, she had no idea what direction she ought to be swimming in.

'We'll have to trust the current,' she said aloud. 'But we might need to just float for a bit and let it find us.'

'Good thinking,' said Harry, who, from the sound of it, was following her. 'Only we must take great care not to drift apart. I know that we will both be trying to keep in the current, but it may have vagaries about which you know nothing. The edges might flow more swiftly, or more slowly than the middle, for instance. And it is growing dark already. We won't be able to see each other for much longer.'

'Have you any suggestions,' she said 'as to how we might do that?'

'Perhaps by simply talking to one another. That way we can check on each other's positions even when it is completely dark. Assuming that it is going to take until well after sunset to reach shore?'

'Probably.' She rolled on to her back and began

to kick her legs gently. 'Although nobody has ever tried this, to my knowledge.' She heard a swoosh to her left, followed by regular splashing sounds. Harry was clearly doing just what she'd done. And never mind whether it was light or dark, you simply couldn't check where anyone else was in the water, when you were lying on your back.

'Usually,' she continued, 'it is inanimate objects which wash up in Whitesands Bay. Objects which have gone into the sea some days earlier. Oh, dear. This isn't going to work, is it?' She felt panic clawing at her insides. 'It took days between Mr Kellet going missing and his body washing up on the beach. And Jenny—'

'Lizzie!' He cut through her mounting hysteria with the one sharply spoken word. 'Don't forget they were weighted down with rocks. And they would have had to wait for the ice to melt before the ropes tethering them to the seabed would have released them. How long do you suppose it would take for a block of ice as big as the one that weasel was fastening round my legs to melt?'

'It…it… I have no idea. But it would account for quite a bit of the time, I should think.'

'Exactly. And we are not inanimate objects, just

drifting, either. We are both alive and swimming. That will speed things up considerably.'

'Harry?'

'What?'

'I just…' She swallowed back a sob. 'I just got a horrid vision of what nearly happened to us just now. Reverend Cottam…' She would have shaken her head in disbelief if she hadn't been swimming for her life.

'Unbelievable, isn't it? That explanation he gave, of how he made his murders look like accidental drownings…'

'He was boasting about it. Gloating.' She shivered. And not just with revulsion and reaction at what they'd so narrowly escaped. She was cold. And her eyes stung from salt water and her throat was raw.

Escaped? They had nowhere near escaped yet.

'You…you understand now, why I was so determined to do whatever it might take, to bring him to justice? Why I… Lizzie, I hope, that is, you…' He sighed.

'Yes. Once he boasted about the way he'd tricked so many people and practically explained how he intended to do away with us, I could see exactly why you felt you had to go to such lengths to stop him.' Not that it hurt her any less.

She swallowed again. Past a lump in her throat that felt like a knife.

'Lizzie? Say something. Please.'

'Something.'

He gave a bark of surprised laughter.

'I do love you, you know.'

She flinched. 'You don't need to say that.'

'Yes, I do. Before it's too late.'

'I would rather you be honest with me. That's what I've always wanted.'

'I am being honest with you. Now there is nothing I need to hide from you. Think about it. What do I have to gain by pretending to be in love with you? When we might never even make it safely to shore.'

That was a fair point. She was so cold. And her limbs felt so heavy. And Whitesands Bay was miles and miles and miles away. And she'd skipped breakfast. The odds were not in her favour.

Nevertheless, if she gave in to despair, Cottam would have won. She clenched her teeth on a growl. She had to survive, if only to tell the world what a horrible, two-faced, murdering swine he was.

'Lizzie…' came his voice from the darkness. 'Lizzie, will you permit me to explain myself?'

'Very well then.' They were going to have to talk about something. And she did deserve an explanation. Which had better be a jolly good one. 'At what precise point,' she said with sarcasm, 'did you fall in love with me?'

'I am not certain.' He went quiet. 'But I started to understand certain aspects of my behaviour while I was lying in the bottom of that boat. It hit me with as much force as…well, as whoever knocked me cold. Though looking back, I think I must have begun to fall under your spell that first day, when you tried to be so mysterious.'

'Mysterious? I never did.'

'Yes, you did. You would not give me your name, remember? Miss Terious.'

'Ah, yes.'

'It was adorable. And then, when we danced together, it felt…'

'As if we matched, yes, you said.'

'And then, when you were in danger… God, Lizzie, why the hell didn't you make a run for it when I gave you the chance?'

'Just how far do you think I would have got down those tunnels when I can barely see my hands in front of my face in broad daylight? I could never have escaped that way. Anyway, what do you take me for? Do you think I could really have run off and left you at their mercy?'

'I wouldn't have cared about that, as long as you escaped. You had to survive. That was all that mattered. Not the investigation. Not a single one of my vows. And then when Bolsover actually struck you, all reason went overboard.'

'Literally.'

'Hah!' He let out a bark of laughter. 'At least I knew you could swim. You told me so, remember? And as we went overboard, I thought at least with them all fighting the sea, they wouldn't have any energy left to try to harm you. I wouldn't have left it so late, if all the time I hadn't been hoping that they meant to kill only me. It had never seemed all that likely, of course, not once they knew your suspicions about the supposed lovers' drownings. But still I hoped against hope that they would do as Cottam had suggested and return you to your grandfather once they'd disposed of me.'

She recalled the way he'd squeezed her foot, as if to reassure her. And wondered if he truly would have meekly surrendered his own life without a struggle if he could have been sure it would ensure the safety of her own.

But it had never come to that.

'Once he explained himself, so fully, that hope died, didn't it? Yes, I came to the same conclusion, when Bolsover took my reticule.'

'I didn't imagine it, did I? That you'd decided to tip the boat over about the same time I made my move?'

'You give me too much credit,' she said. 'I just couldn't bear to think of that man using Sam's telescope when he never got the chance to do so himself.'

'Just as I couldn't bear to lie there and do nothing when he struck you. Still, it just goes to show, doesn't it?'

'Shows what?'

'That we make a great team. We acted as one, without even having to discuss tactics. Together, I shouldn't think there is anything we cannot overcome.'

Except the sea. And the dark. And the awful, creeping cold...

Chapter Twenty-Five

'Lizzie.'

'Unh.' She roused herself to reply, even though all she wanted to do was close her eyes and drift.

'Lizzie!' His voice was insistent. 'Lizzie, listen! I think I can hear waves breaking on a shore.'

She could hear it, too. It wasn't just wishful thinking. She really could hear the rhythmic sound that meant they were drawing close to land.

'Lizzie, we're almost there. Lizzie, please, sweetheart, rouse yourself. Just one more effort and then you can sleep.'

She summoned the last of her strength and forced her legs to kick.

'I think,' he said a few moments later, 'I can—yes, my feet can touch bottom.'

The words had scarcely left his mouth before his arms came round her and he lifted her to his chest.

And, oh, it was heaven to just let him take her weight. She let her head loll into the curve of his shoulder. No more swimming. He was going to carry her to shore.

Though as soon as she got out of the water and the air struck her skin, it felt like being pummelled by shards of ice. She wriggled closer to Harry's big, warm body, no longer scandalised by his nudity. All she wanted was to burrow into the warmth exuding from the slab of hair-roughened chest beneath her cheek.

The water was only to his knees now. He was leaving a wake of glistening foam in his path as he ploughed his way through the deep black waves, though how she could see that when she could see so little else was a puzzle.

'I can't imagine how you have the strength left to carry m-me, either,' she marvelled. He'd made so much of being almost an invalid when she'd first met him, and even here in Dorset, he'd kept on saying he wasn't up to his full strength. Had even that been a lie?

'I haven't,' he gasped, collapsing to the sand with her still in his arms. 'Lizzie, thanks to you, we've made it.' He rolled her into his lap, somehow, and took her face between his hands. 'You have sea-weed in your hair,' he said. Then kissed her.

His lips were as cold as hers. But somehow they warmed her. She wrapped her arms round him, not caring that what they were doing was highly improper. She just wanted to get as close to every manly inch of him as she could, while she had the chance. In case, for some obscure reason, she never got another.

He soon started running his big hands all over her, as though he couldn't help himself.

Or was he trying to get her warm?

For some reason, the thought that he might be acting in a life-saving capacity, rather than a lover-like one, made her very conscious of the fact she was only wearing her stays and the shredded re-mains of a shift. She unwound her arm from his waist, to check that Sam's knife was still where she'd put it for safekeeping. When her hand felt the handle, made from some kind of oriental wood that Sam had carved himself, the relief was so great that a great sob shook her frame.

'Hey, hey, hush now,' he crooned. 'You look ador-able with seaweed in your hair. Like a mermaid.'

'It isn't m-my h-hair,' she stammered through

teeth that were starting to chatter. 'It's…oh, ev-everyth-thing, I sup-pose.'

'But we're alive,' he said. 'And we defeated Cottam.'

And then he kissed her again.

As though he meant it.

And this time she made no attempt to staunch the fire that lit her up from inside. She kissed him back with every ounce of her strength, winding herself round him like seaweed. They were both still wringing wet and cold, but as he bore her down to the sand beneath him she gloried in the feel of his hands roving all over her, stroking, and grasping, as if he felt the need to make sure she was all there. Making her feel as if every inch of her was precious.

As every inch of him was precious to her. And wondrous, in his nudity. She could feel the muscles beneath the satin of his skin. Damp hair on his chest and his legs. And his…

'God, what am I doing?' Harry suddenly jerked away from her as though someone had yanked him away with an invisible cord. 'I need to get you to shelter, warmth, not ravish you on the beach.'

To her disappointment, he knelt up and against the backdrop of a starry sky she could see his outline, his head turning from side to side as he scanned the area.

'There's a light over there,' he finally said. 'A fisherman's hut, or something.' He bent down, scooped her into his arms and got to his feet in one fluid motion. And then he was striding across the sand, with her in his arms like a hero out of a book…

Although, actually, a hero from a book wouldn't be panting for breath, nor weaving from side to side. The poor man was clearly almost at the end of his strength.

'P-put me d-down,' she suggested through chattering teeth. She was far too heavy for him. And if he could walk, then so could she.

'Not a chance,' he grated. Just as the stars began doing something very peculiar overhead. They were all sort of wheeling round. She had to blink to try to get them to stop it.

'Lizzie, stay with me,' he said in a worried voice. 'Don't give up now.'

And then the world was tilting and she could hear him banging his fist against a door. Though she couldn't see him any longer. Couldn't see anything. Darkness was pressing in from all sides.

'Please, mistress,' she could hear him saying,

from very far away. 'Boating accident…lost our clothes in the water…'

'Come you in, then, m'dears,' said a motherly voice. And then a wall of heat hit her. 'We need to get the rest of them wet things off the young lady and get her warm. You, too, me duck. Good Lord, if it ain't Miss Hutton! Such a to-do there's been about you…a boating accident you say, sir?' Harry was putting her down and rough, yet gentle hands were pulling at what remained of her clothing.

'Sam's knife,' she protested as the woman removed her stays.

'Just you let Nan see to your things,' said the woman. 'Dry 'em all out nicely over the fire, we will, and you can put them all back on in the morning.'

She then started rubbing at her with some sort of towelling, before heaving her to her feet, getting her across a packed earth floor, and down on to a bed.

'Get you in, too, sir,' said the woman, just before Lizzie felt Harry flop down next to her. He put his arms round her and then it felt as if the woman, Nan, threw just about every blanket and coat and tablecloth she had over the top of them.

'Is there someone you can send for a doctor?'

Harry pulled Lizzie into his arms and started running his big hands up and down her back. She buried her face into his chest and breathed in the comforting smell of salt and man.

'There ain't no doctor nearer than Peacombe,' she heard Nan saying. 'Besides, he won't do nothing more than what I'm doing. Best to send for the Colonel, if you ask me. Out of his mind with worry he is over this young lady going missing. And his place is nearer, as the crow flies.'

'Do you happen to have a crow handy?'

Nan cackled with laughter. The laughter faded and she heard a door opening and closing.

'Lizzie,' Harry whispered, though she was pretty sure they were alone. 'When your grandfather comes, please let me do all the talking.' He stroked a strand of hair from her face. 'I will tell him everything. But we need to agree on a story to account for what has happened today, to tell everyone else.'

'Is that really n-necessary? C-can't we just tell the t-truth?'

He redoubled his chafing.

'We cannot let the truth get out. It involves too many people who want it kept quiet. Please, can you just trust me on this, Lizzie?'

'But Reverend C-Cottam tried to k-kill me! And he did k-kill Mr K-Kellet. And Jenny. You c-can't want to let him get aw-way with it?'

'He hasn't got away with anything. He's dead, darling. At the bottom of the ocean where he belongs. And no good will come of raking up…'

She turned over so that she lay with her back to him. And shut her eyes.

She felt him kiss the crown of her hair, but it didn't feel the same as it had on the beach. There was thought behind it. Deliberation. As though he was trying to…to *turn her up sweet*.

Which was what he'd been doing since the very day they met.

Even on the beach…it might have felt real…but what did she know? She'd never kissed any other man. And though she'd poured her heart and soul into it, that didn't mean he'd been doing the same.

She bit down on her lower lip, which had started to wobble. And wrapped her arms about her waist. And though his arms were round her, too, it felt as though a distance had crept in between them.

The next thing she knew, daylight was streaming in through a door that had been flung open with a bang. And the familiar outline of Grandfather stood silhouetted against it.

Nobody said anything for a moment or two. During which period she became aware she'd turned over in her sleep so that she was snuggled up against Harry with her head tucked underneath his chin. It had only been for warmth, naturally, but to an outsider, their position, naked as they were, must look utterly scandalous.

'I think we can forget about the money, under the circumstances,' said Grandfather, confusingly. 'You will be married as soon as you can get hold of a licence.'

Harry tensed. Just before he bit out, 'Of course, sir.'

And it hit her, then, like a...like a saltwater wave to the face, that he'd never intended to marry her. All the courtship, all the following her about the place, had all been merely a ruse to find out what Cottam was doing and what his weaknesses were.

Only now, because Grandfather had found them in bed together, he was not going to be able to wriggle free.

Nan, who must have been sitting by the fire, got to her feet. 'So romantic it was, your honour,' she said to Grandfather. 'The way Miss was swooning in his arms as he carried her to my door.'

It hadn't been romantic. There was nothing romantic about almost drowning, after spending hours listening to a madman gloating about how he planned to do away with you.

Nothing romantic about being used as a…as a… well, she wasn't sure what the term was, but Harry had definitely been using her.

'It wasn't romantic,' Lizzie began to object. Only to wince as Harry pinched her arm gently.

'Not now,' he breathed into her ear.

But surely, he wanted this notion of Grandfather's nipped in the bud, before he ended up shackled to her for life?

'But, Grandfather…'

'Not now,' growled Grandfather. 'Captain Bretherton can explain just exactly how you wound up here, to me, *in private*.' There was a hint of a threat to his tone.

'Yes, sir.'

'My thanks to you, Nan,' he then barked, 'but you have played your part. I must get my granddaughter home now, as quickly as possible.' Then he came and sat down on the crude stool beside the simple bed upon which she was lying. 'Lizzie,' he said in a softer tone. 'I thought I'd lost you.' He reached out a hand that was trembling, to brush a hank of salt-encrusted hair from her face. 'When you vanished, I had the militia out, searching for you. My only hope was that, since Captain Bretherton had vanished as well, you were together, somewhere. And he would rescue you.'

'He did,' she said. 'The smugglers—'

Once again, Harry stopped her. 'Do not upset yourself by speaking of your ordeal, not now. You need to rest. To recover.'

'Yes, and you, young man, need to go outside and get some clothes on,' said Grandfather sharply. 'And leave my granddaughter to do the same, in privacy. Close your eyes, Lizzie,' he said sharply, as Harry sat up and scrambled out of the bed. As if he couldn't get away from her fast enough. 'Your man is outside with clothing and such for you, Bretherton. The messenger this good lady sent told us in what case you were found.'

Lizzie closed her eyes, groaning inwardly. It would be all over the area by now that she'd been carried to Nan's cottage by a naked man. And if anyone knew anything about how to help people get over a dunking in freezing sea water, they'd guess she'd just spent the night in the same bed with him, too. The chances she could free Harry from the necessity of marrying her were getting slimmer by the second.

'Lie still,' said Grandfather, when she made one last effort to sit up and fight for Harry's freedom. She flopped back, exhausted, without saying a word. For the truth was that she did feel awfully light-headed. And her limbs and back ached from just that one attempt to sit up.

'Get a move on, man,' said Grandfather irritably, when Harry seemed to hesitate by the door. 'And, Lizzie, you keep your eyes closed. Decency! Harrumph! Let us have some decency to proceedings.'

Which was the sort of stupid thing people described as locking the stable door after the horse had bolted. For one thing, she'd been pressed up against every inch of Harry's naked body, all night long.

For another, even if she opened her eyes and ogled him, she wouldn't be able to see all that much. Just a blurry outline.

Still, Harry meekly did as he was told and, since Grandfather got up and barrelled out after him, she was left alone in the hut with Nan.

The man who'd brought Harry's clothes had also

brought a selection of her things. Or Cook might have bundled them up for her.

Though they didn't feel like hers any longer. She wasn't the same girl who'd worn them before. She'd had her eyes opened, both about the Reverend Cottam and Captain Bretherton.

Captain Bretherton. Funny, in the sea, she'd thought of him as Harry. Had thought of him as Harry right up to the moment when she'd started putting on her clothes.

Only now she couldn't do it any longer. Because he wasn't the man she'd thought he was. The man he'd wanted her to believe he was. He was a…a sort of thief taker, or something. A man who'd been on a mission to root out the evil that had been lurking in Peeving Cove.

And having heard Mr Cottam boasting about his evil deeds, she could—at least a part of her could—grudgingly see why he'd gone to such lengths to expose and defeat him. Indeed, Captain Bretherton was fully justified in using whatever means at his disposal.

And, having reached that very sensible, level-headed conclusion, she promptly burst into tears.

Chapter Twenty-Six

Before she'd fully got her tears under control, Sergeant Hewitt came striding into Nan's hut, wrapped her in a blanket and swept her up into his arms. He settled her into Grandfather's carriage and placed her feet tenderly upon a hot brick. Before she had time to ask what had become of Captain Bretherton, he'd closed the door on her and ordered the coachman to set off.

Grandfather really did want to get her home and as quickly as possible.

When they arrived, Cook came bustling out of the house and would have swept her upstairs, had her legs not given out the moment she got out of the carriage. Once again, Sergeant Hewitt came to the rescue, carrying her upstairs and into her room.

But this time, not before she'd glimpsed a second carriage bowling up the drive.

'Don't you fret about your young man,' said Cook, in between removing her shoes and tucking a mound of blankets over her. 'That feller Dawkins will see to him.'

'Is that what all the noise is about?' While Cook had been getting Lizzie settled, she'd heard what sounded like a herd of elephants in riding boots trampling up the stairs and along the landing to the little-used guest wing.

'That's it. Brought all his things from the Three Tuns the minute we got news you'd come out of the sea in Whitesands Bay. Oh, miss,' she said, sitting down suddenly and clasping her hands together. 'When Billy rolled up, right as rain not an hour after you'd gone out looking for him, and then you disappearing... Lord, how I boxed his ears!'

'It wasn't his fault.'

'No, but he told me about what had gone on in the night. And if he'd never got mixed up with that lot, you would never have gone a-searching for him, and none of this...' she waved her arm at the mound of bedclothes covering Lizzie '...would have happened. And I didn't know what to tell your grandfather...' She wrung her hands.

'What did you decide on, in the end?'

'I daren't tell him nothing. And all night, I've

been afeard I'd sent you to your death…' The woman burst into tears. 'Well, that's that, I dare say,' she sniffed, wiping her nose on her apron. 'I'll lose my job anyhow.'

'No, you won't.'

'You mean, you won't tell your grandfather how you ended up almost getting done in by Bolsover? Coz that's what happened, ain't it?'

'I…' Lizzie paused. She really didn't want to add yet another secret to the mountain which already felt as if it was crushing her. But what good would it do to get Cook into trouble?

'What story,' she asked, hesitantly, 'is going about, at the moment? About why I was in the boat with Bolsover and his men? And Reverend Cottam?'

'Well, nothing yet. I don't think nobody else knows. So far. Your grandfather has just been ranting up and down the moors, getting the militia out and threatening to wring Captain Bretherton's neck if he's allowed any harm to come to you. But we're bound to get visitors today, wanting to find out how you ended up on the beach without a stitch of clothing.'

Lizzie's cheeks heated. 'I don't think anyone

needs to know anything we don't wish to tell them, do you?'

They exchanged a look, loaded with meaning.

'I could say,' Cook suggested hesitantly, 'you're too overset to talk straight. People will come up with their own notions, but once you and the Captain tie the knot, the gossip will soon die down.'

'Ah...' Lizzie began.

But Cook was patting her hand, and looking much more cheerful. 'The doctor will be here soon, to tell us how to get you well, but I've water heating for a bath to get all that nasty salt off your skin and out of your hair,' she said, bustling away to the door. 'Since he'll probably tell me we oughtn't to wash your hair, lest it bring on some kind of fever, we'd best get you done quick. And then by the time he gets here you can be sitting up in bed sipping some nice hot broth, which he surely cannot have any objection to me giving you.'

A bath did sound good. As did sipping some hot broth. And she had no argument with going along with the fabrication that she was too overset to talk about her ordeal.

In fact, for the rest of the day, every time the door knocker sounded and another set of visitors was turned away, she felt nothing but relief. She really wasn't up to talking to anyone. She didn't even have the energy to argue with the doctor, when he decreed she must stay in bed for a day or so and avoid any more excitement. Normally, being confined to her room would have felt like a punishment. But for once, all she wanted to do was drink broth and doze. She'd learned her lesson about skipping breakfast. A girl never knew what would happen later on in the day, not with men like Cottam and Bolsover in the area.

Not to mention Captain Bretherton.

She wondered if he'd received the same orders from the doctor, since the man had gone along the corridor after leaving her room, rather than going straight downstairs. If so, it meant there might be time, before he went and got a licence, to speak to him and find a way to prevent him having to marry her. Because she had no wish to end up shackled to a reluctant groom.

When night came round, as Lizzie had done nothing all day but doze and sip broth, sleep did not come with it. Every time she shut her eyes, her mind was assailed by a variety of horrible scenes. If it wasn't enormous shadows chasing her down dark tunnels, it was leaden limbs that wouldn't move no matter how hard she strove. Or creeping cold making it an effort to breathe. Or the faces of men sinking below the waves, a trail of bubbles streaming from their silently screaming mouths. Even when she jerked awake, the nightmarish feeling didn't leave, because the throbbing in her cheek, where Bolsover had struck her, reminded her that it had all been real.

And there were no strong arms to hold her, no warm chest to burrow into. It was all she could do not to get out of bed and creep along the corridor, and climb into bed with Captain Bretherton.

Only that would be the end of any chance they might be able to wriggle out of marriage.

And he'd probably think she was doing her utmost to trap him.

So she sat up and wrapped her quilt round her shoulders, and tried to think of something else. Sunshine and meadows, and blue skies…anything but the sea and the dark, and the crushing feeling of being trapped underground with a gang of ruthless cut throats.

When morning came, so did the news that Bolsover's body, along with the other three men who'd been rowing their boat, had washed up in White-sands Bay. And then, as soon as it reached an acceptable hour for visitors to call, call they did. In droves.

'So many people coming to wish you well,' Cook panted when she bustled upstairs with a tray at midday.

They were more likely to be driven by rampant curiosity than concern for her. It wasn't every day that a smuggler as notorious as Bolsover met his end in such mysterious circumstances. They'd naturally wonder how a boat full of expert sailors could have capsized in a dead calm. Especially after she, too, had been involved in a 'boating accident'.

She wished she knew what tale Grandfather was giving out.

She wished she could talk to Captain Bretherton.

In fact, she didn't see why she shouldn't. Cook and Sergeant Hewitt and Grandfather were all busy seeing to her so-called well-wishers. Nobody was paying her any attention. Nobody would notice if she just slipped along the corridor.

She set her tray aside, and swung her legs out of bed. Her head felt fine until she put her weight on her feet. And the dizziness passed fairly swiftly.

She wrapped a warm shawl round her shoulders, thrust her feet into some thick socks and shuffled along the corridor until she reached the best guest room. After knocking briefly, she darted inside.

Only to run full tilt into Dawkins.

'Ah, miss, you shouldn't be in here,' he said apologetically.

'But—'

'The Captain is as well as can be expected,' he said, ushering her backwards out of the door. At which point Lizzie flushed. She hadn't spared his health a thought. He'd seemed far less affected by the cold of the water than she. After all, he'd carried her up the beach, hadn't he? And felt like a furnace all night long. And got out of bed and gone outside to get dressed, while she'd needed Nan to help her fumble her way into some clothes.

It was only when she was back in her room that she wondered why he hadn't spoken to her. Why she hadn't had any sense he was even in the room at all.

Had he already set off to fetch that licence Grandfather had demanded he procure? Oh, surely there must be some way to prevent a wedding going ahead? If only she could just talk to him.

But he was as far from her reach as if he'd been still staying at the Three Tuns.

That evening, after Cook brought her tray, there was another knock at her door. Her heart leapt, in the hope it might be Captain Bretherton.

And sank when she saw it was, instead, her grandfather.

'Bearing up, are you?' he asked gruffly.

She was still trying to form an acceptable way of telling him she was not going to be party to marrying Captain Bretherton against his will, just because she'd spent the night in bed with him—without a stitch of clothing between them—when he gave a small cry of distress.

'Your face,' he grated and shook his head.

Her hand flew to her cheek. 'Does it look so very bad?' She'd avoided examining the bruise too closely. But then she'd never been one to gaze at her reflection for very long.

'If that villain was not already dead, I'd…' He worked his hands over the head of his cane, rather than finishing his sentence.

It sounded as if Captain Bretherton had told Grandfather how they'd ended up in a boat with

Bolsover, if he knew how she'd come by the bruise on her face. Which meant she could speak freely.

'Grandfather, I really am unharmed…mostly unharmed. This is just a bruise. Could I not leave my room now? I feel sure that I would recover more quickly if I could be busy during the day, rather than sitting here brooding over it. And I really do need to speak to Captain Bretherton…'

'Hmmph. Brooding. Well.' He bowed his head.

'Please, Grandfather,' she said meekly, knowing that to confront him would only set his back up and make him dig his heels in. 'I am not used to being idle. And with Captain Bretherton staying, I'm sure Cook would appreciate some help about the place.'

'Yes. Yes. And your wedding is going to make a lot of work. A lot of work.'

'Well, and that is another thing,' she said. But he kept right on talking as if she hadn't said anything at all.

'Lord and Lady Rawcliffe will be arriving within a day or so. Thought it best they stay here, rather than at the Three Tuns, what with the Reverend Cottam being her brother. She will want to be here when his body finally, ah…' He shifted from one foot to the other. 'Poor girl won't want to have to put up with the likes of Jeavons at a time like this.

So have put it about that they are honoured wedding guests.'

Well, that would certainly explain to the locals why Grandfather was suddenly filling his house with guests, when everyone knew how much he valued his privacy. He was turning the focus away from the crime and towards her wedding. A wedding which she couldn't permit to go ahead.

However, if she said she wanted to help with the arrangements, at least she would have the freedom of the house again. And she could surely find some opportunity to have a frank discussion with Captain Bretherton and untangle their future in a way that would satisfy everyone.

'I had better come downstairs tomorrow, then, and help with preparing a guest room.'

'Rooms. Because we will also be expecting a Lord and Lady Becconsall.'

'Who?'

'They are friends of, ah, all concerned.' He then mumbled something incoherent into his moustache and made a speedy exit. Leaving Lizzie rather puzzled. Although it didn't take her long to wonder if somebody was using the pretext of throwing her a wedding to gather a group of people together under one roof, in such a way that their true purpose could remain hidden.

In fact the longer she thought about it, the more sense it made. Reverend Cottam had spoken at great length about Lord Rawcliffe's determination to expose him. And what was more, last time Lord and Lady Rawcliffe had come down here they'd rented an entire row of cottages rather than put up at the Three Tuns. And with it being well after the seaside season finished, those cottages were all standing empty. So there was absolutely no need to invite them to stay here.

When next she saw Captain Bretherton, she was going to give him a piece of her mind. She was absolutely sick of him using her to hide his true purpose.

But he could be extremely elusive when he put his mind to it.

The next morning, though it was early when she went to his room to attempt to confront him in private, he'd already got up, dressed and gone out.

Downstairs Cook informed her, with a twinkle in her eye, that he'd gone off to see about that special licence.

Lizzie sank into a chair, her spirits plunging.

Licences were terribly expensive. And Captain Bretherton already had substantial debts. Oh, if only she'd been able to speak to him, in private, before this. She might have been able to save him all that money, as well as his time and effort.

But before she could express her regrets, Lords Rawcliffe and Becconsall rolled up, with their wives in tow. And when she wasn't busy seeing to their rooms, and their servants, and their horses, Captain Bretherton was closeted with his friends in one room or another, talking in low, urgent tones, which nobody could make out even if they pressed an ear to the door.

And then they all rode out to Whitesands Bay to see what the tide might have washed up.

Conversation at dinner on the first night of their stay was stilted, at best. Lady Rawcliffe hardly ate anything and fled back to her room as soon as she could, her handkerchief pressed to her face. After that, Grandfather, Captain Bretherton, Lord Rawcliffe and Lord Becconsall sat over their port for what felt like an eternity while she strove to entertain Lady Becconsall in the drawing room. Lady Becconsall surrendered first, making the excuse that she'd had a long day and wished for nothing more than her bed. And then Sergeant Hewitt came in, and told her that she might as well go up herself, since the gentlemen had called for another bottle.

Though it wasn't port that was keeping them in the dining room, she thought darkly as she went upstairs. It was a conspiracy, that was what it was. A conspiracy to keep her and Captain Bretherton apart. Which would probably go on until the moment they were standing before some hapless vicar who believed he was going to conduct their marriage service.

The next morning, she walked into the breakfast parlour, to an atmosphere she could have cut with a knife.

And then Lady Rawcliffe burst into tears and Lord Rawcliffe hauled her to her feet and half-dragged her out of the room and up the stairs.

'They found Cottam's body,' said Captain Bretherton. 'Becconsall and Lady Harriet, when they went out for their early morning ride. All tangled up in netting and seaweed. He looks…that is, there was no sign of rocks, or ice…'

'If we hadn't known,' said Lord Becconsall, 'we'd have thought it was just an accidental drowning.'

But it hadn't been. It had been the result of his attempt to kill her. Lizzie found she had to sit down, rather urgently. Fortunately, there was a chair to hand, otherwise she might have ended up on the floor.

Captain Bretherton sat down beside her and took her hand. 'Go and get her some brandy, Ulysses,' he snapped, sending Lord Becconsall scurrying off in the direction of the sideboard. She pressed her face into his shoulder, for a moment, drawing comfort from his solid warmth.

But then Lord Becconsall was back and pressing the drink into her hand, and Captain Bretherton was urging her to drink it.

'This must have been a dreadful shock to you, Miss Hutton,' said Becconsall when she gasped as the pungent spirits hit the back of her throat.

'Yes,' said Grandfather, getting to his feet. 'You had best go back to your room and have a lie down. I shall need you, Captain Bretherton. We are going to have a busy day.'

She was about to say that she had no need to retire to her room like a feeble idiot. Hearing that Cottam had finally washed ashore hadn't been that much of a shock. Because she'd been waiting for this very thing to happen ever since the boat had overturned.

Only, her knees were shaking a bit. Whether from the brandy, which she wasn't used to, or the after-effects of snuggling up to Captain Bretherton only to have him skitter away like a scalded cat, or anger that he would allow Grandfather to send her to her room without uttering a word of protest, when Lord Rawcliffe had looked as though he would have leaped mountains to offer his wife comfort, she didn't know.

'Let me help you upstairs,' said Lady Becconsall.

'Fine,' she said, setting the brandy glass down on the table and getting to her feet. And giving one disdainful sniff as she left the room and the men to their important business.

As they mounted the stairs she could hear Lady Rawcliffe sobbing. And the low tones of her husband, who'd had no intention of abandoning his wife to her misery.

'Shall I ring for some tea?' Lady Becconsall asked, when Lizzie slumped dejectedly on to her dressing table stool.

'Fine,' she said again, only this time morosely.

It took only a few moments for Cook to arrive with the tea tray. She laced the first cup she poured liberally with sugar and yet more brandy, and urged Lizzie to drink it.

'Then you have a bit of a lie down,' Cook suggested.

'I don't need a lie down. And I ought to come and help you in the kitchen...'

'Oh, I'm quite handy, you know,' said Lady Becconsall. 'I can help out, I'm sure, if you show me what to do.'

And between them, they got Lizzie into bed and gave her another cup of brandy-infused tea. And almost before they'd gone downstairs, she fell asleep.

It was the sound of someone knocking on the door which roused her. She pushed her hair out of her eyes, stunned to see that the light had swung round so far that it must be getting on for the time to dress for dinner.

'Come in,' she called, cursing the brandy for robbing her of almost an entire day. Although, she hadn't been sleeping well at night. That might also account for her having fallen so deeply asleep.

Though nothing could account for the sight of Lady Rawcliffe, standing in the doorway, head up, chin out, clutching a handkerchief between her long white fingers.

'I...oh, I didn't mean to wake you.' she said.

'Think nothing of it,' said Lizzie warily, sitting

up and grabbing at the mound of blankets and shawls which went slithering in all directions. It was bad enough being caught sleeping at this time of day, never mind with legs on show. And whatever Lady Rawcliffe had to say was not going to be pleasant, to judge from her militant posture. But could she blame her? The elegant little redhead must have formed a very poor opinion of her the first time they'd met, which had been when she and her husband had been staying in Peacombe for their honeymoon. Lizzie had knocked over a vase of flowers and then set fire to a hearthrug. In the space of about five minutes.

And now she'd drowned her brother.

And then spent the entire day in bed in an alcohol-induced stupor.

'I am so sorry,' said Lady Rawcliffe, coming straight to her with her hands outstretched.

'*You* are sorry?' said Lizzie, taking hold of the woman's tiny hands as gently as she could, suddenly understanding Harry's comment about being half-afraid he might snap such delicate-looking appendages. 'No, *I* am the one who should apologise. If I hadn't…'

'Fought for your life,' insisted Lady Rawcliffe. 'That was all you did. And I have been so ashamed of him, and of us, for exposing you to such danger, I haven't known how to face you.'

Lizzie let out a huge sigh of relief. She'd thought Lady Rawcliffe had been avoiding her because she blamed her for her brother's death.

A movement from the doorway caused Lizzie to look in that direction, where she saw Lady Becconsall hovering on the threshold.

'May I come in, too?'

Though Lizzie couldn't imagine what she might have to add to the proceedings, she nodded.

'I haven't known how to face you either,' she said, slipping inside and shutting the door firmly behind her. 'But it is no use trying to steer clear of you in a house this size, is it?'

Oh, she didn't know about that. Captain Bretherton seemed to be managing it admirably.

'So we have decided to grasp the nettle,' said Lady Becconsall. 'And clear the air.'

'The nettle?' Lizzie looked from one lady to the other, in bemusement.

'Well,' said Lady Becconsall as she perched on the end of Lizzie's bed. 'It will sting a bit when we own up to what we've done. Only we did it to spare you, truly we did.'

'Yes,' said Lady Rawcliffe, nodding vigorously.

'When we heard the plan our husbands came up with, to snare Archie's killer, we knew we had to do something to protect you from real harm. Especially as it was my fault they thought of using you. I… That is, after we met… I might have…' She winced as Lady Becconsall jabbed her in the side with one finger.

'That is, I *did* tell them,' she said, twisting her hanky between agitated fingers, 'that you had access to Lady Buntingford. And that if anyone could reveal what had been going on in her house over the last few years, it would be you.'

'Only then my husband got involved,' said Lady Becconsall grimly. 'Actually, he was involved from the start. Which was my fault. You see, it all began when my uncle discovered that some of my aunt's jewellery had been replaced with fake stones.'

Yes, she'd heard all about that, from Cottam himself.

'Uncle Hugo,' Lady Becconsall continued, 'accused her of doing it to pay gambling debts. But she swore she hadn't. Things between them grew rather unpleasant. And because I owed her a great deal, I vowed to prove Aunt Susan innocent. And, in the course of my investigations, I discovered that something similar had happened in Archie's family. When his grandmother died, they found that some of her jewellery was paste, too.'

'Archie?'

'You knew him as Mr Kellet. And the old lady who died in Jenny's care was his grandmother. That was why he felt so strongly about coming to see Lady Buntingford, to find out how she was involved.'

'You thought Lady Buntingford was involved?'

'She had written the references that got Jenny into the house of both Archie's grandmother and my Aunt Susan,' said Lady Becconsall.

'But she couldn't have done,' said Lizzie. 'At least, not recently.'

'No, Atlas explained about the seizure. And when we checked, we found out that all those references were written after she'd had it. Once Clement—that is, my brother,' said Lady Rawcliffe with revulsion, 'took charge of her correspondence.'

'Oh.' Lizzie felt a bit sick. The man had been using Lady Buntingford's helpless state to introduce thieves into the houses of other vulnerable, older ladies.

'Archie must have found out about that, too. And that is why they killed him. Oh, Miss Hutton, you should have seen how devastated our husbands and

Atlas, too, all were when they found out. They… they lost all sense of reason. They swore they'd go to any lengths to avenge the death of their friend.'

Lizzie already knew that much. Captain Bretherton had confessed it.

'Yes. They weren't thinking rationally when they came up with the plan to send someone to go to Bath so they could, um…'

'Seduce me?'

The ladies nodded in unison. 'Well, naturally, we couldn't have that,' said Lady Rawcliffe indignantly.

'No, absolutely not. Only we couldn't openly defy our own husbands. Especially not when we could see how…um…'

'And that's when I thought of Atlas. Captain Bretherton, I should say,' explained Lady Becconsall. 'When I first met him, you see, even though the others forgot to behave like gentlemen, he never did. Even though he was as…well, inebriated as the rest of them.'

'Besides,' said Lady Rawcliffe, 'we thought it would do him good, too. He'd been sort of drifting—'

'Sinking, more like,' muttered Lady Becconsall.

'Yes, so we thought that if only he could get involved in our husbands' scheme, not only would it do him good, make him feel as if he had a purpose in life—'

'That is, to avenge Archie's murder—'

'And he would behave with complete propriety toward you, which nobody could guarantee if they hired someone to get close to you so they could find out if Lady Buntingford really had become some sort of criminal mastermind who trained girls to get into the houses of rich ladies so she could amass a huge pile of rubies.'

'Hire someone?' Lizzie's stomach had been lurching as the two ladies babbled out a tale she could barely comprehend. Suddenly, Grandfather's mention of money at Nan's cottage crept into her mind. But surely he couldn't have known... He would never have allowed... Lizzie's thoughts swirled sickeningly. But, no. Bretherton might have betrayed her, but her grandfather would never have gone along with such a thing. Bretherton must simply have told him that he was going to come into some money, conveniently leaving out the terrible reason why. To think that she'd *trusted* him. Lizzie shuddered with revulsion. 'You mean, your husbands were going to pay someone to pretend to... to want to...marry me?'

'I know, it does sound awful when you put it like that—'

'Which was why we let Atlas know what was going on. So he could put a stop to the madness. They'd been keeping it all from him, you see, because they didn't think he was interested—'

'So we had a very loud, very indignant conversation about the plan, right outside the room where he was sitting.'

'And just as we'd hoped, he was so angry that he went charging off and took the job himself.'

'Oh, please, don't be upset.' Lady Rawcliffe started patting her arms, which she discovered she'd wrapped round her waist.

'How many men…had they asked about… seducing me?'

'Oh, none! That is, they assembled some likely candidates, but they did not tell them exactly what they were being interviewed for.'

Lizzie let out the breath she hadn't realised she'd been holding in. It wasn't as bad as they'd made it sound, to begin with.

Nor had Captain Bretherton taken part in the actual planning of her…humiliation. Her stomach roiled again.

Captain Bretheron, she had to remember, had

only become involved because these two ladies had dragged him into it at the last minute and he'd done it to save her from being callously used by some other, nameless, faceless men...

But that didn't alter the fact that in the end, he was going to be financially rewarded for deceiving her. Something inside her went hard. For suddenly she had another explanation for his determination to avoid her the past few days. His estates. His mortgaged estates.

'I...well...thank you for coming to tell me,' she said stiffly. 'If you would not mind, I need to get up now and dress for dinner.'

The two ladies looked at each other.

'Oh, but you do forgive us, don't you?'

Lizzie looked down into Lady Rawcliffe's up-turned little face. She'd just lost her brother. And was terribly upset. Yet she'd steeled herself to come in here and make a heartfelt apology for the part she'd played.

'Of course I forgive you,' said Lizzie. After all, they hadn't been the ones who'd planned to treat her like some kind of disposable pawn in a bigger game. On the contrary, once they'd found out about the scheme they'd done what they could to ensure she came to as little harm as possible.

They couldn't have known she'd fall in love with the man they'd assumed would protect her. A man who had such a warped sense of honour, he would actually go through with marriage to a woman he'd compromised and accept payment for doing so!

Chapter Twenty-Seven

Nobody was eating much dinner that night.

In the case of Lady Rawcliffe, Harry could understand it. Her brother's body had washed ashore only that morning. The only wonder was that she'd dragged herself down here to dinner at all. She really was a brave, proud little thing.

But he could not fathom why Lady Becconsall could not meet anyone's eyes.

And as for Lizzie...ah, Lizzie! She'd been growing more dejected by the day. No doubt at the prospect of having to marry him. He couldn't blame her for loathing him, now that the truth had come out. It had only been what he'd expected. But he'd never imagined he wouldn't be able to walk away from her, leaving her at least with her dignity intact.

Now that they'd spent the night together, though,

she had no choice. With the result that she'd lost her appetite.

With the ladies doing little more than pushing the food round their plates, it seemed heartless for the men to tuck into the chicken, succulent though it was. In the end it was Colonel Hutton who brought the curtain down on a performance that wasn't satisfying anyone.

'We may as well all adjourn to the drawing room,' he growled, tossing his napkin on to the table. 'And discuss the matter which is occupying so many minds to the detriment of my cook's finest endeavours.'

He stalked out.

The ladies all abandoned their cutlery with evident relief and followed him from the room, which meant the gentlemen all had to get to their feet as well. Becconsall scooped one more forkful of chicken fricassee into his mouth the moment his wife had left the room, while Rawcliffe snatched two decanters from the sideboard.

Harry grabbed as many glasses as he could fit between his fingers and they all trooped to the drawing room as well.

As Harry walked in, it struck him that this was the first night they'd all gathered in the same room like this. Up 'til now the awkwardness of the situation had meant that at least one person had been avoiding at least one of the others at any given time.

The Colonel was correct. It was high time to get everything out in the open.

'May as well start,' said the Colonel belligerently, while Harry was setting the glasses out on the mantelpiece, 'by informing you I've reached my decision.' He glowered at Lord Rawcliffe. 'I agree with Your Lordships that the entire affair ought to be hushed up. Completely.'

Harry's sigh of relief was cut short by Lizzie's cry of protest.

'You surely cannot wish to sweep murder and attempted murder under the carpet?'

Harry strode quickly to the sofa on which she was sitting and took the chair next to it. 'Reverend Cottam has paid for his crimes, though, hasn't he?'

'And there could not be a punishment more fitting,' drawled Lord Rawcliffe, 'than for him to get tangled up in the ropes he meant to employ to drown you and Atlas with.'

'Divine justice, that is what it was,' said Becconsall from the mantelpiece where he was busy filling the glasses from the decanter he'd snagged from Lord Rawcliffe. 'Begging your pardon, Lady

Rawcliffe,' he said as her husband sat down beside her and took her hand.

'No need to beg it,' she retorted. 'He was wicked.' She let go of her husband's hand to fumble in her reticule for her ever-present handkerchief. 'Wicked!' She blew her nose with more feeling than grace.

'But—' Lizzie began.

'No, my mind is made up,' said Colonel Hutton gruffly. 'It is far better for him to have ended the way he did, than for me to have arrested him and put him on trial. A man of the cloth, behaving like that.' He grimaced in disgust. 'Would have brought the church into disrepute. And you would have had to testify, Lizzie. Your name would have got into the papers and become the topic of vulgar gossip.'

Lizzie was shaking her head in disbelief.

'If you understood it all,' said Harry to her gently, 'you would agree—'

'How can I understand,' she said, rounding on him, eyes burning with hurt and indignation, 'when you have deliberately kept me ignorant of so much? For so long?'

'It wasn't his fault,' put in Lady Becconsall while Harry was still reeling from the way she'd expressed a reaction he might have known she'd have. 'My aunt and uncle, as well as Archie's family, were the ones who made us promise to act with extreme secrecy. They didn't want anyone knowing anything about the thefts. If it had got about that family heirlooms had been exchanged for paste, people would have been bound to start wondering whether their financial position is secure. And they didn't want my cousin Kitty's chances of making a good match spoilt.'

'And to tell you the truth,' said Lady Rawcliffe, 'I don't want the truth about Clement getting out, either. It won't do either of my other brothers any good in their careers. It's bad enough just being his sister, without everyone knowing what a villain he was. And perhaps saying that Rawcliffe only married me as an excuse to get close to him—' She broke off sharply. 'What?' She looked at her husband, who had just given her a sharp nudge. 'Look, Miss Hutton understands how you came to set Atlas on to her. And she understands, don't you, Miss Hutton?'

Everyone turned to look at Lizzie.

'I understand that people wanted to prevent anyone knowing about the theft of their jewels,' she said, through tight lips. 'And I can see how poor Mr Kellet's friends became so angry over his murder, they vowed to avenge him. I even understand why Lady Rawcliffe and Lady Becconsall...' She trailed off as both ladies tensed up. 'Well, never mind that. I just mean to say that they have helped me to understand why you all swore you would go to any lengths to bring Reverend Cottam to book. And when I think of all the evil he has done—' She broke off, shaking her head.

Lord Rawcliffe cleared his throat. 'I had long believed Cottam was behind it all, Miss Hutton. But without proof, we could do nothing. He always stayed behind the scenes, sending others to do the actual deeds.'

'Which was why I suggested,' said Lord Becconsall, 'we send someone down here, under cover, to get conclusive proof of his villainy.'

Harry winced as Lizzie shot him a wounded look.

'It is more important to undo the evil he did, my girl,' put in Colonel Hutton, 'than let the world know about it. Oh, I'm not saying we will ever recover the jewels he had stolen and copied. They are long gone. But at least we can do something about Lady Buntingford.'

Lizzie's eyes flew to his. 'What do you mean?'

'All that nonsense about her not wanting any visitors,' he growled. 'I never would have believed it if it hadn't come from the lips of a clergyman. Why, she was the nosiest old busybody it has ever been my misfortune to...' He pulled himself up short and cleared his throat. 'What I mean to say is, she thrived on gossip. Would never have cut herself off like that. Even if she couldn't spread any, she'd still want to hear it. So, long and short of it, I forced my way in, as soon as Captain Bretherton apprised me of the way it really was. Never seen anyone so glad to see me as the poor old girl.' He chewed on his moustache for a moment, a suspicious sheen glowing in his eyes.

'And you don't need to ask how I could tell. She might not be able to say much, but her eyes can still shine with pleasure right enough. Even the two words she can say, she can say with such expression that you know *exactly* how she's feeling.' He tapped on the floor with his cane to emphasise his point. 'Took me deuce of a long time to write the letter to her family to let them know they would be welcome to come and visit whenever they wished, though. Could not bear to let them know that they were all hoodwinked by that rogue. Cannot credit I fell for his nonsense myself. Didn't want to see anyone, indeed,' he growled.

'I am glad she will have a bit more company from

now on,' said Lizzie. 'I never felt I was the person she would have chosen, somehow, to be her only link to the outside world.'

While everyone else in the room seemed pleased with her response, Harry felt saddened, because she had such a low opinion of herself. How could she assume the old lady would have preferred any-one but her to bear her company?

'You keep saying you understand, L—Miss Hut-ton,' he said. 'But you have not yet said that you forgive us for embroiling you in this affair. For put-ting your very life in danger.'

'For those things I can easily forgive you all,' she said. But then her lower lip began to tremble. 'What I find harder, though,' she said turning to him, 'is the way you…you…toyed with my affec-tions. The way you are *still* using me to cover up the reason for you all being in the area at all.'

Everyone went still. It was as though the whole room was holding its breath.

And then everyone began talking at once.

'Lizzie, I thought you understood,' said Harry, leaping to his feet.

'Now, see here, young lady…' Grandfather said.

'Now the fat is in the fire,' said Lord Rawcliffe.

All at the same time.

'Might I have a few moments alone with Miss Hutton?' Harry spoke to the others, though he never took his eyes from Lizzie's downbent head. 'And there is no use saying it isn't proper, Colonel Hutton,' he added when the man took a breath as though to voice an objection. 'You've made me stay away from Lizzie for days now and this is the result. She's started to think I don't care!'

Something about Lizzie's posture altered, slightly. She still wouldn't look at him, but her shoulders were no longer slumped quite so despondently.

'Very well, you've made your point,' said Colonel Hutton, before ushering everyone out of the room. Everyone but Harry, that was.

'Lizzie,' he said, the moment the door closed behind the last of them, 'I didn't toy with your affections. I explained it all, that night. While we were swimming. Don't you remember? I told you I loved you. Didn't you believe me?'

'I almost did,' she said. 'Until I worked out that you must have just been saying it to…give me hope. Or calm me down. I was almost hysterical at one point, so it isn't as if I can blame you for employing such desperate measures.'

'No, Lizzie, it wasn't like that,' he said, dropping to his knees at her feet. 'Think, Lizzie. Think about what happened the moment we got to shore. The way I kissed you. Why did I need to do that if I didn't mean it?'

'Relief, I dare say. You might have got carried away for a moment or two. But that doesn't mean you have to marry me. I know you don't want to. And if it wasn't for the money…'

'Money? Money has nothing to do with it!'

'But you will get rather a lot, I believe, for marrying me.'

'For marrying you? No.' He got to his feet. Took a step back. 'I can claim a reward for discovering Archie's murderer. And for settling his hash. Not that it had any bearing on why I took on the case. Hang it, I'd give it all away if it wasn't for the fact that we *are* getting married.'

'What do you mean?'

'Lizzie, I can't afford to keep you as I'd like, without it. But if I accept it, I can set you up in style, wherever you wish to live. And you will be a countess, don't forget, with all the social opportunities that go with the title. I want to make sure you have the means to take advantage of them all.'

'I don't care about money or titles,' she said mulishly.

'But you deserve some recompense for all I've

put you through. So I mean to ensure that you never want for anything, for the rest of your life.'

'I don't want some...*reward*,' she said, her nose wrinkling in disgust, 'for just...' She waved her hands vaguely. 'I didn't *do* anything.'

'You saved my life,' he pointed out. 'If not for your warning, I'd have tried to swim straight to shore and ended up drowning from exhaustion trying to fight the current, or dashed to pieces on the rocks.'

'Oh...fustian!'

'I don't believe this,' he said, thrusting his fingers through his hair. She was slipping through his fingers. The way mermaids always did once a sailor dragged one ashore.

He had the fight of his life on his hands if he didn't want to see all that they'd been through turning to sea foam and blowing away on the breeze.

'Look, Lizzie,' he said wearily, 'I know you must hate me. I know you cannot wish to marry me. I wish I could give you the freedom you want. But we were discovered in that cottage. Unclothed. What kind of a man would I be to simply walk away and leave you to face all the gossip and ridicule alone?'

'It's so silly,' she said gloomily. 'When nothing happened.'

'Lizzie, you spent the night in my arms. Naked. What's more, my girl, you...' He braced himself to do what was necessary, since soft words had been getting him nowhere. 'You plastered yourself to me. And kissed me back on that beach, might I add! Like a...'

'I admit, I got a bit carried away on the beach. But that was before I realised...' She stopped, her shoulders slumping again.

'Realised what?'

'Nothing,' she mumbled. 'It doesn't matter.'

'Of course it matters. My whole future is at stake.' He couldn't stand still. He had to take a pace or two about the room.

'Very well, Lizzie, what will it take? Name your terms. And I will give you a new life. A better one than you've had under your grandfather's guardianship, that I promise. If you cannot stand the sight of me, I will go back to sea as soon as we've signed the marriage lines and never bother you again, but the protection of my name you must and shall have.'

'Is that,' she said in a small voice, 'what you want? To go back to sea?'

'What *I* want?' He couldn't help laughing, a touch bitterly. 'If I told you what I want you'd run screaming from the room.'

'But at least you would be honest, for once.'

'Honesty? Is that what you want? Very well then, here it is.' He leaned back against the mantelpiece and crossed his arms across his chest. 'What I want is to have the right to kiss you, the way I kissed you on the beach. Whenever I feel so inclined. To hold you in my arms all night long with not a stitch of clothing between us.'

She didn't raise her head, but her cheeks went pink.

'And what's more, I want to see you...' He searched for the right word. 'Blossom. I'm sick of the way people treat you as if you are of no account. Mocking your height and making you try to be smaller than you truly are. Even robbing you of the ability to see your way about clearly. Which is why,' he said, reaching into his pocket, 'I bought you this. I want you to have it, even if you won't have me.'

He tossed the gift he'd bought her into her lap.

'What is that?' She eyed it with suspicion.

'Some spectacles. I know how you hate not being able to see anything clearly, at a distance. And I'd like you to always feel as confident and capable as you were in the water. Which you cannot do when you cannot see properly.'

She turned the box over. Shook it. Her fingers actually went to the latch. But then she set it down and shook her head.

'I cannot take a gift from a man to whom I am not betrothed,' she said. 'It wouldn't be proper.'

'I know I'm not the man you would have chosen, Lizzie.' He thrust his fingers through his hair again and turned away. 'What woman in her right mind would choose me?'

'I…' she said hesitantly. Then cleared her throat. 'I might have chosen you, if I'd been certain that your feelings were…sincere. If you'd actually proposed to me, rather than being compelled to marry me just because Grandfather found us together like that.'

He strode across the room to stand over her.

'My feelings are sincere, Lizzie. And in spite of what you think, I've never lied to you. The way we met might have been…contrived. And I may have withheld some facts from you. But I do love you.'

She gaped at him.

'Damn it, why can you not just believe me when I say I love you? Why can't you believe yourself worthy of love? Damn your grandfather and every-one else who has ever made you feel unworthy and unlovable. Including me. I should have…when we both came back here I should have…but you see, I wanted to tie up all the loose ends. Needed to make sure that none of it would have a lasting effect upon you. And I had to summon Zeus and Ulysses, be-cause they needed to be in agreement with my plans. And then I had to make arrangements for poor Jenny to have a proper Christian burial. Aye, and pick up the spectacles I had made by one of the finest oculists in Bath. And all I achieved was to make you think I was staying away from you because I didn't care.' He sighed.

'What can I do, or say, to convince you I'm tell-ing the truth? That I want nothing more than to be your husband and devote myself to making you happy, for the rest of my life?'

She shrugged. And turned the spectacles case over and over in her hands.

'You might try actually proposing to me.'

'Lizzie, please marry me,' he said at once.

But she didn't even raise her head from the spec-tacles case, let alone say yes.

'Lizzie, you have to marry me,' he said, planting his fists on his hips. 'You are a woman of integrity.

You are never going to be able to spend the rest of your life with the memory of being kissed senseless by a naked man, to whom you were not married, seared into your memory.'

'It was only one kiss. Well, two, to be precise,' she corrected herself, blushing. 'And it isn't as if the memory will be *seared*, exactly, into my memory, since I never saw anything much.'

And suddenly, he got an idea. Because he was almost sure he'd detected a wistful note in her voice when she'd denied having seen *anything much*. And she'd certainly been keen to *feel* every inch of him. Her hands had been all over him. If he wasn't very much mistaken, she wanted to believe he loved her. She just lacked the confidence to reach out and seize what she wanted.

'If you had been able to see me, would that have made a difference?'

'I don't see what good it will do splitting hairs. The point is, I didn't see you and so—'

'Then it is time to remedy the situation,' he said, shrugging his arms out of his jacket. 'I don't think you are the kind of girl who could humiliate a man by refusing to marry him,' he said, ripping his neckcloth free, 'once you'd seen him in his natural state.'

'What,' she said, her eyes growing round, 'are you doing?'

'I'm stripping,' he said, undoing the buttons of his waistcoat. 'I am going to bare my all, again,' he said, tossing it aside.

'You can't,' she protested as he sat on the edge of her couch to tug off his shoes.

'Watch me.'

She squeezed her eyes shut. 'This isn't the answer. If anyone comes in…there would be such a scandal. Oh, please…'

'We've already had one scandal,' he said, dealing with his hose. 'What difference will another make? I'm done with being proper and sticking to the rules where you are concerned. You are not the kind of girl who ought to live by rules made by mere men, anyway.'

Her eyes flew open.

'I cannot see you clearly, anyway,' she said, blushing as he undid the buttons at the neck of his shirt, then stood up to pull it off over his head. 'So you are wasting your time.'

'You have the means to see me,' he countered, pointing to the spectacles case. And then began to undo his breeches.

She licked her lips, as though her mouth had run

dry. 'You must not,' she said huskily. 'If anyone were to come in…'

Actually, that was a good point. He did not want anyone to interrupt them, not at such a crucial juncture. So he went to the door and, not finding a keyhole, took a straight-backed chair and wedged it under the handle instead.

She gave a little gasp.

'I am going to turn round now, Lizzie. I am going to stand before you, stark naked. To prove that I love you, that I will never keep anything hidden from you, ever again. That I want nothing more than to marry you and spend the rest of my life making you happy.'

He turned.

For a moment, she gazed at his face, her own glowing scarlet, even though he knew she'd be unable to make out more than his outline, from all the way across the room.

There was a beat of silence.

Two.

He'd never felt more exposed, or more vulnerable in his life.

'Lizzie, for pity's sake… I've bared myself to you here. Not just my body, but my very heart and soul. If you won't marry me, sweetheart, what am I going to do with the rest of my life?'

Lizzie bit down on her lower lip. Fumbled with the package on her lap. Drew out the spectacles and hooked them over her ears.

And he knew it was going to be all right.

* * * * *